WED IN HASTE
TO THE PRINCE

Heba Helmy

MILLS & BOON

First published in Great Britain 2026
by Mills & Boon, an imprint of HarperCollins*Publishers* Ltd,
1 London Bridge Street, London, SE1 9GF

www.harpercollins.co.uk

HarperCollins*Publishers*, Macken House, 39/40 Mayor Street Upper, Dublin 1, D01 C9W8, Ireland

ISBN: 978-0-263-41867-5

01/26

MIX
Paper | Supporting
responsible forestry
FSC™ C007454

This book contains FSC™ certified paper
and other controlled sources to ensure responsible forest management.

For more information visit www.harpercollins.co.uk/green.

Printed and Bound in the UK using 100% Renewable Electricity
at CPI Group (UK) Ltd, Croydon, CR0 4YY

For M., second but born with main-character energy.

Also, here is me putting it in official ink: you're a dork.

I love you.

Chapter One

Adnan

Cairo, Egypt, May 1883

Prince Adnan Ahmed Ali glanced at his new bride and thought miserably, *What have I done?*

Yes, Lady Olive Whitmore was breathtakingly beautiful with her curly blonde hair pulled back in fine ribbons beneath a lace veil. Yes, her blue eyes shimmered with a kind of passion that might have been infectious if Adnan were the sort prone to the influence of others. *If.* He was not. The shade of blue, however, was interesting. Darker than the sky on a sunny day—*if* Adnan were the sort to waste his time staring at the sky. He was not.

And, yes, Olive Whitmore had the sort of full, pink lips that any man whose blood ran hot might enjoy kissing. Adnan's blood was certainly heated, but he'd also seen the pout of those lips. Heard the insolence of the words that came from them.

He certainly did not want to kiss them.

Olive Whitmore was a spoilt young woman, and witnessing her disrespectful attitude towards her father over the last few weeks certainly didn't bode well for the kind of wife Adnan always pictured himself having.

One who was soft-hearted. Kind. A good home-maker. *Bint balladoo.*

Not only was Olive not his countrywoman, but she was none of the other things as well. She was too rash and reckless. And what was the likelihood of a pampered noble English lady knowing how to keep a good house?

He thought again, *What have I done?*

The sheikh at his mosque would say that Allah's destiny overrides people's wills. Adnan believed it, but destiny had beaten his will too many times and sometimes too harshly over the years.

Learning his father was actually the khedive of Egypt at the formative age of fifteen had confused him, and the subsequent anger he'd bottled up towards both his parents for the deception was only dampened by the kinship he'd gained with his siblings, especially his younger half-brother, Saleem, and older half-sister, Nawal, during his regular visits to the palace.

It was good that he didn't come to live here full-time, that he didn't leave his mother entirely and that they'd all agreed that the khedive wouldn't publicize the fact that Adnan was his son. It was not a secret among those in the know here, but outside of the palace and noble circles, there were only rumors around the fact he was a Prince of Egypt, rumors that Adnan didn't feel a pressing need to confirm or deny.

He was glad to move about relatively freely, unrecognized in public spaces, and maintain minimal guards in those places where scrutiny was higher. Saleem was the heir and had learned from Adnan's ways enough to seal himself and his new wife off at the Lodge in Alexandria.

Yet he knew that when it was time to step into the role of khedive, his brother would be ready to serve Egypt. As for himself, he was grateful to not have such a responsibility. Adnan was content to be at his brother's side, helping wherever and whenever he needed— *but* having the option to return to his own home at the end of each day. His was a home he'd built not with the funds from any inheritance but from his own hard work. When Adnan had learned he was a Prince of Egypt at fifteen, that was also when he decided that he'd never call upon his title to forge his life's path.

He'd believed it the right decision for the most part, wavering only when his mother got sick. The khedive's reach was such that he could bring in specialists from top European hospitals. But illness doesn't distinguish between the mother of a prince or a pauper. The doctors said her leukemia was incurable and that she would not live much longer.

Adnan had been overcome with regret about all the time he'd wasted being angry at her. He'd learned then that if he could not escape Allah's destiny, at least he would try to not accumulate regrets. And a hasty proposal and marriage to Lady Olive Whitmore?

That, he feared, would end up being his biggest regret.

Adnan prided himself on being measured, deliberate, thoughtful. He weighed risks before deciding on actions. The strategy worked for him in the job he'd taken with his father's office and in the business ventures he'd begun that now gave him monetary freedom from that job.

And though he'd not made any decisions on when to marry or start his own family, he'd planned to do so once Saleem was settled. His brother was heir, after all, and the pressure was on him from their father. But when Saleem put his foot down, marrying Elise Clifton—for love—rather than her best friend, Olive Whitmore, whom the khedive planned for, Adnan found himself foolishly proposing to be Olive's groom instead.

He remembered that proposal now. Olive had been slumped in the leather chair in the study at the Raseltin Palace, looking utterly dejected and embarrassed because she'd not known about Elise and Saleem's love. It seemed her pale blue gown was drowning her, her blonde hair a mess, her eyes wide and wild. And maybe because of all that had happened with his mother, Adnan could not help but look at a lone woman in distress with empathy.

In any case, his faculties took a leave of absence.

Although Olive agreed to Adnan's proposal at the time, he consoled himself by thinking that the wedding would never happen. But now that it *was* happening, Adnan could only believe that the marriage was a farce that could not last.

Olive made no qualms about the reason why she wanted to marry him. She did not want to go back to England with her father, Lord Whitmore, but rather to stay in Egypt. And for that, she needed a husband. Maybe once Lord Whitmore left, Olive would realize her mistake and ask Adnan for a divorce. Fickle as Olive was, it was the most likely outcome.

It serves me right! It had been a foolishly hasty proposal that he was too damn gracious to back out of. *At least, I need not put in the effort to play her husband.* He would spare himself the inconvenience.

Nawal grabbed his elbow and shook, drawing his attention. His sister hissed, 'Are you physically unable to stop frowning, even on your wedding day?'

He grunted in response, but she was undeterred. 'The wedding festivities have yet to begin, but you're sure to frighten the guests in the ballroom who've agreed to attend on such short notice. Not to mention your bride, the *miskeena* poor girl who'll be on your arm—imagine the fright you'll cause her when she sees you looking like such a brute!'

Adnan avoided looking at Olive, sitting across from him but out of earshot. 'We have signed the papers, made the marriage official. What more is necessary? I do not know what we are sitting here for, simply waiting for the *festivities* in order to make a grand entrance. I dislike entrances, grand or otherwise. As for the guests—who could refuse an invite to the khedive's palace with all its finery, the chance to show off their best costumes and rub elbows with the country's elite? I do not feel sorry for them, sister. Still, I am here, am I not?' He scowled. 'I am ready to be paraded as befits a Prince of Egypt. Can we not go in now and get the party over with? Who are we waiting for?'

It sounded less grateful than Adnan would've liked considering his sister was the party planner, but Nawal knew him and she did not take offense. 'It is a wedding, you goat. I only have two brothers and since I was denied arranging Saleem's altogether and yours happened so quickly, you will suffer me. This is minuscule in comparison to what I would have done had there been more time.' She grinned mischievously. 'Or are you that eager to steal Lady Olive away? You understand women like to be romanced before…' She cleared her throat suggestively.

'You've no shyness whatsoever? Where is that husband of yours to rein you in?'

Nawal winked. 'My husband understands that watching the children whilst I am busy is the best way to romance me.'

Adnan shook his head, then smiled, despite himself. His half-siblings had a way of catching him off guard; he was used to that. But when, across the room, Olive's gaze locked on his after noticing the change in his demeanor, Adnan dropped his smile.

He was not used to her.

She frowned, and whatever curiosity was in her face disappeared as Olive turned to say something to her best friend, Elise.

Which prompted Adnan to ask, 'Where has Saleem gone? What could possibly separate him from his new bride?'

Nawal gestured with her chin in the direction of the foyer's doors. 'He was bringing *who* we are waiting for to get the party started.'

There his brother, dressed to match Adnan—black trousers, white jacket and the blue-and-gold insignia accessories that marked the regalia of the Princes of Egypt—was hunched over a wheeled bath chair. One which contained Adnan's mother.

She sat in it, looking frailer than she'd been this morning when he kissed her goodbye.

'She did not tell me.'

'Elham knew you would not agree,' Nawal said.

Adnan's voice rose. 'She is not supposed to be out of bed! The trip to the palace and then back home? All the people in the ballroom? What if one has a cough or something worse? Her condition means she cannot handle catching anything.'

Nawal's expression softened. 'Your mother insisted, Adnan. She contacted us and said you are her only child. Her *own words* were that even if she was guaranteed to die this very night, she would still want to be here.'

Adnan exhaled, forced his frustration to calm, then strode towards them. He thanked Saleem, relieving him of his chair-pushing duties.

'It is my honour to escort *umm al 'arees* to her son's wedding.' Saleem spoke with a flourish, crouching respectfully to touch Elham's knees.

'The sly, secretive mother of the groom.' Adnan planted a gentle kiss on the top of her shawl. It was plum-coloured like the dress she wore—one he'd gifted her a few Eids ago. It had been fitted well then, but was now ridiculously loose on her. And, he feared, much too thin of a material to be warm enough in the vastness of his father's palace.

'You look beautiful, *ummi*. But do not think you

got away with this. I will take you to task when we are back home.'

She waved her bony fingers dismissively. 'I wish to meet the girl blessed to have captured the heart of my dear Adnan.'

It was not exactly true but he would not tell his mother that. She needn't fret over his heart with all her other worries. Were this a slower, more traditionally timed wedding, Elham should have met and got better acquainted with her future daughter-in-law long before now. Another regret for Adnan to add to his list.

Nawal waved Olive over and as she made her way to them his mother called her *amar*—the ultimate compliment for beauty in their vocabulary, to compare a person to the moon.

Maybe this was why he'd asked Olive in the first place, signed the contract to finalize it. His mother was dying, so everything *had* to happen quickly. Elham's contentment was what he could gain from this marriage, short-lived as both may be. Adnan could almost believe that, subconsciously, he'd asked for Olive's hand because he wanted his mother's happiness. Marriage, love, family: those had always been his mother's dreams for him.

And when Olive bent to greet Elham, clasping her hands as his mother cupped her cheek, Adnan watched and decided here was a moment he'd always treasure.

But as was sure to happen with their marriage, Olive

quickly ruined it with the careless words that came out of that frustrating mouth of hers.

In her broken Arabic, she said, 'It is my pleasure to meet the beloved nursemaid.'

'She is my mother.' Adnan spat the reprimand in English. When Olive flinched, he nearly regretted it, but really, what was she thinking, blurting whatever came to her mind? To a woman who was her mother-in-law and obviously ill as well.

'That cannot be...' Olive muddled, searching around, until her eyes landed on Ulfat Hanem. 'Is that not your mother?'

Elise had come to stand by her friend and her husband. She gave Olive a quick shake of the head and explained, 'That is the khedive's wife, mother to Saleem and the sisters, not Adnan.'

Olive's eyes widened. 'I had not realized. I am very sorry.'

He wasn't sure who she was addressing. Still her apology would have been fine, forgotten even, if she'd ended it there. Instead, Olive chuckled sheepishly and announced, 'Prince Adnan does look very *different* than the rest of you.'

Adnan wasn't sure what to make of her use of the word *different*.

Saleem interpreted it in his typically positive manner, instinctively attempting to cover for an offense another might have caused. 'Adnan is the handsomest of us, yes.'

Nawal chimed in with a teasing 'He's also the darkest among us.'

And though Adnan was more tanned, with nearly black eyes, his sister was speaking of his disposition. Olive, however, did not know Nawal well.

'I'd read about harems,' Olive remarked. 'Does it mean there are many more princes and princesses and *mothers* I've yet to meet?'

'Enough.' Adnan was grateful at least that his mother did not understand the conversation since it had been in English. 'Foreigners may be unfamiliar with the concept, but we have a praxis *you* should familiarize yourself with as a woman in the harem—if one has nothing pleasant to say, then it is best to say nothing at all.'

Olive smarted, haughtily pressing her lips together. Why was she so doggedly intent on irking him even while seeming to heed his advice?

Nawal lightly added, 'Clearly, you have not heard the harem's gossips, brother.'

Saleem urged, 'Happier moods should prevail at weddings,' just as their father approached with his mother, Ulfat Hanem.

Beyond knowing that his mother was the daughter of workers in the khedival palace, Adnan never learned how his parents got together, married, then divorced. He had never asked for the details. At first it was because he was too angry, and later it was because of his pride. Nawal and Saleem spoke of their mother being hurt by it though she herself had had a father with multiple wives.

None of that was apparent now. Both his father and Ulfat Hanem civilly greeted Adnan's mother as if she was, indeed, a beloved nurse. They congratulated her on his marriage. Ulfat Hanem put a gentle hand on his mother's shoulder and the khedive asked, 'How are you feeling, Elham?'

Adnan chafed at the use of his mother's first name without any honorific.

'I am well, Ahmed,' she said, emphasizing the khedive's name without his title. Adnan wondered if it was her way of putting herself on par with the man she'd once been married to or if true affection for him lingered after they had gone their separate ways. Again, it was a detail he wasn't privy to.

His mother continued, 'Congratulations on the marriage of your son too.'

She wasn't referring to Saleem; she was talking about him. And wasn't that the epitome of Adnan's position? The two sides from which he was born were so utterly separated that he himself could not be a whole person. The two parts of his identity were ever warring. On one hand, he was the royal son of the khedive, comfortable in the palms of ostentatious luxury, but on the other hand, Adnan was the son of Elham, a divorced mother who'd raised him in one of the poorer Cairo neighborhoods. He'd had no choice but to harden in the toughness of its streets, to become his own man.

'Shall we enter the ballroom to greet our waiting guests?' The khedive's question was more a demand, one he followed with further direction: 'Adnan, take Lady Whitmore's arm and smile. There are diplomats gathered.'

Adnan relinquished the handles of his mother's chair to Nawal and she wheeled her to one side whilst the familial procession to the ballroom doors lined up. First were his father and Ulfat Hanem, then Elise and Saleem, followed by his other sisters.

Adnan and Olive were last, presumably because they were the main attraction of the show—*show* being the right word. He steeled himself with each step; it had never been easy for him to feign joy, to pretend he was pleased when he was not. Adnan's moods were written on his face so plainly that the best he could do to hide them was to neutralize the facial muscles. The result made him seem reserved, withdrawn to others. *Unapproachable.* He liked that.

His new wife, however, had no issue with approaching him.

Olive pushed her arm through his and muttered, 'Elise speaks of how noble Saleem is and I've decided you must be the same. She says I must think of you as a friend firstly. And since you did, after all, make a gallant offer of marriage when I most needed it, I am willing to ignore all else, Adnan. I will graciously tolerate your irritability.'

He couldn't get in a sharp 'thank you' or any other word before she continued, 'Perhaps this day throws into relief how *attached* we are to be and you have regrets. I assure you, however, as soon as I do what I came to Egypt to do, we can go our separate ways. You will get on with your life and I shall be out of your hair. No harm, no foul. Not even any need to not have fun today!'

She was already planning her escape then. Yet for her to take divorce so casually…? He'd already thought about it, so why did Olive admitting it bother Adnan? Before he could answer his own question, the ballroom doors opened with a flourish and the *zaffa* began in earnest, drowning out everything but the music.

Nawal had hired a traditional band for the march. As the family procession splintered to different sides of the ballroom, he and Olive were flanked by at least ten men. Each man wore an ornately embroidered vest and loose *sirwal* trousers. Each carried some manner of drum or tambourine instrument, all of which were being played at the same time. A few of the men were singing, but it was hard to make out who while the guests clapped along and two women with great lungs let loose *zargootas*. Before Adnan's ears had adjusted to the noise, a middle-aged, turban- and *gala-baya*-wearing man pushed his arms out and came to stand at the march's centre. He was a Hegalla dancer who wielded a large stick, swinging it above his head and twirling like an acrobat, kicking his legs in a diz-zying manner.

Adnan had to laugh.

This was the kind of wedding *zafaa* that would hap-pen on a side street of his Cairo neighbourhood home or Egypt's countryside villages. It wasn't the kind fit for dignitary guests, many of whom were foreigners, nor was it at all suited to what was probably the most grandiose palace on this side of the African continent.

His father must be embarrassed!

How had Nawal got the khedive to agree? Likely, she'd used her daughter, Maysoon, their father's fa-vourite grandchild, as a distraction to hide her plans from him.

His sister had quite the sense of humour and Adnan was grateful for it.

He sought her out over the din and the head of the dancer and saw she'd brought his mother across to get her own unencumbered view. Nawal whispered something to Saleem about him and the two of them laughed and waved as he gave them a nod of acknowl-edgement.

They understood him.

With his siblings at least, he was fully Adnan.

But these festivities were not for him alone. Beside him, Olive's body began swaying to the band's music. He didn't mind it—it was a natural reaction to the *zaffa*'s liveliness, even if it was surprising for an Englishwoman. What Adnan did mind was how she was taking advantage of all this planning, his family's optimism, their joy.

Him.

Only to have her fun.

He minded that once Olive did what she'd come to Egypt to do, she would leave without sparing a second thought for the trouble they'd all gone through today.

Chapter Two

Olive

Olive Whitmore should most certainly *not* be moved by the music, not in such an undemure manner. Her personal rejoinder to stop dancing, however, had come before Adnan threw her a look of disgust. And that just made her want to continue.

'Miserable man,' she said, tapping his shoulder and mouthing the words to make sure he would see the sentiment even if he could not hear it over the music.

Olive had just claimed she'd not let his irritability bother her, but the truth was that despite his gallantry in proposing marriage, she was most utterly and profoundly infuriated with him! And she'd been so ever since she'd met him in Rasheed weeks ago.

She'd only just secured the house rental, when Adnan came barging in on her, calling her impetuous and cruel to leave her friend Elise and not meet his brother Saleem, who had been expecting her.

After that first of many such lectures, Adnan had gone silent, waiting for her to answer him as to why she'd done it. He'd asked, 'What is your excuse, daughter of Lord Whitmore?'

There'd been an instant then, when as he stared at her, his thick brows furrowing over his deep-set dark eyes, Olive nearly told him the truth.

The horrible, shameful truth about her real father.

And that she wasn't the daughter of a lord.

Olive stifled the truth at the last second, something she'd been doing for months since the terrible night when she first found it out herself.

Maybe that's why my body acts of its own volition and the ill-timed things I say are regarded as impetuous. All were an attempt to stifle the truth before it could be spoken aloud.

Indeed, remembering that horrible night caused Olive to sober now, even amid the vibrant wedding party. It was never far from her mind.

Elise's father, Thomas Clifton, had visited their London house the week before he was found dead. Olive loved Elise as a sister but had long ago guessed there was something clandestine about Elise's father's acquaintance with her own. Thomas Clifton was considered by many to be a gangster, and Olive's father, Alfred Whitmore, was a respected member of parliament. The two men should not, by any stretch of the imagination, have had any interactions. And they didn't, for the most part, since Mr Clifton would rarely accompany Elise to the house when she visited.

The fact that Elise wasn't with her father made that dark night even more odd. The men must have believed her asleep, as it was late, but Olive liked to experiment in the kitchens at night when Cook wasn't there to watch over her.

She heard the men talking on her way back to her room.

Thomas was distressed about a matter. Olive didn't know what at the time, but after Elise's recent ordeal with her former suitor and uncle, she now knew it had to do with her friend's inheritance. At the time, her father said he'd do whatever he could to help Thomas. It was the next part of their exchange that still haunted Olive.

Thomas said, 'None would believe our friendship started by me blackmailing you over the man from Rosetta.'

Then her father—nay, *Lord Whitmore*—had actually laughed as though something was amusing. 'It wasn't really a bribe. You wanted me to welcome Elise into my home and she has become like my own daughter and Olive has grown to look quintessentially English, so that none would believe her father was an Egyptian man paid to bed my wife.'

It had taken all of Olive's might not to scream, not to rail against both men right then.

It was shame that stayed her tongue, forced her to sneak back to her room.

With every strained step, she'd realized how each facet of her existence had been a sham.

Olive was not a lady, daughter to a lord. Neither was she the orphaned daughter of a loving, gentle woman whose heart gave out not long after giving birth to her. Even if Olive's mother wasn't part of the plan and did not know about her husband's paying a man to seduce her, she was still a woman who'd allowed herself to be seduced.

All that Olive had once valued and believed came crashing down on her head that night.

Worse still was that she'd no one to talk to about it. She thought to confide in Elise, but her best friend was in Manchester at the time. Then, days later, the news that Thomas Clifton had died shocked them all.

When her father told her, Olive expressed her disbelief. 'He was only here a few nights ago!'

Lord Whitmore had looked at her oddly and though he didn't say anything, she understood that he guessed she'd overheard them.

It had been cold between them since. Maybe it was his own shame that stayed his tongue as well, for he could no more broach the subject with Olive than she could with him.

When he mentioned having received a letter from his old friend the khedive, she'd been excited for the

chance to correspond with Prince Saleem only because he was in Egypt. Asking Elise to write to him
instead felt like the right thing to do. She had come to
stay with them after her father passed and because she
was grieving, Olive thought the distraction would do
her a world of good. And she must have done a good
job since the invitation to visit Egypt came soon after.
When the prospect of the two women travelling to
Egypt was broached, Lord Whitmore didn't want to
let them travel alone, but he eventually relented.

'I will to Rosetta,' Olive had said.

'There is nothing there. The Rosetta Stone is now
in the British Museum, and it is merely a stop on the
Nile Delta. Prince Saleem will meet you and Elise in
Alexandria.' Her father knew why she'd brought it up
and, by the look on Olive's face, must have understood
he'd never again have sway over her decisions.

Olive had always been spontaneous but since she'd
found out Alfred Whitmore wasn't her true father, her
actions had become foolhardy even for her.

She decided that she'd come to Rasheed to find her
birth father. Hear his side of things. Those were Olive's
goals, but abandoning ship when she did—and Elise…
Well, she didn't need Adnan's lecturing to know she
was wrong about that.

Still, things worked out for her friend; Elise had
found love with Prince Saleem!

But when Lord Whitmore arrived in Egypt and it

was clear Olive could no longer stay in the country alone to accomplish her goals, she'd agreed to marry Adnan.

The foolhardiest of decisions ever.

To marry Adnan, of all men? He'd made the days in Rasheed unbearable for her. All he could talk about was 'protocol' and 'duty' and how it wasn't the place of a lady to live on her own and what would her father, the esteemed Lord Whitmore, think?

Adnan's words had prodded Olive's wounds and she must have said the most ridiculous things to hide her true reactions to them. He surely believed she was a rash ninny; yet somehow, miraculously, just when she thought all hope was lost and she'd have to go back to England not having met her real father, Adnan had proposed marriage.

Maybe it was a princely thing. Elise had spoken of Saleem's nobleness too. The difference was that her friend and the Prince were in love, and they would live happily ever after. Saleem and Elise were well matched, him with his sunshine ways and her with her pragmatism.

Adnan was gruff, cynical. A man of few words.

And Olive? Well, she didn't even know who she was anymore. Not really.

Maybe she'd had a sense of it *before* but learning the circumstances of her birth had changed everything. Olive had once believed that the love between her

parents was the kind to transcend death and mourning—why else had her papa never remarried? She'd
imagined having a similarly great romance, a fairy tale
featuring a dashing groom with whom she'd spend a
lifetime of joy and adventures.

But that Olive was long gone. She *could not* think
about falling in love, sharing a life with anyone, until
she found her real father and heard what he had to say.
She *could* hope the 'man from Rosetta'—for she knew
no other name for him—would say or do something
magical enough to release the shame which had con-
sumed Olive for months. Maybe then she could think
about what the rest of her life would be.

Adnan let go of her arm when they reached the dais
where two throne-like chairs awaited them. When the
music suddenly stopped, Olive had the misfortune of
hearing his incredibly huge sigh of relief.

She tried to ignore it.

Adnan looked as though he wanted to help her sit,
either a result of his princely manners or a realization
she'd have trouble doing so in her wedding gown without falling on top of him.

And Olive wouldn't like to ruin the gown that she'd
grown fond of.

After a few lengthy—considering the little time they
had—meetings with dressmakers that proved fruitless,
Adnan's sister remembered the dress in her closet.
Nawal had been gifted it years ago from a potential

suitor's family and when she chose a different husband, she'd never returned it nor had occasion to wear it. She'd offered it to Olive with an apologetic explanation: 'The groom's family farmed pearls from the Red Sea, a strange process called "culturing," which they insisted was the best and most modern way to attain pearls but…surely the rareness of a finding a pearl is the magic of it? Still, if you do not mind "fake" pearls, then the gown itself is very lovely, and I think it would be perfect on you.'

Who was Olive—not the true daughter of a lord despite being called 'lady'—to refuse anything fake?

The gown was beautiful. Its pearls gleamed flaxen and blush pink and had been sewn into the lace overlay, subtle from the bodice, to spill heavily onto the full skirt, which required both corset and crinoline. The veil was thinner, an exquisite tulle held down by a full pearl crown and a train that trailed long behind her. Olive had decided she wanted to wear her hair looser. Not let her curls—which she now understood were her due to her Egyptian side—completely free, but tame them with the oils she'd found in the palace hammam.

'I could paint you again—you are a picture of perfection,' Elise exclaimed when she saw her earlier.

Olive took it as the highest compliment and even looked forward to seeing her groom's reaction. Although she'd never felt more beautiful, Adnan's reaction turned out to be a troubled frown.

It bothered her how much she would like to be the one to solicit a smile from him. It was a rare sighting indeed and only ever seemed to emerge when he was with his siblings.

As was illustrated just then when Nawal approached to help seat Olive.

'I tried to figure it out,' Adnan said with a grin, referring to Olive's gown.

'It is quite hard.' Nawal tsked as she demonstrated. 'It is heavy. You have to lift it like this, sweeping it to one side like that, then remain holding it as the lady backs gently and bends into her seat.'

Olive followed the direction and was soon seated comfortably. 'This ballroom is prettier than the Queen of England's drawing room,' she complimented Nawal, knowing it was her planning.

'You were there for the British tradition of being presented at court, I assume?'

'Yes.' Olive remembered how she'd felt like a princess in the white gown she'd worn. Then she was a nobody and didn't know it. Funny how she was now actually marrying a prince and about to become a princess, and yet, she *knew* she was still a nobody. 'All the yellow roses you've included are divine,' she remarked, changing the subject.

Adnan supplied, 'They were a symbol of royalty and

prosperity in ancient Egypt, associated most with the sun god, Ra. The khedive likes his traditions.'

'The khedive wasn't the planner,' Nawal crooned. 'I chose the shade of roses to mimic Olive's hair.' She stared pointedly at her brother, then pulled a rose from a nearby vase. She held it up to Olive's cheek. 'Look, Adnan. Surely, even your austere eyes can see your wife's beauty.'

Olive allowed his sister's tilting of her chin towards Adnan. When she lifted her eyes to his, she couldn't help but be fascinated by the storm she saw brewing there. Maybe it was a play of the palace lights or her own turbulent mind, but the brown pigment whirled as if it contained a tempest. Adnan clenched every muscle in his face, in full control of what he revealed to her, but he could not control his eyes.

Still Olive, alas, could not read them.

It took longer than it should have to break their locked stare. Adnan was saved from commenting on Nawal's statement by the influx of guests lining up to offer their congratulations to the new couple.

He rose to greet many of them and Nawal whispered to Olive that she didn't have to do so. 'They will understand that your gown would need to be constantly readjusted.'

Olive followed that advice, but when Lord Whitmore passed through the line and lifted her hand awkwardly from her sitting position, Adnan interjected, 'Your *father* has come to congratulate us.'

She managed a small smile and a flippant 'Has he?'

'I set sail tomorrow, Olive darling,' Lord Whitmore said, 'but I shall return by summer's end to...visit with you. If you need anything in the interim, you must write.'

She said, 'I likely will not. Need anything, I mean.'

He nodded. 'You look lovely, dear. Your mother would have—'

'Thank you.' Olive cut him off, not wanting to hear anything about what her mother would have liked or how proud of a father he was. She'd heard enough of such lies her entire life.

When he'd gone, giving up his place for the next in line, Olive relaxed. It was hardest to keep her shame contained in his presence.

'He does not deserve to be treated so terribly by you.' Adnan had been lecturing on fathers' rights over their daughters since they'd met. Why should he stop on their wedding day?

Olive was about to tell him as much, then she saw who was next in line. 'Yasser!'

She stood, shook his hand heartily, forgetting all about her dress and ignoring Adnan's reproachful look. Yasser had been a godsend when she first ar-rived in Rasheed. As the proprietor of the Rosetta Car-riage Company and grandson of the town's *eumda*, or mayor, he proved a real help in securing a cottage for her on a local estate when she realized she'd not have enough money for a long-term stay at the city's hotel. Not only that, but through his helpfulness, she'd learned that Yasser had a thorough grasp of the city's history and its people. If Adnan hadn't found her as soon as he had, Olive would have questioned Yasser about whether he knew any local men who'd gone to England twenty years before. She would have devised some excuse as to why she didn't have a name—perhaps even allowing a hint that he was a *friend* of her mother's before Olive was born and since her mother had passed, Olive had never got his name. Rasheed was small enough that surely Yasser could point her in the right direction, put her on the path to find her true father.

'Congratulations, Miss Whitmore,' Yasser said as he shook her hand. 'Or is it Mrs Whitmore? Mrs Adnan? I do not know the English custom after marriage.'

'She will keep her father's name,' Adnan spoke brusquely and as if she was not there. 'Egyptian customs are what should matter in our country.'

And what father's name would that be?

Olive's annoyance with her new husband was nearly enough to distract her from the question she needed to ask Yasser. She'd not expected to see him here and did not want to miss the opportunity. It was neither the time nor place but if she could manage to pull him aside…

The men had switched to a quick-paced Arabic. Olive tried to make out their words as she did with all conversations in her proximity. Her command of the language was improving. The books she'd studied had made Arabic seem more difficult than her experiences with the Egyptian dialect, which proved easier.

It was a genetic disposition, she supposed.

'You may sit.' Adnan leaned in to whisper, 'Unless standing is a better position for eavesdropping?'

No one else had heard him, and Yasser had slipped away while Adnan was crowding her. She didn't appreciate the way his breath near her ear sent shivers to her stomach.

'Why do you insist on being contrary? I have tried to be pleasant, accommodating.' She might have gone on but the ripple in his jaw, the intensity in his gaze, which she really could not read except to know that it made her feel like she'd been dunked in a vat of ice water, confused her. She sighed. 'I wished to speak to Yasser about Rasheed, but you drove him off.'

'What about Rasheed?'

Olive clamped down the words *my father* and offered the first thing that came to her mind in its stead: 'My place there.'

'What place?'

'Three months' rent was paid for the cottage I stayed

in when you found me there in Rasheed. It is where I plan to return to as soon as possible.'

Rather than offer a retort, Adnan pressed his lips together and resumed his seat, leaving her standing there to figure out how to resume hers on her own.

The line of guests receded to allow for a new round of entertainment. A servant offered them flutes of bright red *sherbat*. The drink was sweet and strawberry-rose flavoured—a flavour she rather enjoyed. From the corner of her eye, she saw Adnan hadn't touched his. In fact, she doubted he'd do much more for the rest of the wedding day festivities except grumble to himself.

But what, Olive couldn't help wondering with trepidation, *would the wedding night bring?*

Chapter Three

Adnan

The khedive patted him once on the shoulder to pull Adnan from his seat. He led him to a far corner of the ballroom, to the place where his prized gold harp—a purchase from when the Kingdom of Italy converted the Medici Palace to governmental offices—sat abandoned.

'Nawal has cleared the west wing apartment for you upstairs. It will be one night, then in the morning, *late* morning,' he emphasized, 'you and Lady Olive will ride the royal train to Aswan. There, you will have use of a private luxury riverboat. You can decide your itinerary once there, but know that it is a *honeymoon* per English customs, but also in a place where our ancestors ruled supreme. It will be a chance to show Lord Whitmore's daughter the glorious history of our country. To demonstrate our culture.'

Adnan's father was blunt, barking orders as if commanding a battalion. It was how Adnan knew, the first time he met him at age fifteen, that the Khedive was indeed his father. They were too alike. *You'll come to the palace. Take Saleem, my heir, under your tutelage. Because you are a good man and he will be too, but he is yet a boy with too many sisters.* Even as Adnan was reeling from the knowledge that his father—a louse he'd dismissed as dead after divorcing his mother—was alive and was the khedive to boot, the compliment felt…*nice.*

'I cannot leave my mother,' Adnan replied now. He watched as the wedding's guests were circulating the buffet table or daintily picking from the boxes of cake and sandwiches that had been pre-packaged. Nawal had gone out of her way to consider what might be served at a *baladi*,or traditional, wedding. So rather than have individual place settings that were waited upon, it was each man or woman for themselves.

His sister had said that he and Olive would be expected to cut the cake together later, when she'd brought them their boxes a short while ago. Adnan had eaten the dried-meat *bastarma* and fried-egg sandwich from his box, whilst Olive picked daintily at the *malban*-filled buttery *ka'ak* from hers. He'd heard her telling Nawal it was ingenious to fill the biscuits with Turkish delight and it made him glad. Adnan was not sure why, but he did like to see Olive eating. Anytime he'd been with her at meals, she always seemed to want more but would hold herself back.

'Your mother can stay here if you are worried about leaving her alone,' the khedive countered. 'The doctor will maintain a live-in arrangement until your return.'

Adnan shook his head stubbornly. 'I have lost much time with her over the last few weeks.'

'This is a sensitive time for your marriage, Adnan. Ensure it starts off right. If your wife is satisfied with you, more British doors, more European ones, will open for us. You must learn their ways, circulate in their spheres. Miss Whitmore is learning Arabic and is welcoming of our traditions, and you must do the same. It is what I wanted for Saleem…but his choice was his…choice. He has charm, it will carry him well enough, but with you by his side, as *cultured* as him? The two of you together will be an unstoppable force. It will be a true legacy for our family. Egypt will be for both your sons.'

While he appreciated his father's rare display of affection and the acknowledgement of any future children he might have, Adnan was not going to raise his family with any sort of identity conflict. Not the same as he had. And he certainly wasn't going to have them with Olive, who would likely not be present in their marriage long enough to even begin to think of having children.

He turned to his father, tried to ignore the downturn beneath his thick moustache, the grimace that perpetually existed there.

Should I tell him that the marriage will not last, soften what is sure to be a shock in the near future?

'Khedewy...' Adnan called him 'my khedive,' the term closest to 'father' he'd ever uttered. He tried to appease the khedive. 'Perhaps there will be a honeymoon in the future, but inform whoever planned it that the trip to Aswan must be cancelled at present.'

The khedive raised his voice as he replied, 'I thought you would immediately agree to a chance to check on your nearby sugar cane holdings in person. Your company in Sohag is growing exponentially, is it not?'

The pinch of his father's brow said he already knew the answer.

'I have workers who report to me. You needn't monitor its activities.'

'We should discuss nationalizing sugar cane as we did with cotton.'

Adnan pulled at his collar, tried to loosen it. He did not see eye to eye with his father about the cotton industry and he certainly did not want the same for sugar cane. And everyone in his employ felt the same. 'Yet you passed on the chance to invest in it despite my recommendations, do you recall?'

'I do not wish to steal from your accomplishment, Adnan. I am proud of you for building it as you have, your foresight in the endeavour you started whilst in my employ.' The compliment was conditional, for the khedive made it sound like he was, in fact, the reason why the business was successful. And although the travel and observations he'd made during his work with the khedive's office impacted his investment, the sugar cane company was entirely Adnan's. He'd purposely created it as the very opposite of what the khedives of the past did with cotton. It was why his workers were happy. And he owed it to them to keep them so. He brought in machinery to make their lives easier, and implemented policies to keep the money flowing throughout the year, outside of harvest times.

Most importantly, Adnan hired workers and gave them decent salaries, rather than forcing them to 'invest' in the company and suffer any losses with him if the commodity slumped in the marketplace. That's what nationalizing sugar would entail, which was why Adnan would fight his father as adamantly as he could.

'This is neither the time nor place to discuss that,' the khedive conceded, then leaned in closer. 'I see that that Yasser Tal'at from Rasheed is here. If you recall, I'd cautioned you about him to protect Saleem. I did not expect you to befriend him as well.'

Adnan recalled Olive's reaction to seeing Yasser earlier and pushed back a twinge of jealousy. The truth was that he'd talked to Yasser about buying the *ezzbah*, or estate, land when he'd led him to her weeks ago, discussed his plans for expanding his sugar cane business to Rasheed. Yasser had moved quickly to broker the sale of it for him and had been delivering the final papers to Saleem's office in Alexandria when his brother invited him to the wedding to deliver them himself.

'Yasser poses no threat to Saleem. I made sure of that. And his grandfather is the *eumda* in Rasheed—surely he answers to you.'

The khedive cast him a pointed stare. 'No leader can always manage everyone in his own house. Intelligence tells us that the *eumda*'s son, Yasser's *father*, who was exiled from Rasheed and has not been seen in the city for years, is a member of a revolt group. We were able to quell the disturbances of years past with French and British aide but the *aryaf*, the countryside outside of the larger cities, are unchecked. They are places where discontent can flourish. What if Yasser is helping his father and the two are using my own sons against me to do it?'

It was such a ridiculous suggestion, Adnan nearly laughed. 'If his father hasn't been seen there, then they are not in contact. And you can rest assured that your sons are not dimwits to thus be used.'

The khedive strummed a sharp note on the harp. 'Some might say that you, in particular, have cause to be discontented with your father.'

His father used to use this tactic on Saleem, subtly suggesting that his heir harboured resentment towards him. He'd never bothered to use it on Adnan and that made him unsure of how to respond now.

Given that the khedive wanted to nationalize his business interest and use his marriage as a vehicle to widen opportunities, any son would be discontented.

Adnan could barely conceal his frustration when he questioned, 'And are you one of those "some," *Khedewy*?'

Before his father could answer, Nawal came between them, carrying her daughter, Maysoon, May for short. May was the only one, it seemed, who could immediately shift even the foulest of the khedive's moods.

She pulled out of her mother's arms to jump into his. '*Gidoo*,' she said, calling him by the Arabic for *grandfather*, rather than the title everyone else in the family used, 'how do you like the ribbons in my hair? We got them from China!'

'Perfect ribbons for a perfect girl. What an honour for the ribbon-maker!'

Nawal took the granddaughter-grandfather encounter as an opportunity to pull Adnan aside. 'What was that about? The two of you looked like you were about to start a war in this very corner.'

'Did anyone notice?'

'Your mother was watching. She sent me, knows you and our father, I suppose.' Nawal pointed Elham out at the table, sipping from a glass of water. 'She's getting tired, however. Saleem thinks he should take her home but she wants to see you and Olive cutting the cake, feeding each other from it.'

'Cake-feeding is one tradition all Egyptians like to partake in, correct?'

Nawal grinned. 'You appreciated the research conducted? Al-Azhar University should grant me a bachelor's degree.'

He held up his hands. 'I don't want to know *how* you did it, considering that even the older servants in the palace are woefully removed from commoner Egyptian society.'

'I'm not about to divulge my secret ways of knowing to you.' She nudged him playfully, then pointed to an empty table covered in a lace cloth. 'I'll have the cake brought out now. Go, claim your abandoned bride and take her to stand there.'

Nawal was gone before Adnan could tell her he'd take his mother home, rather than Saleem. His family might expect him and Olive to consummate their union in the palace apartment, but Adnan would not be intimate with a wife who planned on ending their marriage. Hadn't her little speech about returning to her cottage in Rasheed as soon as possible put to rest any doubts of her intentions with regards to their marriage?

There was no need for Adnan to stay with her this night. Better he sleep in his own bed.

He marched to Olive and barked, 'They're bringing out the cake. The party is almost over.'

'All right.' She did not move but twisted those round, forlorn-looking eyes of hers on him. 'What would you have me do with that knowledge?'

'We need to cut a piece of it together,' he explained. 'Feed each other a bite. Is that not a British tradition as well?'

'Ahh.' She rose too quickly, stumbling upon the train of her dress.

Instinctively, Adnan took her hand, held it as she straightened. Her hand was soft in his. He was used to the frailness of his mother's hand, but Olive's was delicate in a different way.

'*Shukraan*,' she thanked him before yanking it back.

At the designated table, a servant handed him a wedged knife and plate as the cake was placed before them. It was three-tiered, covered in a sheet of royal-white icing, a piped design that was decidedly not Egyptian but more likely the work of his father's favourite French patisserie. It must be Nawal's only concession to the wedding's theme.

Guests clapped their encouragement but Adnan wasn't sure where to cut into the cake. Olive guided him to a spot between two piped flowers in the lowest tier, and while he supported the plate, she slid a sliver into it easily.

'You've done this before.' He meant it as a compliment but even to his ears, it sounded like a question.

'Cut a cake? Yes.'

The next moment was strange for Adnan, nearly like he was separated from his own body. The act of feeding Olive, the way her lips parted for the fork and then closed over it. Him, opening his own mouth to accept her offering, the sweetness of the cake, despite how the fork was slightly askew. Perhaps she was nervous, for when the fork left his mouth, her thumb was there on his lips, fixing the lopsided bite. The applause in the background was jarring because he'd forgotten that there were others in the ballroom too—not just him and Olive.

Then, most important of all, he recalled that his mother was there. Adnan turned in her direction, anticipating he'd see joy on her face, but when he caught sight of her, it was only a look of being startled.

Then, she collapsed.

'Her heart was overburdened and that is not surprising for an ill person in her state. She should be recovered within a few days, no worse off than she'd been this morning. I would recommend that she not be moved, however. No more excitement.'

Adnan was grateful his mother's doctor had been a wedding guest; it was good thinking on Nawal's part.

His frustration, however, would not be restrained. 'She should not have come.'

Saleem put a hand on his brother's arm, and as per usual tried to find the positive. 'Let us be thankful she was with us and not alone at home.'

Adnan looked around the apartment, one he'd never before been inside. Nawal explained it was the one they'd readied for him and Olive: 'Because it was the most private, with its two chambers, its own bathroom. *Insha'Allah*, your mother will be comfortable here.'

Adnan knew that his sister was probably feeling guilty and he knew what that was like. He wouldn't be the one to add to such a burden. 'Thank you.'

'It's separate from the central harem too,' she added, with a small smile, 'so there won't be too much gossip.'

Although the more common understanding of the harem was fading from the Egyptian vernacular because it was more in line with the Turkish tradition of noble rule, the upper levels of the palace remained the domain of its women. The room his mother was now resting in had plush carpets, a number of small side tables loaded with conveniences, like porcelain washing bowls, and beneath the burgundy-velvet-draped window, a chaise chair that looked comfortable enough. He walked to it, saw that it had a good view of the main bed where his mother lay, much too small. Her bed at home was small enough that she didn't look so much out of proportion.

'Very well, I shall sleep here tonight. There's a nurse that comes to our house but if you can send your most competent one from the hospital, Doctor?'

When the man nodded, Adnan looked to those gathered.

'We will not stay here for long, I will take *Ummi* home where she is most comfortable as soon as she is better,' he announced in Arabic first and then in English for Lord Whitmore's benefit, who stood next to the khedive and his daughter.

Adnan avoided Olive's gaze but he could not avoid his father's disappointment.

Surely, the khedive wouldn't blame him for refusing to leave for a honeymoon now?

He added, hoping it would be in dismissal, 'I understand you are all concerned for my mother and do apologize for ending the wedding abruptly, but perhaps it would best to let her rest now.'

He turned to the doctor standing alone behind him and threw him a look that urged him to agree.

'That is right. We should let Mrs Elham rest,' the doctor affirmed, gesturing to the apartment door and leading everyone out.

Everyone save for the khedive, who took no orders from anyone. He stepped outside of the room and into the foyer, gesturing for Adnan to join him after he'd bid his farewells to Saleem and Elise, who were returning to Alexandria early the next morning.

Adnan removed his suit jacket as his father dug his shoes into the carpet.

He said, 'Take care of your mother now but do not imagine that our earlier conversation is over. You must find it in yourself to learn how to be cultured, a worthy husband to a fine English lady. I will allow for a postponement of the honeymoon, a shortening of it even, but not for long.'

Adnan seethed at the challenge, the insult to his ability to be a good husband to a woman of culture. 'Cancel the honeymoon. I am not going.'

'And what of your bride standing outside with her father whose return trip to England begins tomorrow? What shall I tell him? That his new son-in-law is preoccupied with his mother and must therefore ignore his wife?'

'What would you have me say?'

The khedive huffed and waved his hand about. 'You think that marrying is only a piece of paper signed and your task done? What of Olive? She may be alone tonight, but tomorrow, the day after? What are your plans for being a real husband to a lady?'

Adnan stopped short of calling his father a hypocrite. Had he not ignored—nay, *abandoned*—Adnan's mother, once the khedive's wife, in a much worse way?

It had been a long day after a few long weeks since his proposal in Alexandria. Adnan was angry at his father, afraid for his mother, and was convinced that he shouldn't spend any emotional energy on a wife who'd ask for a divorce as soon as she was free from her father's presence and done what she'd come to do in the country.

'I have no plans for the cultured Lady Olive! House her here or send her back to England with her father tomorrow—it's all the same to me.'

Adnan had raised his voice to his father in anger, but it was not a scolding from the khedive that silenced him. It was Olive's stricken expression.

She was outside the apartment door and had over-heard his outburst.

Chapter Four

Olive

Olive was not the only one who'd heard Adnan. Lord Whitmore had been standing behind her and although he didn't understand the language, the reaction from the two women who she assumed were Adnan's cousins come to check in on him was enough to show her father that all was not well in her young marriage.

The first woman fawned over her, making excuses in English: 'Adnan heavy burden, he worry for mother.' The second woman's words were dipped in pity as she commented, 'Are you very disappointed? Is it terribly awful to hear such a thing on your wedding night, no less?'

Worst of all was Adnan going back to his mother's room and shutting the door. He must have known she'd overheard, yet he clearly did not regret embarrassing her. Nor would he make any attempt at amends.

'I am scheduled to leave with Prince Saleem and

Elise on the train to Alexandria's port tomorrow morning,' Lord Whitmore addressed thc khedive, 'but perhaps I should delay.'

Olive squared her shoulders, forced a smile. 'There is no need. The khedive, I am sure, and his gracious family will host me while my *husband* sees to his mother's health.'

'Without any doubt,' the khedive reassured Lord Whitmore. 'Olive is now my daughter in front of God's eyes and the laws of both our countries. Trust she will be taken care of, friend.'

The khedive spread his arms and circled the foyer. 'In fact, we'd prepared this wing of the palace for the new couple to stay in as long as they want. Two plush and private rooms, a fully modern water closet with warm water through the pipes.' When he opened the last door, a small kitchen, he remarked, 'My granddaughter Maysoon informs me that she herself chose the tea set and snacks that are stocked in here.'

Olive spied a stove.

Lord Whitmore had seen it too. 'Olive will have a jolly time with the stove. I used to tell her that if she were not daughter to a lord, she'd have been apprenticed to the finest chefs in London.'

Olive swallowed as she watched her father's face fall. He'd spoken without thinking on how his words would be taken. Before that horrible night when she'd overheard the truth of her parentage, she'd believed him the best papa in the world who more than made up for not having a mother. Lord Whitmore had never left her wanting for anything. He was generous with warm hugs and encouraged all her pursuits. He'd played the eager and willing taste-tester to a fair share of her ridiculous escapades in the kitchen.

She stiffened, forcing herself to not crave one of those hugs now. Instead, Olive imagined what she might do after all was settled with her real father in Rasheed. Maybe she would apprentice to a chef.

The khedive pointed to a bell by the door. 'The maids are aplenty. Olive need only ring and they'll be here with whatever she requests. We had planned on hiring a lady's maid but thought we had a few more weeks, er…after the honeymoon…to find someone suitable. I will prioritize that.'

The khedive smiled kindly at her, but Olive wanted nothing more than to be done with this farce of a night. To tear off her wedding dress and veil, to forget the shame of the truth she was continuing to hide. A lady's maid should work for a lady, not for her. And damn the nerve of Adnan for making her seem pitiful on top of it!

'That is most kind, Your Grace, but there is no need to rush. I am proud of Olive's self-sufficient nature.' Lord Whitmore had saved her from commenting and then added, 'Perhaps we should let her get some rest after the excitement of an otherwise wonderful wedding.'

'Yes, it was wonderful and I shall have much more thanks to give when I am better rested.' Olive was grateful when Lord Whitmore, in his diplomatically gracious manner, ushered the khedive and the two cousins from the apartment.

Before he himself left, he pulled an envelope from his inner suit pocket. Olive caught a glimpse of his clamshell pipe case, recalled how, as a child, she played with it often. She'd broken her fair share of them, but he'd quietly replaced them so that she wouldn't feel bad about it for too long.

He put the envelope in her hands, then squeezed. 'Read it later. When you're alone. I hope you will find it in your heart to forgive me, Olive, for I love you and you have been my life's greatest joy.'

When he leaned in to kiss her on the forehead, the lingering aroma of the tobacco he used was *too* familiar and for a moment she forgot how angry she was with him.

He was gone before she remembered it.

Finally, Olive was alone, letter in hand.

What would it contain? An admission? An excuse? An apology?

Olive basked in the silence, heavy, utterly complete. The walls of the foyer were draped in a brocaded silk but beneath it was the palace's concrete. *This is what being in a cave must be like*, she thought. It wasn't the same in their London home, where the walls were covered with flowery paper and the brick was on the outside. Beautiful as the Whitmore mansion was, it was never quiet. In the evenings, there was the creaking of floorboards as the staff moved about, the soft snoring from her father's room across the hall, the crickets chirping away beneath her window. Save for that one time when she'd overheard a life-shattering conversation, Olive used to love the noisiness of it all.

Here? The silence was unnerving. It meant she was alone with her thoughts. Her mind volleyed between the shut door of Adnan's mother's room, and her father's letter in hand.

Which was causing her more anxiousness?

Olive strode into the bedroom that would be hers for the night. The four-poster bed was wide and high enough she'd probably need to vault to get atop it. Its cherry-wood frame exuded opulence and its maroon silk sheets were strewn with yellow rose petals, the same variety that had been abundant in the ballroom. On either side of the bed were table lamps, each with a stained-glass butterfly design on its shade, and emanating an ethereal glow.

The closets held all the clothes she'd brought with her from England and then some, gowns and skirts pressed along with all manner of undergarments, shoes and gloves. To one side of the wardrobe was a white silk nightgown and matching robe for her, next to a folded pajama set which Olive assumed was meant for Adnan.

Next to it was a disproportionately large number of towels.

She flushed when she realized what those were for. Clearly, it was expected that she and Adnan would do what a husband and wife did on the night of their wedding.

She decided against ringing for a maid to help her undress. What if everyone assumed Adnan would do it? Olive did not want to encourage any gossip. She examined her reflection in the large looking glass, trying to figure out how to do it herself, but she could barely focus on anything save for Lord Whitmore's letter still in hand.

She tossed it to the bed, then struggled to undress herself so as not to tear or lose a single pearl from the gown. When, much later, she was done and stood before the mirror, naked, a question leaped to her mind.

Would Adnan have wanted to make love to her?

Did she want him to?

It did not matter. Olive's lack of sexual experience or any desire to acquire it should not be a priority.

She was determined to find her real father and until she did, nothing else—including her grumpy new husband—mattered.

Olive decided that a bath would calm her, help her

sleep. She retrieved the letter and wrapped the largest towel she could find around her naked body. The bathroom's lamps were warming and illuminated what was quite the sanctuary, a room that married the convenience of a water closet and the opulence of a Turkish hammam. The floors were tiled with turquoise marble, a complement to the geometric painted pattern that adorned the ceiling. There was potted green shrubbery along with other decorative accents throughout, and the washing basin was a bright brass. The bathtub water wasn't as hot as Olive might have liked but it was tolerable enough for a short, cooling cleanse. Careful not to let her hair get wet because that definitely would require the sort of attention she did not have the capacity for, and holding her father's letter, Olive slipped into the tub.

Too late, she realized she'd forgotten to lock the door.

No matter, she wouldn't be here for long.

Taking a deep breath, she braced herself and unfolded the single sheet of paper. By its size and colour, she recognized it was a page he'd carefully torn from the journal he often carried.

His name is Tal'at Sharif. He was a determined man I'd met whilst he was working at a traveler's club. Your mother and I had been trying for too long to conceive and though she'd given up, I knew how desperately she wanted a child. Tal'at was handsome, passionate and when he told me of his plans to leave England, arrangements were made for him to give your mother what I could not. He needed to finance his return to Egypt and I told myself and your mother that 'he is leaving anyway' and then it will be done and we can forget how it happened. It was a lie. In many ways, your disappointment with me now is a relief, a kind of liberation of the guilt I've long suppressed. I will not apologize for what was done, for the result has been my greatest joy. I only hope you will find it in your heart to one day forgive me for my cowardice in not admitting it.

Olive gaped at the words for too long. She felt both grateful and frightened. It was more than she ever imagined her papa would tell her about her real father. And it should be enough information. How hard would it be to find a Tal'at Sharif who'd been to England and worked at a traveler's club, in a place as contained in population as Rasheed? If Lord Whitmore had given her the letter earlier, Olive could have easily asked Yasser about him and got an answer.

But what if Tal'at didn't want to meet her? Didn't want to have anything to do with her? Her husband certainly didn't.

Adnan was upset over his mother, as he had a right

to be, but Olive was not oblivious. She had sensed his regret from the start, practically since he had first proposed marriage. She had managed to ignore it because it was what she needed in order to stay in Egypt, but it was not easy to feel utterly unwanted whilst keeping such a shameful secret.

Now that Olive knew the truth about her parentage, she wondered if she'd always fear rejection.

Not having had a mother had been devastating growing up, but Lord Whitmore had been Olive's haven. Any hurts she suffered, any assurances she needed, he'd been there, solid, loving, wanting only for her to be happy once again. But what if, as he alluded to in his letter, that too had been him trying to assuage his own guilt?

If only Papa hadn't lied to me from the start, I could have been reconciled to it.

Olive had known of at least two young ladies among the *ton* with scandals in their parents' past. And was not her friendship with Elise nurtured outside the confines of London Society?

She tossed the letter to the towel she'd abandoned by the bath then smashed the water with both fists.

Her hot tears came then. She was alone—she could allow it—but they also brought into relief how long she'd been there, how cold the water felt now.

She rose, just as the unlocked door opened.

Adnan.

His trousers had been rolled up at the knees and his shirt, though not completely off, was unbuttoned so that with a small push at the shoulders, it would have been. There was a smattering of black hair across his chest, broad but narrowing at the waist as if sculpted with a precise knife. Olive had never seen a bare-chested man before—or if she had she could not recall them being as *enticing* as the one before her.

'I didn't know you were in here.' He sounded apologetic, even *kind*—which gave her pause.

When Adnan averted his eyes, Olive realized that if he were half naked, she was entirely so.

He rushed to grab the towel she'd dropped and wrapped it around her, covering her body. 'You'll catch your death with cold.'

'No. It…is…fine.' Despite her best efforts, the words emerged between chattering teeth. She disliked proving him right.

He snapped, 'How foolish are you?'

When she'd gained her composure and warmed a bit, she said, 'I'd rather be foolish than cruel.'

That was enough to silence him. He helped her step out of the bath, and she caught a glimpse of her father's letter on the floor. She reached for it instinctively, then crumpled it and immediately tossed it into the tub so that its ink would fade.

She wouldn't need to refer to it again. Olive knew exactly who she was looking for now.

'There is a rubbish bin outside.' Adnan began to admonish, but then must have felt her cold skin for he quickly led her outside and to her room.

Or more precisely, what should have been *their* wedding night suite.

Awareness crossed his face as he took in the closet she hadn't shut with his clothes. And hers.

'Put on the warmest thing you have and come with me to the other room—there's a fire there already.'

'I don't want to disturb your mother.'

'You won't.' He turned around while she slipped the warmest dress over her head to cover herself. She'd have said it was enough but her teeth were starting to chatter. A fire would be nice.

When she was ready, she turned to find that Adnan had buttoned up his shirt and rolled down his trousers.

Probably for the best.

They walked in silence across the foyer. When they entered the room, at the sight of his mother looking so frail, Olive held her breath and waited for the sound of Elham's light breathing, guessing that Adnan had done the same. Her gut clenched for mother and son.

She settled near the fireplace where a pile of plush pillows had been gathered. He'd been here; she could smell his lingering cologne: a soft but deep scent, with notes of clove and pine.

After rearranging what she'd disturbed, he sat next to her. Folding his long legs beneath him, the movement had Olive looking away because it was oddly intimate.

'You've been crying,' he said.

'Not because of you,' she countered.

He grinned. It wasn't a smile like those he saved for his siblings but it felt like she'd bested him a little bit.

'I am glad because no man should make a woman cry.' He cupped his perfect knees. 'What you over-heard, what I said... I am sorry, truly. It is no excuse but my father was pestering me, has been all day and didn't stop even when my mother—'

'About what?'

Adnan pursed his lips and the fire's amber glow hit his clenched jaw. He'd shaved his beard for the wedding but the stubble was coming in now. He'd had nearly a full beard when she first met him in Rasheed and just then she rather thought she'd like to see him in it again.

'A honeymoon. He'd planned a trip. I'm supposed to show you Egyptian culture in Aswan, a romantic riverboat cruise along the Nile.'

Olive didn't know what to say to that, so she remained quiet. And Adnan, with his unrivalled ability to not feel the necessity of filling in a lull in conversation, said no more either.

Who would break the silence first?

Apparently, she would, for Olive didn't like what

otherwise might come out of her mouth. 'Your mother. What's her diagnosis? Her prognosis?'

'A cancer, in her blood. She has been sick for a few years, seen by the best doctors. Last winter they said she would not survive it.' He shook his head. 'Every extra day since then feels like thievery. Or a gift. And then I wonder who is, in fact, being robbed?'

There was a truth to Adnan's words that pierced Olive's very being.

'*Allah kareem.*' She'd heard it being said in Rasheed. It seemed fitting now. It meant that God was generous.

Adnan gave her a nod of agreement. 'She was happy today, believing me settled, married. I am grateful for that.'

Olive wasn't sure if he was thanking her for being a part of it or for something else. And, as per his norm, he did not elaborate further.

'I cannot imagine the impending sense of loss,' she said.

'Can you not? You lost your mother as well.'

'I was but an infant. I did not have a lifetime of memories. Or any, for that matter.'

Adnan examined her for a long minute, his finger on his temple. 'It is late but we will talk more tomorrow morning about what you said at the wedding, what you want to do in Egypt before you leave here. I will grant it, Olive, and we can go our separate ways thereafter. I only wish to prioritize my mother's peace for a little longer.'

Adnan was being a gentleman, telling her he'd heard her and would grant Olive's request. Why then was she fending off yet another wave of disappointment? Might it be the bit about them separating? Did he mean that they would get a divorce? She might have been first to mention going their own paths, but she'd assumed that he, of all people, would not accept the idea without any argument to the contrary.

Olive swallowed down that increasingly familiar lump of rejection forming in her throat. She turned to look back at the sickly woman in the bed. 'Your mother's health is most important.'

Adnan stood. 'Stay here for a short while until I start the fire in your room. You will sleep comfortably there.'

Olive leaned back. She must have been more exhausted than she thought, for when she next opened her eyes, the fire had burned out and dawn's sun was peeking into the room.

Adnan had covered her with a blanket, but she had spent their wedding night alone.

Chapter Five

Adnan

When his emotions ran high, Adnan went running.

Seeing Olive in the bath when he certainly didn't expect her there? *Breathtaking.*

Then, after he'd gone to warm her room, returning to find her asleep at the foot of his mother's bed? *Heart-wrenching.*

He'd thought of carrying her back to her room, but feared she'd stir and he'd not want to leave thereafter.

If their marriage was going to end, best keep away from any *intimate* relations beforehand.

Instead, Adnan had returned to what would have been their wedding night suite. He too had slept on the floor near the fireplace, weary of disrupting the scattered rose petals on the bed. It would be an irritant for whoever would have to clean them up. Adnan supposed it would have been a thoughtful detail if marriage matters had been conducted as they normally might have, and if his mother wasn't lying ill in the next room having taken a turn for the worse. In truth, he'd barely slept and kept on checking on her throughout the night.

He filled his lungs with the crisp morning air now. His heart raced as his feet pounded the perimeter of the garden, appreciating the outdoors of the palace after spending the night stifled inside of it. And he didn't expect it would get less stifling until they left. While the apartment Nawal had prepared was private, members of the family would descend on them soon enough. His mother surely wouldn't like the fuss or the feeling that she was at all beholden to the khedive and his chosen family.

He'd ask her as soon as she was awake. And although he'd dismissed it yesterday, what his father had said about taking Olive's needs into consideration gave Adnan pause.

Her father had left this morning and whether Adnan liked it or not, she was his responsibility now.

'*As Salam alaykum, ya ameer,*' the palace gardener, Raaouf, greeted him. He was a middle-aged man who Adnan often ran into since he liked to take the fruit tree path into the palace rather than the formal gates with all their pretence and saluting guards in uniform. He'd had conversations with the gardener about how the land differed across Egypt. Raaouf came from Upper Egypt and was a wealth of knowledge. He was a diligent worker and trustworthy. Raaouf was one of his brother's first hires, a menial task their father had given him, but one that proved Saleem had good instincts.

If it hadn't been for that fact, Adnan would have lured Raaouf away to come work for him. Adnan didn't believe his instincts were not as good as Saleem's, but he differed in that he usually made decisions *after* careful deliberation. That was probably why Adnan was conflicted about asking Olive to marry him when he had: there'd been no deliberation on the matter whatsoever.

'My tolerance for palace gossip is limited,' Raaouf claimed, reaching for a basket behind the trunk of a date palm, 'but I heard there was a wedding which happened yesterday. A thousand congratulations!'

He handed Adnan the basket. 'For your bride—*mish mish* from my tree. Tell her that apricots are rare this early and do not last long when they are ripe so best hide it from any she'd not want to share with.'

Adnan thanked him, '*Shukran*, I am sure she will enjoy them.' He remembered what his mother used to say about apricots and why they were her favourite fruit because 'their season is short and forces us to enjoy them.'

Her season, her life, was nearly over and Adnan had been angry with her for too long.

As he'd been out of the palace for too long.

After shaking Raaouf's hand, he ran back, thinking he'd have time to bathe before Olive was awake. But to Adnan's chagrin, when he entered their apartment, it was clear that any privacy they'd enjoyed thus far was over.

All three of his sisters were there along with two of his cousins and one of the maids. The latter stood near the door to the room he had slept in, looking unsure of her role.

The wedding night bed with all those rose petals had not been disturbed. Surely the palace residents would not gossip about whether he and Olive consummated their marriage after his mother had taken ill?

Speaking of which, where was his new wife?

'You've been running,' Nawal observed, with a teasing wrinkle of her nose.

'Why are you all here so early?' he quipped back. 'I thought you woke up in the late afternoon.'

'We wanted to check on Elham Hanem,' his youngest sister said, adding the title out of respect for his mother, then greeted him with a kiss on the cheek.

His cousin said, 'We brought *fitoor*, but your *wife* said our style of breakfast wouldn't do.'

Adnan noticed a toasty smell from the apartment kitchen, which he hadn't thought was equipped for cooking. 'How "wouldn't do"?'

'See for yourself.' Nawal angled her head towards the room but he was already crossing the foyer.

His mother was sitting up in the bed and Olive was feeding her something from a bowl. They were talking, even laughing at something out of his earshot. He tried to ignore the depth of warmth and gratitude he felt not just at seeing his mother awake, but that Olive was with her.

'*Ummi*, how are you feeling?' he asked, forcing himself to not just observe from the door and make his way to her bedside.

'Grudgingly, I will say, better.'

'Why "grudgingly"?'

'Because she does not appreciate the breakfast I have prepared for her which is meant to make her feel better.' Olive's Arabic was careful, broken, but that she'd understood the words and known how to respond was impressive.

Adnan dug a finger into the bowl, and found it like a thick pudding, sweetened with milk and honey. He tasted it and it was…*nice*. 'You made this?'

A look crossed Olive's face, one he could only describe as akin to bashful.

'It is called porridge,' she said, 'and it is a properly nourishing English breakfast. It is meant to be made with oatmeal or barley but the maid said the kitchens only had semolina.'

Adnan reprimanded his mother, 'Why do you not like it? It is delicious, comparable to *mahalabiya*.'

'Exactly! A dessert for those with no teeth. Give

me fried eggs, fowl with *baladi* bread, a plate of salty, crunchy beet-coloured pickled turnips.'

His mother's sullenness was in jest but Adnan was concerned Olive would be upset by it, considering the work she had done. She had been crying in the bathtub last night, after all.

When had he started to notice that she had feelings?

Maybe his concern was because he wouldn't have expected the daughter of a lord to know her way around a kitchen at all.

It dawned on Adnan that there was much he didn't know about Olive. And that maybe he wouldn't mind getting better acquainted with her.

'Those foods upset your stomach with their heaviness, *Ummi*,' he told his mother. 'The doctor says as much, the nurses as well. I nag you about it.'

Olive smiled. 'Thank you for supporting me.'

His mother scoffed, 'Adnan is your husband. If he does not support you, then no man will. Clearly, not even one's own son.'

Olive chuckled, and that initial feeling of warmth spread in Adnan.

'Why are you not as funny as your mother?' she asked, cocking an eyebrow at him.

'Adnan takes things much too seriously. Perhaps he will learn to ease now he is a married man.' His mother pointed to the basket in his hand. 'What's that?'

'A gift from the gardener's home. He heard about

the wedding and sent it for Olive.' Adnan lifted the handkerchief to show them the apricots inside.

'*Mish mish*.' His mother clapped. 'It is my favourite fruit.'

'Would you like me to cut one up in your porridge?' Olive asked but his mother had already grabbed one and was digging in.

'It is your gift but perhaps we should offer some to the ladies outside, send them on their way?' Adnan asked, switching to English. Olive nodded appreciatively. It was nice to speak to someone in a way others could not understand. It had been necessary in certain situations with Saleem, but with Olive it felt more intimate. And Adnan could grudgingly—there was that word again—admit to himself that it was more exciting too.

Lowering her voice, Olive said, 'It was kind of them to ensure all is well…but they were asking very many *questions*.'

Her cheeks reddened at that last word and Adnan did not need to ruminate on the wide-ranging line of questions. He loved his sisters but they could come off as intrusive to those who did not know them.

'I will ensure they do not bother you again.'

He kissed his mother's head, then taking the fruit that remained in the basket, he closed the door and offered them to his sisters and cousins. '*Ya'Allah*, Nawal, lead everyone back to where they came from.'

'You're lucky I insisted on only us. There are many more in the east wing eager to visit. I had to quell a wailing Maysoon,' Nawal explained as the others filtered out.

He chuckled. 'As she should have. May equals all of you put together. Next time send my niece alone.' He hugged her goodbye. 'Pass along that there is no need to worry. My mother seems better and Olive is...' He wasn't sure how to finish that sentence but his sister didn't need him to.

'We're concerned for you, brother. This was not the best way to start a marriage. It was already happening too fast and then the bout with your mother at the same time...'

Nawal had a parting word before she left. 'One piece of advice? Bathe. The maid drew a fresh bath and so you know because none will tell you—goats don't always need to smell like goats.'

'I was running,' he protested as she scurried off with a laugh.

He bolted the door behind her and proceeded to take said bath. Of course, he couldn't help remembering how Olive had looked there.

I hope the water is cold.

Adnan needed sobering.

When he was done and feeling refreshed in a newly pressed shirt and trousers, he returned to the room to find his mother telling Olive a story about her youth.

One he'd never heard.

Adnan held his breath, afraid she'd stop if she knew he was listening.

'...there we were, in the middle of Cairo, lost. Me, Elham, the lone daughter of a widowed housekeeper, and her friend Ahmed, who also happened to be the Prince of Egypt but was wearing his sleeping clothes because he'd run away from his father out of anger so that none recognized him. But that wasn't good either because people in the street were not in awe of him at all. And he was mad about it! Very mad.'

'How old were you both?' Olive asked, sounding mesmerized.

'Twelve or eleven even. We had no monies on our person, no bodyguards or any adults to help us. And it was getting dark. Ahmed had the idea to climb to the top of the citadel to map out the city and see our way back home. "Elevation makes the path clear," he said—already sounding more like his father than he cared to admit, but it was a smart thing to do. We found our way back here, depending on each other, taking breaks when our feet felt like they would fall off. And even though we thought we would starve before we arrived, a vendor took pity on us and gave us paper cones filled with *lib*, roasted watermelon seeds. It was the best meal I ever had. Ahmed too.'

Adnan didn't feel comfortable eavesdropping on

their conversation and it was Olive's next question that had him interrupting, for fear of hearing the answer.

'Is that when you and the khedive first fell in love?'

Adnan cleared his throat, drawing attention to himself. Olive turned to him with that same look he'd seen at the wedding. What was it exactly? Her words were never that measured but she looked nearly afraid that she'd said the wrong thing.

Adnan wished he knew her better, wished he could understand what was going on in her mind when she did say things despite knowing she'd regret them.

'You did not tell me that tale of adventure, *Ummi*.'

'You never asked.'

'I'm sorry if my question brought up bad memories,' Olive said.

'Not at all, my dear, that was one of my fondest ones,' his mother said, a comment which, were he honest, pained Adnan. What did it say about their mother-son relationship that he wasn't privy to her memories so near the end of her life?

Because he was sure that his question wouldn't be as brazen as Olive's, he asked, 'Do you find it hard to be in the palace now? Would you rather go home? We could leave immediately if you feel up to it.'

His mother stifled a yawn. 'I think it is an immediate nap I need, but I do not mind staying here, Adnan. You leave me, take your new wife out, for my sake.

She should not be cooped up with a sickly old woman so soon after her wedding.'

'I cannot leave you.'

His mother wiggled downward and deeper into the bed. 'Show Olive the citadel, a felluca ride on the Nile. For me, the way I did it once with your father. The two of you can sneak out without any guards following. I insist so that you can narrate your version of my story when you return and I wake from my nap rested enough to hear it.'

Chapter Six

Olive

It was the same sun the world over, yet its mysterious effect on Olive's being in Egypt could not be denied. She marvelled most at its willfulness. Winter was decidedly over and summer had not exactly begun but the sun in Cairo seemed not to care for the seasons.

She tried to explain as much to Adnan. 'It does not heed convention—it is an independent entity.'

'A hellish one then,' he said, squinting at it, then wagging a finger to the sky. 'And this isn't even its worst. A few more weeks and Cairo will be unlivable and there will be none to blame save for that sun up there. Anybody with any means will try and escape the city.'

'Where to?'

'Alexandria or anywhere else along the Mediterranean or Red Seas. The salty breeze from them fights the sun's wrath. Even if it is not always successful then it is a good distraction.'

'What an odd way of describing it!' she argued. 'The sea is beautiful in its own right. Think of its turquoise waters glittering under the sun. It is inspiration and healing for the soul, not merely an escape or a distraction. We can swim or frolic there, use it as a means of travel. A conduit for the exchange of goods.'

'How is it that you sound both like Saleem and my father at once? Ever hear of the sea's stormy waters or her tempests? Ships and *lives* are lost in it.'

He'd smiled to imply it was spoken in jest but Olive had to ask, 'Must everything be antagonistic with you?'

'I am a realist. I prefer truths, boldfaced as they may be.'

They'd come to the felucca, a rickety sailboat, which looked much too small to hold both of them along with the boatman who'd get them across the Nile. Adnan held out a hand to help her board and when Olive took it, she nearly blanched at the all-too-vivid and recent memory of him seeing her naked last night. *The picture of him, half so himself.* Then came the thought that she would not mind seeing that again.

In the sunlight.

Fearing he'd read her thoughts, she lowered her gaze, focusing on her skirt as she lifted it with her free hand. The wobbling made her unsteady but Adnan held tight, his grip unwavering. He placed a foot into the boat to further stabilize it, then waited until she was seated before releasing her hand and taking the seat beside her.

The bench was snug but especially so when the boatman hoisted a lateen sail and took the opposite bench with its attached oar.

Adnan said something to him that Olive didn't quite catch, but then the man shuffled around so that his back was to them.

'We can't have him watching you the whole time,' Adnan huffed in English. 'It is good you are dressed in the style of local women. Otherwise the men who stare at you would not cease. They see a beautiful woman and utterly forget their manners. Are English men the same?'

'With me? No.'

Was Adnan being protective? Was he saying she was beautiful or was he actually...*jealous*? She hadn't noticed the boatman but he was probably Adnan's age, perhaps a little younger. It struck her that she'd no idea her new husband's age.

'How old are you?'

Adnan threw her a shake of his head. 'Why are you asking?'

'We got married so quickly and I do not know it. I do not know much about you.'

Adnan watched the horizon as the boat set on its

course, moving away from the banks until they were in a deeper channel of the Nile. 'How much do you need to know if our marriage will not last for long?'

Olive did not know how to feel about how candidly he'd asked it. 'Would it be terribly awful if we were to become friends for the duration?'

'I do not subscribe to "friendship" as others might.'

She watched him, the way the sun and shimmering water played on his face whilst he refused to even squint. He seemed introspective, yet he was wrong about himself in this. She had seen Adnan with his siblings. Was that not friendship?

'You know I wanted to marry to stay in the country, Adnan, but why did you ask me? What do you benefit from our time together?'

She gripped the boat's gunwale, steeling herself for some insult or another, but it wasn't forthcoming. In fact, his voice softened and he took a moment to carefully craft his words. 'I have asked myself that too. I witnessed how you were that day in Alexandria, pushing to marry my brother, who was clearly in love with Elise—'

'I have apologized and feel bad for not seeing it.'

'Everyone saw it, Olive. I'm not saying it to place blame on you, but to explain that you were oblivious because you were…distraught. And I could not disregard a lady in such a predicament.'

'Is it because of your mother?'

He thought about it. 'Because she is sick, you mean? Perhaps yes, but also because she was alone in the world with me after her and my father divorced.'

'I am sorry for being rude when I met her, for not properly understanding the past relationship with your father.'

'In truth, I have yet to understand it myself.'

Olive waited for him to say more but when he didn't, she sighed. 'It is a shame she is so ill. She's a lovely woman, strong willed. Funny.'

The movement of the oars, cutting through the still Nile waters, filled the somewhat awkward silence that followed.

Finally Adnan said, 'You asked what I would get out of our marriage. I want my mother's happiness. You were good to her this morning, kind. I would ask that you continue to be like that with her, ensure that she dies knowing that her son is settled. Happy, even.' He turned to her with his whole body, his knee brushing against her thigh. 'It goes against all I believe about truth and lies, but can you pretend to be my wife?'

Olive was tired of duplicity; she didn't want to pretend anything. 'You mentioned it last night, prioritizing your mother's peace, and I agreed. There is no lie, Adnan. I am your wife.'

'On paper, yes, but by Egyptian laws, which are influenced by Islamic jurisprudence, until a marriage is *consummated*…a woman retains her rights.' Adnan studied her face until she felt herself flushing with the intensity of it.

Olive knew what he meant by 'consummated' but replied, 'I am unsure what you mean by "rights." Will you explain it to me?'

'Until a husband and wife lie together in a carnal way, a formal divorce with all its detrimental effects would not be an issue. When a couple who have not been intimate—and therefore there is no possibility of the woman being pregnant—decide to separate, their marriage would be considered an annulment, a broken engagement even. In Islamic law it is called *fasakh*, and I believe that Christian faiths have a version of it as well.'

She had been so intent on marrying as a path to staying in Egypt that Olive hadn't thought about the ramifications of divorce. She'd pushed the possible scandal, and the shame society doles out to divorced women, to the back of her mind because of the grander shame that came with knowing that her father wasn't Lord Whitmore. A scandal that would surely be worse were it to be revealed in London.

'We would both be virgins still. Do you see?'

'I do *see*,' she answered because Adnan was waiting for a response and she didn't want to think too much about him being a virgin too. She hadn't thought of him as a rake and knew that Muslim men were supposed to only be intimate with their wives, but Adnan was a prince and Olive believed that such men wrote their own rules. And she certainly did not want to dwell on the fact that if they'd had a proper marriage, she would have been his first.

His brow furrowed. 'Is that not your plan, to go back to England? Remarry, have a family?'

She nearly scoffed at the absurdity of that. 'Until I do what I came to Egypt for in the first, I cannot bring myself to think of a future at all.' She hastily added, 'I can, however, offer support to your mother in the meantime. I am happy to be a daughter to her.'

'Thank you.' He swallowed before shifting his body to face forward again. 'That is all that matters.'

His gratitude was nearly corporeal, reflecting the love he had for his mother. It was there in the tenseness of his shoulders, the way he gripped his knees. Olive found it touching, enough that she needed to stop herself from reaching out and squeezing his hands with her own.

She settled for saying 'You are a good son.'

He shook his head. 'I have not always been. I was mad when I found out who my father was, the lie I'd grown up with, but since turning on him was hard to do because of his position as leader of the country, she suffered me. I treated her poorly. Not outright, she is my mother after all, but our relationship was altered. The fact that the khedive kept up with my news, knew what kind of youth I was growing to be, that information could have only come from her. It meant that even after they divorced, they communicated in secret and I had a hard time forgiving that.'

'I understand.' If Olive knew anything, it was something about altered parental relationships.

When Adnan turned his neck so that his face and hers were inches apart, Olive's gaze was drawn to a tiny mole over his right eyebrow. It was the blackest of black, as if he'd been pierced there, branded, with the prick of a burning pin.

'Can we agree then,' he said, 'that ours will be a marriage of mutual convenience to be annulled after my mother…passes? Your presence will keep her happy until then and I will offer you the standing to pursue what you want to in Egypt.'

She appreciated that Adnan did not ask her about what she needed his standing to do.

'Shall we shake hands on it?' she asked, holding out hers. He took it and held it for longer than he probably should have, and she felt the loss of it when he let go and then blurted, 'And no intimate relations!'

'No! We will have none of that.'

She tried not to dwell on the brusqueness of that response and how he wrinkled his nose as he said it. He added, 'Whatever you need to do is in Rasheed, I presume?'

'It is, yes.'

He waited a minute, perhaps expecting her to say more. 'Would it be all right if there is a…delay?'

He did not know when his mother would be gone and just like he'd not wanted to go on a honeymoon, he did not want to leave Elham's side now.

'I can wait until it is possible.' Olive had wanted to return to Rasheed as soon as he'd taken her from it the first time, and it had been weeks since then. But she did feel sorry for Adnan, knew that it was more important to spend the time with someone who was dying than someone Olive had not even known existed for most of her life.

She decided that she could indeed wait a bit longer to find her father. Spending time with Elham would be good for Olive too. It would give her perspective, give her the chance to reflect on the future which would come after she and Adnan separated. 'What I wish to do in Rasheed can wait.'

'You can tell me what it is, if you like. Perhaps there is more I can do to help?'

Olive bit her lip, wondering if she *could* tell Adnan about learning that her real father was an Egyptian named Tal'at. It might be a relief to tell somebody. But by his own admission, Adnan was not the friendship sort and if they were headed towards an annulment after his mother passed, then it was best she not get too attached to either one of them.

Could Olive expose her shame to him? She had a

feeling that Adnan's reaction to learning she wasn't Lord Whitmore's daughter would further devastate her.

Still, if she gave him a hint of it, maybe it would ease some of her burden.

'There is a man in Rasheed I wish to find. He knew my parents, my mother, in England, before I was born. I am hoping he can tell me more about her.'

Adnan's eyes roamed over her face, searching. Olive's only reprieve was to look away. She didn't want to know what he might be wondering about her or her mother but all he asked was 'Do you have a name for this man?'

'Enough of one that I believe Yasser of the Rosetta Carriage Company would be able to help find him.'

'That is why you were glad to see him at the wedding?'

Something in his tone gave Olive pause. Why did the prospect of Adnan noticing her actions move her? Like his reaction to the felucca driver, she wondered if it was jealousy. She supposed Yasser was a handsome man, but Olive did not find him attractive. If she were being honest, it was Adnan's interest that excited her more, likely because he was a hard man to stir.

'I did not expect him to be there for it hadn't seemed like you two were *friends* in Rasheed, and given what you've recently told me about your position on friendship, I was right.'

He smiled. 'Yasser was delivering the papers for a business venture of mine in his city.'

Olive wondered why a Prince of Egypt would ever need to be a businessman as well.

Before she could ask, the boatman announced they'd arrived. 'Wasalna.'

As they stepped out on the banks of the Nile any conversation that might have continued between them was supplanted by the sounds and sights of midday Cairo.

Rasheed was quite small, everything was fairly close to the single train station and Olive got a handle on its terrain from the first day. And while Alexandria was a much bigger city and she'd not stayed there long, she could immediately tell it was very different to Cairo in terms of the layout. During Elise and Saleem's wedding at the coastal palace they called the Lodge, she'd gone for a stroll to the highest peak and could practically see the whole of the city from it, how it winded like a road along the sea. If Alexandria was long, it was not very wide.

Nothing like what sprawled before them now of Cairo.

Adnan hailed a *hantoor* carriage and told the driver that they wished to go to the citadel. As they rode on, he drew her attention to the height and magnificence of the pyramids dotting the skyline, but told her that they were actually quite far from them. 'We can visit another time, but today we're here per my mother's request and should get back sooner rather than later.'

She wondered whether there ever would be another time considering they'd already shaken hands on the utility of their marriage. No recreational activities—carnal or otherwise—were a part of their deal.

Streets and pathways branched in all directions, and ancient palm trees watched guard over young-limbed shrubs, some of which were fluorescent pink dahlias, while others were white flowering hawthorns. Tall, modern buildings with apartments and balconies were being built next to traditional homes with *mashribiya*-latticed wooden screen shuttered windows and iron pillar gates as doorways.

Everywhere were the sounds of life *moving*. Merchants noisily selling their wares, parties of people gossiping, horses clomping in the traffic alongside donkeys who trudged with their loads. Bells on bicycles, shouting from a football game along the sidewalk.

When they reached the citadel, Adnan told her that it was built on hills called the Mokattam. After a long upward trek, Olive was amazed to find it was walled in the manner of medieval-era forts. From her position in the carriage, she could not tell what was inside its walls and that must have been their purpose for she doubted any would know until they were past them. Rising above it, however, was a structure with multiple and majestic minarets and domes shining silver.

'The Alabaster Mosque,' Adnan named it, leaning over to peek outside of the carriage window, 'although some call it after the khedive who renovated it years ago—the Muhammad Ali Mosque.'

When the *hantoor* halted at the gate, Adnan helped her out, then guided Olive to an inconspicuous corner. He looked left and right, as if ensuring it was safe enough for her, and then said, 'Wait here.'

She followed his form as he walked. His stride was quick, long, as he moved towards the citadel guards. She saw Adnan reach into his pocket to give the one standing the farthest away from the group what she assumed were monies. The latter took it and ran off whilst the others remained speaking to Adnan. They were out of earshot but Olive could tell that even as he was listening to them, his watchful eye on her did not falter.

His care for her today, when last night he'd shouted the very opposite sentiment, was jolting. Adnan had apologized, said that it was his father's pestering that caused it—but why was he so different now, away from the palace, with none to witness it?

Adnan strode back to her, his arms pumping, his chest tight. The stance of a runner.

She'd noticed it when he'd come back this morning. Ladies would stroll along the promenade near their London home and she conformed to that slower pace, despite Elise's constant pestering to go faster. Olive had always thought it wouldn't befit her station as a lord's daughter.

Now I'm not that, perhaps I'll take up running too.

Who was she fooling with that thought?

'Ready for some physical exertion?' Adnan asked when he returned, sensing her thought and then having one of his own. 'I mean to say that it is quite the long climb to where we are going.'

'Oh.' Olive was distracted by the intimate suggestion of 'physical exertion'. But since they were safe from that possibility, she was struck with a touch of flirtatiousness. Had not his mother insisted that today was supposed to be fun?

'If you will take it slow with me.'

Adnan nodded stiffly, catching her meaning and reddening when he did.

'You are blushing,' she said, to which he had no reply.

He had his revenge, however, as she huffed and puffed her way up what seemed like the world's longest staircase. It was old and dusty, steep with parts the hem of her skirt would snag upon. Adnan kept turning to check on her, telling her they could go back. When she refused, he encouraged her by saying it would be worth it.

'How much further?' Olive asked one last time, ready to give in for surely going down would be easier.

'From what I can see, three more stairs.' True to his

word, a minute later, Adnan opened the door to the highest point of the citadel. The rooftop had a gathering of stone lions at its centre.

'This tower is called Burj al Siba, named for those very lions,' he said.

Olive ran a hand along the stone mane of one. 'It is as if they have come from across the land to contemplate on the city's fate amid a threat only they are privy to.'

Adnan examined them to see if there was merit in her fanciful statement. Rather than dismiss her fancifulness outright, he said, 'I could not tell you since I do not know much about the building. A proper tour guide or historian would go over the history of the citadel but I did not want to take more time than we have.'

Olive barely heard what he was saying. She found she was drawn to the edge of the roof and strolled there to discover how spectacular the view of the city was. All of Cairo was before her. 'It is as if the best and most detailed of maps has come alive,' she marvelled.

This time, Adnan did not humour her. 'Be careful. The ledge is not high.'

But he relaxed when he came to stand by her, his elbow touching hers. He pointed out a spot near to the west. 'You see that bright tent, the white one? It is an alleyway in our neighbourhood. At first it was rarely brought out, erected only for the biggest occasions when people needed to gather, but the city has grown so much that it is now rarely taken down. Eid celebrations or community Ramadan iftars. Weddings, funerals.'

He is thinking about his mother. To distract him from his sadness, Olive asked about the brightly coloured flags in another street and he told her they were actually a little medieval trick in lieu of fancier street lights that were expensive and troublesome to upkeep. He talked about the different shops that were there, the mosque that he often prayed in, a large old tree that children avoided walking near because they were convinced it was a portal to the world of the jinn.

'What a thriving area of rich culture.'

'It is,' he agreed. 'My father believes my upbringing there was a detriment, that it made me uncultured. That being married to an Englishwoman will make me less so. Did I mention the trip we were supposed to take to Aswan?'

Adnan was clearly still angry about it.

'You did,' she said. 'It would have been a nice trip, but a terrible reason to take it.'

He watched her for a minute so that Olive almost believed that she saw something in her that was working to quell his anger with the khedive.

It made her feel *needed*.

'Was Lord Whitmore the same with you,' he asked, 'trying to make you into his image? Turn you into who he wanted you to be?'

'No.' Olive dipped her head and thought about how Lord Whitmore would be boarding his ship soon. When would she see him again? The thought that she didn't have an answer gave her pause. Was it sadness?

'Papa let me lead the way often. He called me "head-strong" certainly, but always in a loving, gentle way. Accepting. Even encouraging. He put in protections when he was not sure I would be safe. Elise, whenever she was around. One of the responsible older maids whenever she was not. And now, I suppose, he trusts I will be safe with you.'

When Olive angled her face to look at him after she'd said it, Adnan's smile seemed somewhat, but not *exactly* identical to, the kind he reserved for his siblings.

Chapter Seven

Adnan

It was hard to admit but Adnan was starting to see how wrong he'd been in his presumptions about Olive. She was kinder, even more sensible than he'd thought—but what she'd said about her relationship with her father puzzled him the most.

She was hiding something, but he'd had enough lies to last a lifetime. He did not know how long he could suppress the need to know, but right then he felt grateful to Olive for agreeing to be a daughter-in-law to his mother in her last days. Going against his nature of wanting all the knowledge before he embarked on something was the right thing to do. Maybe too, Adnan thought, it would be nice if Olive were to trust him, to share what she wanted to in her own time.

'I don't know much about you, *husband*.' Olive tore him from his thoughts 'Tell me more about who you are. This business you've mentioned. Your favourite colour. Your age—I believe I asked you that earlier and you did not enlighten me with an answer.'

'Not much, you say? Do you know anything about me at all?' He was trying to tease her because her calling him 'husband' stirred something in Adnan he did not want moved. For Olive's part, however, she took the question seriously, her brows knitting in an endearing manner.

'Do you need more time to think about it?' he asked.

She threw up her hands with a laugh. 'All I know is that you're a grump.'

'A grump? Yes, you've called me that before.' He angled his head and shrugged. 'If facing matters with seriousness as per their due is perceived as grumpiness, then I cede it. But I can relax sometimes.'

'Yes, you do have that one smile reserved only for your siblings. I've seen it with Nawal and Saleem. It is like you forget for just a minute that you are carrying the world on your shoulders. The burdens disappear and you're not entirely sure what the lightness means but you give yourself permission to not question it. It is remarkable to witness, like a midday eclipse, a change in your entire being, a—' Olive had been lost in the description and when she noticed him staring, she abruptly realized all she had said.

Adnan couldn't help but frown as she looked at him to see the effect of her words. What could she read on his face? Even he didn't yet understand how he felt about them.

Her own face reddened. 'And there is the frown! Adnan, I do not mean to make you conscious of… Never mind me. I say foolish things…without thinking beforehand.'

Adnan didn't want to make the moment between them more awkward than it already was. 'Sugar. Green. Twenty-eight.'

'Huh?'

'You asked what I do for business. I invest in agriculture, sugar cane crops in particular. I bought a piece of land in Sohag, built a company there that is doing well and I am looking to expand in areas like Rasheed, which has traditionally been more used to cotton crops as you might have noticed in the *ezzbah* you were at. Green is my favourite colour, the shade of trees, grass, because it means the earth is healthy, thriving. And I am twenty-eight years old. Now you know a few more things about your grump of a husband.'

Adnan crossed his arms over his chest and though he would not smile, he wanted Olive to see that he could be fun as well.

'Well, I do like sugar,' she said.

'I know.'

'How?'

'It was all you were choosing to eat from the assortment offered in the food parcels at the wedding.'

'Very well. Do you also know my favourite colour then?'

'Blue.'

Olive gaped. 'Someone must have told you.'

He shook his head. 'I wasn't entirely sure of that one but you confirmed my theory that those with blue eyes like that colour best.' Adnan pressed his lips together lest he say more about how the shade of blue of her eyes might cause him to amend his favourite colour.

'You will not know my age.'

'You turn twenty-three in—' Adnan made a smug show of counting on his fingers '—exactly three weeks to the day.'

'What day is it?' Olive did her own count and found he was right. She groaned, 'How could you possibly know that?'

'Some of us actually read marriage contracts before we sign them. Consider the details.'

'Sounds like what grumps are wont to do.' Olive wagged her finger in his face and Adnan had the urge to grab it, bring it to his lips. What was wrong with him? Wasn't 'no intimate relations' a condition to the marriage deal they'd agreed?

Thankfully, they were interrupted by the guard he'd paid to bring them food.

The man seemed to want to ask questions about who they were, but Adnan had honed the art of silencing any discourse and getting things done to his satisfaction. It started by choosing the quieter people—it had been his experience that they were the smarter ones in a group, or at least the less arrogant—and posing a direct question to ascertain if they were suitable to the task in question. In this case, if the man knew the location of the bakery. Then Adnan paid double the price of said specific task, and stressed that his directions needed no additions or improvisations. As the task was being completed, he would keep one hand in his pocket to indicate that a tip was forthcoming. The result was that people did what Adnan wanted and they did it in efficient silence.

Adnan wasn't as rude as his father, who demanded obedience because of his position; neither was he as nice and forgiving as Saleem, who retained his charming demeanor in spite of his position as heir to the khedive. Even before he knew who his father was, Adnan had had to cultivate a tough exterior in his dealings with others—his wasn't the easiest of neighbourhoods, and a divorced mother was more often than not a favourite subject of gossip.

Olive, however, was oblivious to his art. As the guard was setting up the food, she thanked him in Arabic and then mentioned how wonderful it smelled.

'And look at that steam, it is hot too!'

The guard giggled at the comment, perhaps because he was nervous in the presence of such a beautiful woman or by her manner of speaking in Arabic. Either way, what kind of self-respecting man giggled?

Adnan responded by shooing him away. '*Khalas*, leave it. We can handle the rest.' The additional tip was not given.

At least Olive hadn't realized she'd disrupted his method, wholly focused on the food as she was. He said, 'You need to tell me when you're hungry.'

'I am fine.'

'The breakfast tray meant for two was untouched when I ate it all myself—and even I am peckish now.'

'You're a man who's been running. Women have to be more careful with their bodies.'

'It is not care when you do not eat, Olive. Rather, it is neglect. Besides which, your body is perfect.' He was stating it as a matter of fact but she flushed. Wanting to show he wasn't always grumpy, he added, 'You can be sure I am right because, as you may recall, I have seen it.'

'Adnan!'

Something about the tone she took in admonishing him made him fear that he might begin blushing, giggling like the guard, so he set to cutting her a piece. 'Custard and powdered sugar *fiteer mishaltit*. It is from a place that doesn't include paper or utensils to eat with, but if you protrude your face outward as you bite in, your clothes will remain clean.'

He watched as she did so per his instruction. Her

eyes closed for an instant and she practically moaned, 'Oh my goodness, that is delicious. The buttery, paper-thin layers of dough, the way it flakes and yet melts in my mouth. And that filling? Custard, you say? I have never tasted one so divine.'

'I think they add fresh *eishta* to it, what the English call clotted cream.' Adnan would let her eat all the sweet but he preferred the savoury cheese and sausage. He lifted a bite to her mouth. 'This should be more satiating. Try it.'

She took a bite and swallowed. 'I like the other better.'

'Of course you do.'

As they ate and enjoyed the view, Adnan told her about how he'd stumbled upon the *fiteer* maker a few years ago, before the man's bakery was famous. 'Now the line stretches the whole street.'

'How did the guard bring it so fast?'

Adnan tossed her a smug look. 'I told him the secret word that would allow him entry into the back.'

'Is it not terrible now the guard knows it, what if he tells others?' Olive asked, but from the way she bit her lip, eager to hear his answer, it was clear she wasn't asking for the guard.

Adnan was not dense; he knew she had a secret, but as before when it came to not questioning her about the relationship with her father, he didn't want to speculate. He could squelch his nature to be curious and cautious and he could empathize with burdens people needed to sometimes carry on their own. Was that not his plight?

'It is not terrible,' he said. 'It only means that the shop owner and I will have to find a new secret word when next we meet. I go there often enough that it should not be hard to do.'

They finished eating fairly quickly and he was about to announce that they should get back to the palace when Olive asked if he might take her to a market-place beforehand. 'I don't want to rely on the kitchens having the right ingredients. I'd like to make dinner for us. Your mother and you. Maybe proper porridge in the morning as well.'

'Really, dinner?'

'Don't look so flabbergasted. Consider it a thank-you for today.'

'There's no need for thanks, Olive. We have a mar-riage deal, remember? You are kind to my mother while she's alive and I will be your husband so that you can stay in the country and find who you're look-ing for, the man who knew your parents.'

There was no need to repeat the details, except to re-mind himself that the soft sentiment that was between them wouldn't last. Adnan should not get accustomed to having a wife—not one who made him dinner.

'Marketplaces are a hobby of mine, a favorite pas-time of mine in London, ranking each for which was best and for what items. I was quite looking forward to doing the same here but since you bombarded me in Rasheed, I have yet to visit a single one. You owe me a marketplace, Mr Grumpy.'

It had hurt Adnan's pride to have to stay with his mother at the palace until he could take her home. At least this way, they'd not have to rely on the khedive's staff for their meals as well. He could have brought in his own domestic help but it would be awkward to do so when the palace was filled with them. Olive had given him a way out of that; surely none could blame her for wanting to make him and his mother a meal here and there.

'All right, *wife*, you shall visit the marketplace. But you'll have to hold my hand the whole time and not talk to any merchants at all. They'll increase prices and give us the worst of their products if they sense a hint of non-Egyptian blood. That is the thing you need to know about our marketplaces.'

She argued, 'How will you know what I want?'

'You point and whisper the amount in my ear.'

Olive gave an exaggerated sigh of exasperation, but when she offered up her hand, he knew she'd accepted the directive. Now it was up to Adnan to keep his wits about him as she whispered in his ear.

He guessed that would probably be the hardest part of the near perfect day, but as it turned out, the hardest was when, whilst Adnan was paying for a bunch of parsley and radishes, Olive sauntered away and he feared he'd lost her in the crowd.

His mind throbbed with the horrible things that might happen to a beautiful woman alone. There were men who acted like hungry dogs hiding among the horde, searching for prey.

Then Adnan's distress turned to annoyance. *Must Olive be watched like an errant child at all times?*

When he spotted her at a shop selling decorative furnishings, he rushed to her side with a lightness in his steps, as if a disaster of monumental proportions had been averted.

And it had all happened in the span of a few moments.

'What is it called?' she asked, oblivious to Adnan's fretting. She pointed to an ornamental game board sitting atop a table with two chairs straddling it, 'I saw the older men playing it in the cafes in Rasheed but it is unlike chess, which I am definitely not good at playing. All the moving parts and skill sets of each piece, the thinking ahead.'

At that last bit, Olive grinned with self-deprecation. *Endearing*, indeed.

Adnan focused on the games, understanding the differentiation she was making with regards to their strategies. 'This game is called *tawla*, much like the table it sits on. It is a version of backgammon, somewhat more straightforward, yes, than what we call *shata-rang*, or chess—but the end goals of both are similar.'

He wanted to say he could teach her if she liked but he wondered what use it would be, how much time they would have together anyway.

So Adnan said nothing.

It was late afternoon when they finally sneaked back into the palace, managing to enter through Raaouf's garden shed off the back of the kitchen. They covertly ran up the winding staircase with their bags, avoiding both the hallways that led to the harem and his father's working offices. They did bump into two maids and a butler but Adnan knew how to handle them.

After the last, Olive laughingly asked, 'What was that look? The widening of the eyeballs along with the one-two shake of your head. Are you asking them to be discreet or threatening them?'

He realized it must look ridiculous and he had to smile at her description. 'After I learned who my father was, I used to come and go here to visit my siblings. That was one of the looks Saleem taught me, because he was always getting into trouble.'

'So you were boys then but now you're grown men and still doing it.'

She laughed again and it was a pretty sound to listen to.

Still, feigning grumpiness, he remarked only 'Except you're going to ruin it because you cannot keep quiet.'

Finally, they made it to the stillness of their apartment and while Olive got started on their supper, he went to check on his mother.

She was up but looked more tired than when he'd left her.

'Your bride will fret over that worried expression,' she said. 'You're supposed to be a happy groom despite your dying mother.'

If only she'd seen him minutes ago.

Adnan sat down beside her, took her hand in his. 'Do not speak of that.'

'That I will die? We both know it is true, my son. We were weary of saying it aloud before but I can now, glad there is a future for you after it. A family of your own. A wife. Many children, *insha'Allah*.'

His mother's content smile was further proof that Adnan had made the right bargain with Olive. Whatever sadness that would come after she was gone or anger he'd face from his father when he and Olive ended their marriage would be bearable knowing his mother died thinking her son was happily set for life.

She asked now, 'Where is your wife?'

'Olive is cooking you supper but made me promise not to say anything about it until she can add her perspective on the meal.'

'*W'Allah*, I like her very much! When you told me about marrying her, I worried. It didn't seem like you wanted it. The haste I could understand because of me but I was sure you'd never want to be with an Englishwoman who was originally intended for your brother. But Olive, she seems very much like an Egyptian woman, very much like the sort of woman I'd always pictured you with.'

Adnan didn't want to dwell on his mother's words, the agreement she knew nothing about. Instead, he pulled out a bag of roasted seeds. 'We brought you this from the marketplace. Olive said it would be in honour of your first outing to the citadel. Let me split them for you.'

She managed a few before yawning and telling him he should wake her again when their dinner was ready.

'Go, help your wife cook for it is the pinnacle of romance when a man enters the kitchen to serve his woman.'

It occurred to Adnan that if Olive was there, she might have asked what story his mother could tell about how she'd come to that knowledge.

And though he wouldn't ask on her behalf, it was a thought that—dare Adnan admit it—made Olive's reckless tongue more tolerable, perhaps even admirable.

He would have liked the answer but he knew better than to dwell too much on her tongue, especially at a time when his feelings towards his wife were heightened.

They'd agreed to no intimate relations, after all.

Chapter Eight

Olive

They fell into a routine over the few next days. Adnan's mother, who insisted Olive call her Elham, seemed to feel better with the porridge she'd make her in the early morning. It gave her a few hours of energy which Adnan enjoyed alongside them, Elham telling anecdotes or giving advice and Olive trying to soak up all her wisdom. Then, while Adnan went to his work, Olive would read or tidy up while the nurses bathed or administered any medications his mother needed. When Adnan returned in the late afternoon, they would eat a heavier meal, an Egyptian *ghada*, or lunch, but earlier than a typical English supper. A few times these meals were per Elham's direction— 'so that my son will always have his mother's meals on hand'—and other times Olive would cook what she felt like eating. A pot roast with root vegetables one time, and another time a cottage pie.

She wrote down Elham's recipes for lentil soup and an aubergine accompaniment called baba ganoush. Olive's favourite to make was the *macarona bil bechamel* with its ground mince and pretty penne-cut pasta that had been dried and then imported from Italy. It was baked in a rich cream-and-butter sauce, which contained Elham's secret ingredient of nutmeg.

Adnan would grunt his pleasure and, when reminded to by his mother, offer her compliments. It didn't come naturally to him to do so, but that was all right. Olive knew the food tasted good by how he eagerly he ate, how he cleaned his plate. More than once, he'd catch her watching him eat to see his reaction and he'd slow down and get—dare she say *bashful* about it. And bashfulness was definitely not in his nature!

Perhaps his reaction to her watching him had to do with her comment about the smile which Adnan reserved for his siblings. Ever since she'd mentioned it that day on the citadel's rooftop, he'd been more conscious around her. She had regretted letting it slip at the time, but the look he gave her now instead—a half smile, nearly a smolder—well, that made her regret it less. Olive fancied *that* non-smile was one he reserved for her.

And it heated her body in a way that was not at all unpleasant.

Adnan would encourage Olive to *kuli*, or eat, right after each such smirk, which was a word that took on a whole different meaning, particularly when she was alone in her bed at night, thinking about it. Thinking about *him*.

He routinely built a fire for her in what should have been their shared bedroom, then left her alone to return to his place at the foot of his mother's bedside.

Olive sometimes even *nearly* forgot her mission to find her father in Rasheed. She nearly forgot her shame too. Nearly, but not quite. It assailed her when Adnan's relatives from the harem came to visit. Some would look at her with what Olive perceived as ill judgement, or make comments about how very 'Egyptian' she was becoming as if it were an unfortunate occurrence. Where she wanted to practice her Arabic, they only wanted to talk English or French, which had never been her strong suit. And God forbid she let her hair free in front of them. One of Adnan's cousins rudely pointed out that 'Those are the curls of a country maid. You need to spend time in the bath, put oils, and iron it out!'

Olive haughtily replied, 'My husband likes it.'

She hadn't known where that came from; Adnan certainly hadn't said anything about her hair. But the cousin snorted a laugh and whispered a word that Olive didn't know but it must have been bawdy for it garnered a scolding from Nawal. Amid the reprimand, Olive did understand the cousin's defense of her comment: 'It was in jest for the maids say they have not yet shared a bed.'

The next morning after breakfast and, while his mother was resting, Adnan came to Olive in the tiny quarters of the kitchen.

'Nawal told me how our cousin was rude to you yesterday. She wants me to convey their apologies.'

'It was nothing I could not handle.'

She wondered if his sister had also relayed to him the rumors surrounding their marriage bed. She might have asked but was stunned to silence when he let his gaze circle the frame of her face as if following the hands of a clock. He picked a loose strand. 'Your hair is perfect. Any who say otherwise cannot see clearly.'

She didn't know how to respond to that, but Adnan quickly let it go, went on as if he'd not held it between his fingers, as if he'd not said anything at all. Had she misheard him?

'I have said that none should visit but they wait until I am gone to defy my orders. Today we shall thwart them for I will not leave you at their mercy. I only have a short meeting downstairs with my father's ambassador to India. After it, we can go to the pyramids. We talked about it that day at the citadel. We can throw in a camel ride whilst there—it's the best way to see them and it means no walking up a thousand and one stairs. No rickety felluca ride across the Nile. Nothing to tire you.'

'Are you mocking my lack of athleticism, Prince Adnan? I may not be a runner like yourself but I do not mind a good stroll at a steady pace now and then.'

He held up both hands. 'I only wish to do what is comfortable for you.'

'I used to ride horses when I was a girl. How difficult can a camel be?'

'They're very different beasts, but you'll see that for yourself.'

'Very well. Shall I get ready?'

Adnan was standing in her way, a distracted look on his face.

'There is one other thing. I think it is time for us to leave the palace. My mother's doctor is coming to check on her tomorrow morning and if all is well then, we'll go. Would you like that? Our home is not the palace but it is comfortable—no unchecked visits from others at least. The kitchen is certainly larger than this one too.'

He placed a hand on the counter and she could feel the intimacy between them, the warmth of the stove in the cramped quarters.

Olive couldn't help but feel pent up with his nearness. It wasn't an unpleasant feeling but one she knew she ought to fight. Adnan, however, was not making it easy.

He was taller than her by a good foot but when he stepped closer, and looked down on her, it was almost as if their heights were on par. Perhaps it was the curl in her toes that urged her to rise up on them when he was near.

'Would you agree to come with me, my mother and I, I mean...to leave here, with us?' he asked, stumbling a bit on his words at the end. Then he straightened. 'You are free to remain here if you would rather.'

'Hmm...a larger kitchen would be appreciated.'

Adnan laughed. She had caught him off guard and it was...*nice*.

'Good. I shall take that as a yes. Go prepare for that camel ride then. I will return for you shortly.

Olive had no idea what one wore on such an outing.

She rifled through her things, remembering that, having seen photographs of tourist activities in Egypt in one of the newspapers back in London, she'd packed boots and leather gloves in her travel chest. She pulled them out now and though they would likely be hot, she thought that those in the pictures would have been the same. If they could manage camel riding in such get-ups, so could she! She rang for a maid to help ensure her breeches and safety skirt were on well enough, Olive then donned a blouse and long coat. It was appropriate wear for riding side-saddle.

When the maid left, task completed, Olive stepped out of her room with a large brown hat. She angled it over her head and managed to lower the organza veil that surrounded its brim. It was the most fashionable part of an outfit but yet, Olive felt frumpy in it regardless.

She was altogether rethinking the outfit when Adnan returned from his meeting.

'Will you not be hot in *all* that?' he asked, lifting his brows to indicate the hat in particular.

It was the smug look on his face that made Olive say 'It is meant to protect one from the sun. I shall be fine.'

As they descended the stairs to the waiting carriage, Adnan offered his arm. 'In case you cannot see past the…what would you call that? Mosquito net.'

It was pure stubbornness on her part that made Olive stick to the spiraled railing and say, 'I can see fine, thank you very much.'

She would not admit Adnan was right, even if she thought the roads which led them to the pyramids seemed to have been paved upon a desert inferno. She tried not to display her discomfort nor complain and whilst Adnan did not say he'd told her so, he did toss her a smug look now and again.

Funny how she could sense *that* beneath her hat.

Nevertheless, his princely side triumphed over whatever pettiness he could have doled out, for the first thing he did when they arrived and before she'd even descended from the carriage was to hail down a juice seller.

Adnan handed her the cold drink he called *erq sous*. 'It's made with licorice root and mint—an acquired taste but sweet enough for you, I think. It will help you face the sun best.'

Olive lifted the netting and took one sip and then another. It was refreshing enough that she downed it almost immediately. Adnan helped her out of the carriage and then pointed out the seller, a colourfully costumed man—not too different from the members of the band at their wedding. He had a gallon of the juice strapped to his back from which he poured into drinking glasses that were upon a block of ice. 'I have to give the cup back to him but would you like another?'

'Perhaps on our way back.' Olive had become aware of the magnificence of their surroundings. No picture she'd seen in a newspaper could have done the place justice. The pyramids of Giza were a city in and of themselves, no wonder she could see them in the skyline from the other side of Cairo for they were huge! A single stone on the bottom level of the middle pyramid they'd stopped closest to was taller than a carriage and as wide as one.

'What a marvel,' she exclaimed. 'They make you feel so small, so insignificant.'

Adnan got a faraway look in his eyes. 'My father brought me and Saleem here a few years ago, said he wanted to show us our birthright, the leaders we descended from, to inspire us to be greater. He cleared the entire place so we could walk the length of it, even had an archaeologist give us a tour of the inner chambers of the smallest pyramid. Most of the treasures and preserved bodies had been removed but there were a few left there. We did not learn the lesson my father intended, but both of us were moved by the experience, to be sure.'

Maybe because she'd been denied it from her real father, Olive was curious. 'What lessons did you learn?'

'For Saleem, it awakened a love of history, a desire that all Egyptians should learn about their past and have access to it. When he studied at university, his interests and ties were always with the professors who had a hand in archaeology. I have never seen him as excited as when they discovered the catacombs of Kom El Shoqafa in Alexandria.'

Olive watched Adnan's expression, how it softened when he spoke of his younger brother, and she had the sudden thought that he would make a wonderful father one day. She imagined him to be the type to nurture each of his children's individual interests and share in the joy they'd get from them as if they were his interests too.

She reprimanded herself for thinking of Adnan being a father when she wouldn't be in his life for very much longer. 'And what of you? What lesson did you derive from that visit to the pyramids?'

'That the arrogance of man is limitless and we should fastidiously fight it within ourselves.'

And then he started reciting a poem she'd not heard

of but it was magical listening to him stating it by heart. If Olive were focused more on the lines, she might have got the gist of the poem better but she only caught it was about a king named Ozymandias and lone sands.

Adnan searched for her gaze beneath the organza veil. She hoped he could not see her stricken face, the enchantment she was feeling. He said, 'It was written by Percy Shelley.'

Olive couldn't recall the name but managed, 'The Englishman?'

He nodded just as his name was being called by someone in the distance.

'Adnan! Adnan Ali Ahmed! Woohoo!'

They both turned towards the direction of the bellowing. Olive lifted her veil to see clearer and was struck by the vision of a woman with rich auburn hair catching the sun's rays, a green-and-gold *galabaya* lassoing it so that it haloed around her.

Olive's heart sank to the bottom of her heavy equestrian boots.

The woman looked like a Cleopatra coming to claim her Anthony.

Chapter Nine

Adnan

'Dalia, meet Lady Whitmore. Dalia's eldest brother manages the sugar factory in Sohag,' he told Olive by way of introduction. The two women shook hands in a manner friendly enough, but Olive was looking at Dalia oddly and he did not think it was his place to disclose that Olive knew how to speak Arabic.

Dalia said to Adnan, 'What a fortuitous day for you to make the trek up to the pyramids.' She pointed to the people lining up to be photographed at the base of the farther pyramid—a relatively new venture but one that was engendering a visitor economy across the country when their photos were published along with their writings on Egypt. 'Is the *hanem* a diplomatic guest looking for a souvenir of her travels?'

Adnan felt Olive's eyes on him. But he couldn't admit to Dalia that he'd got married. She'd mention it to her brother in Sohag—and while he knew Adnan was a Prince of Egypt, he had kept it a secret. He didn't want to have to explain an annulment to him.

'We are here for a camel ride around the pyramids but I have not yet asked the lady if she'd like a photograph.'

Dalia tugged at her *galabaya*, then lifted it to show how loose it was. She gave a quick shake of her hips and said, 'This is what a woman needs to wear to get up on those camels, not *that*.' She gave Olive's outfit a once-over.

Olive huffed, in English, 'What a ridiculous display and yet we are here standing talking to her, even whilst away from your ill mother. Or have you forgotten?'

He bristled, not needing the reminder. 'Apologies, Dalia, but I must take the lady for her camel ride. Give my best to your brother when you return to Sohag.'

He turned but Dalia tugged on his sleeve.

'Forget the camels,' she implored. 'There's a better way to see the pyramids. The Englishwoman will get the ride of her life and when she returns to her country she will tell all how grand Masr is, that we are Umm al Dounia.'

Egypt, Mother of the World. Adnan disliked thinking that his father would like that line and he should remember to share it with him. 'No, thank you.'

Adnan was starting to walk away but Dalia tugged his arm.

'My cousins are with me—we travelled all the way

to start a business venture of our own. Please follow me.' She pointed towards the back of a collection of carriages.

'Another time, perhaps,' Adnan said even as Olive started walking in the direction.

Dalia clapped happily, urging her onward. Adnan rushed to catch up with her. 'What are you doing?'

'Seeing what she has to offer.'

Was that a note of jealousy in Olive's tone? Adnan tried not to make too much out of it, might not have even recognized it if it wasn't for something in her stance that reminded him of himself whenever other men were around Olive.

Behind the carriages, a large basket was squared off with sticks in the sand that formed a fence. There was a big contraption behind it and a pungent odor in the air. It took him a minute to realize what it was.

'A hot-air balloon!' Olive exclaimed.

He'd never seen one in Egypt. Never been in one. Saleem had when he'd visited Turkey a few years ago and said it was a good time but he'd never want to do it again. Try Everything Once was his brother's mantra. It was not Adnan's.

'I want to go up,' Olive said, surprising Dalia with her Arabic. Before he could refuse, Dalia ran off to set it up with her cousins.

Adnan had never sought out such adventures. Not from fear, but simply because they didn't appeal to him, but something about Olive's doggedness was catching. It made him suddenly want to throw caution to the wind. Adnan would not allow Olive to accompany him. He didn't want to put her in any danger. He recalled that moment when he thought he'd lost her in the marketplace a few days earlier. The horrible feeling. This could end up much worse.

'It is dangerous. I will go up alone to test the safety,' he decided.

Olive pouted but he marched to where Dalia and one of her cousins were, unwilling to hear any protests.

'Unfortunately,' the cousin said after he'd pocketed Adnan's piastres and explained the basic mechanisms of the balloon, 'we need two people in the basket for the stabilizing effect.'

'I will accompany you.' Dalia gestured to the people standing around, waiting to see the balloon in action. 'A woman with a thimble of courage shames even the bravest of men. And there are only cowards here.'

She marched towards the balloon whilst he turned back to Olive. 'The ride will not take long. You can wait there and if all is well, I'll take you up next.' He pointed to where Dalia's cousin would be managing the contraption, deeming that the man would be cognizant of her in the hopes he'd earn an extra tip.

'No. I am coming with you,' Olive declared. 'The balloon ride was my idea.'

'Exactly. I am merely testing it for you.'

Olive pointed to Dalia, who'd hiked up her dress and was getting inside. 'You would go up with her instead? Is that proper, being alone and in close proximity with a woman who is not your wife?'

Where had that come from?

Olive marched ahead of him, but he didn't like to be told what was proper. He did have his own barometer for that.

'Dalia,' he said, 'perhaps I should go up with your cousin instead. Your parents surely haven't sent you here to be—'

'Come now, this is modern Cairo,' she tutted, 'not the confines of Sohag where everyone knows everyone and a girl would be shamed for spending any time with a boy.'

'Perhaps the confines are there for a reason then, because we should not change *who* we are when we change *where* we are,' Adnan countered with one of his own personal beliefs, albeit one he struggled with most considering the rift at the very core of his identity between Prince and the man raised in one of the city's roughest areas.

His tone quieted Dalia, but Olive did not care. She edged her way to the top of the basket.

'I will go with him—you leave us.' she declared in Arabic. 'Adnan is my husband.'

Dalia looked shocked but it was Olive, struggling to get in with her convoluted skirt, who required Adnan's full attention. He moved to her side, grabbing her by the waist and sweeping her off her feet before she hurt herself. In one quick motion, he had stepped over the rim of the basket and lifted her inside.

With them both, it was close quarters. Very close.

'You can set me down now,' Olive remarked, a bit breathless.

Adnan wasn't sure he wanted to. She felt right in his arms. Like she belonged there. And while his carrying of Olive—overdressed as she was for the excursion—spoke to his strength of body, why then was he experiencing a weakness of the knees?

'I said, set me down,' Olive demanded. She was not, however, wriggling to free herself.

'And I said that you need to go back and be safe.'

But then the shouting from Dalia's cousin commenced and the top of the balloon was being inflated above their heads and that noise drowned out everything else. The skin of the balloon was a bright red that was almost as much of an eyesore as staring directly at the sun might be.

There was no way she would be safe under that thing.

Even as he squinted to try to find a way to get Olive out of the balloon, they began floating upward. They were off the ground, a few feet and then some more. Dalia's cousins were managing ropes attached to each corner of the basket. Long ones. *How high up were they meant to go?*

As their basket lurched and bobbed, Adnan finally set Olive down for fear he'd lose balance and she would be hurt.

'You stubborn, reckless woman. You should not be here. You should be sitting side-saddle between the humps of a camel down there, posing for a picture.'

'While you go gallivanting with other women?' Olive yelled over the hissing gas. Or was she yelling because she was angry? She swayed and he took her hands, tried to guide her to clutch the rim of the basket. But she was more interested in poking him in the chest. 'Why did you not tell that woman that I was your wife?'

Before he could answer, Olive swayed with a sudden movement of the balloon, toppling onto him. He held her close, their gazes locked. When had she removed the hat's veil? Why were her eyes outdoing the blue of the sky? Why was it that he feared she could read his every emotion, what was behind every smile or frown, as if they were written in ink on the pages of a book?

He reprimanded himself for the trail of his thoughts.

He needed to stay alert. This required more focus than the felucca ride on their way to the citadel. This would not be a dip in the Nile if things went wrong. A fall here could mean the difference between life and death.

Adnan twisted Olive around, leaned his body over hers, made her clutch the rim and gave her no room to do otherwise.

'You're stubborn,' he repeated in her ear, whilst trying not to deeply inhale the perfume of the jasmine flower that her hair carried beneath that ridiculous hat.

As the balloon rose higher, everything got smaller, more insignificant. People had gathered to watch but their cheers faded with the distance and the hiss of the balloon.

Adnan could easily believe that they were the only two people in the world.

Olive's heart strummed so hard, he seemed to feel it through her back and in his own chest, pressed as hard as it was to her body.

She turned her head so that the side of her cheek was near his mouth. 'You can let go of me, Adnan. I will not jump.'

'Will you promise to hold onto the rim?'

When she nodded, he moved back, releasing his grip on her and, to his chagrin, having to quell his desire so that the lingering *effect* of their nearness would not be noticeable.

For the next few minutes, they said nothing to each other, each taking in the view of the pyramids from opposite ends of the basket. The hiss of the gas, the heat it generated seemed to diminish and the higher up they went, the more incredible it became. Cooling too.

It was one thing to see the magnitude of the pyramids from the ground, but another from this level. It was nearly like they were eye to eye with those who'd built them and he wondered about the men who'd placed the last stone on the top of the largest of the pyramids. Adnan knew they must have been slaves but he also could not help but think they must have experienced a sense of great wonderment and accomplishment. They would have felt like they were the kings of the world.

'The Sphinx,' Olive mouthed.

From their angle, it was hard not to see it as the stone body of a lion rising from the bedrock, its mane the human head of a pharaoh. Around it, the camels circled like bored ants around a mound of food that had long dried out, no matter the enthusiasm of their riders, which Adnan assumed they had.

Adnan tried to enjoy it, to let the experience of being higher than he'd ever been fill his senses, but his mind leaned towards criticism. He thought about how he'd steer the balloon properly so that it would be a smoother ride. He'd hold tighter to the ropes, ensure those who held with him were the same build so that those going up would not experience the jerky movements. If Adnan were in charge, he'd make balloon rides safer.

'It feels like flying.' Olive removed her grip on the rim of the basket and spread her arms wide. She closed her eyes, then threw away her hat, and laughed as she leaned over and watched it flying in the sky.

He held his breath. Tried to remain still. *One sudden move. She wouldn't dare try to retrieve it!*

'You broke your promise,' he said, sure she wouldn't hear.

'And you didn't tell that woman you're a married man,' she admonished.

'Why does that bother you, Olive? I did not tell a lie.'

'You kept a secret and I hate when people pretend to be who they are not.'

He would have told her the reason why, admitted he wasn't sure how long they'd be together once his mother was gone and Olive had done what she'd come to do in Egypt.

Instead he asked, 'Are you having fun, Olive?'

For wasn't that the goal of the outing?

'I am not Olive.' She whooped, 'I am a bird. A biiirrrd.'

Watching her being free, being privy to her as she soared…? Adnan had to admit it was a perspective that he was most grateful to witness.

Chapter Ten

Olive

Something shifted in Olive after the balloon ride concluded and they'd touched the ground again. She'd thrown away her hat, basked in Adnan's nearness, was giddy with the way he watched her, the desire in his eyes, and though she'd tried to hide the fact, she'd noticed his body too. They'd returned to the palace in silence, their gazes locked for most of the trip and only when they'd passed the gates did he remember:

'We forgot about the camel ride.'

'I suppose you owe me another trip then.'

He smiled in response and Olive had to quell every bone in her body to not cross over to his side of the carriage and beg him to hold her. Kiss her.

Take her.

She blanched beneath the flint in his eyes, the perfect shape of his full lips, his chiselled jaw, the controlled tightness of his entire body. She imagined what it would be like to be the one to make him loosen, unwind his rigidness. How would it feel to have Adnan's tautness and rigidity inside of her?

It was not safe to be around her husband anymore.

Olive had to keep focused. And, she reminded herself, Adnan wanted an annulment. Though he didn't always seem like it, he *was* a Prince of Egypt and she was the illegitimate daughter of a lord. She was no lady. Even if by some miracle their marriage could turn into something real, the khedive would not like to know his eldest son was married to a nobody. There was already a rift between Adnan and his father; she'd not be responsible for worsening it.

Especially when she still had hers to find.

She suspected that Adnan had intuited the shift as well, since for the next few days he made sure to spend the majority of his time away from the apartment, timing his presence to align with when his mother was sure to be awake.

Still, there were instances when it felt like he struggled as much with his desires and that it might be harder for him to be alone with her.

'Did you tell Adnan about your seamstress's apprentice in England?' Elham asked the next evening as she was bidding her goodnight. 'All the things she did to get pregnant?'

Olive was proud that Elham had liked one of the stories she'd told because she'd heard much more from her. She said to Adnan, 'Her name was Marta and she'd been married for a few years without conceiving. She always fancied she'd be a mother to many by then. She would ask all of the customers that walked in for advice—and word spread far and wide. I'd be at the marketplace and overhear women I'd never met asking on Marta's behalf for any new tricks. She visited midwives and apothecaries, took medicines meant to increase her husband's "appetite" but ended up turning her face blue so that he could barely stand to look at her alone...'

She'd begun the story without realizing that part would be more sensitive and even when she was first telling it, Elham lingered on that aspect. Had her mother-in-law been trying to initiate a discussion about when Olive and Adnan would have children?

Adnan's glance bobbed between her and his mother, as if wanting to interject and say something but thought better of it.

His silence forced Olive to finish the story. 'Marta even dragged her husband to Stonehenge, to undertake a strange pagan fertility ritual she'd heard about. He was arrested and spent a whole month in jail before the judge visited to hear his case. He was made a laughing stock.'

Elham chuckled and Adnan smiled. When he finally spoke, it was to ask, 'Did Marta get what she wanted in the end?'

'A baby?' Olive nodded eagerly. 'Triplets in one stomach! Nobody knew what was the winning formula in the end, but that way, at least three of the women whose advice was given could claim success for one of the babies.'

His mother laughed as heartily as she had the first time Olive told the story. Tired out, she quickly fell asleep thereafter.

She watched Adnan tenderly plump his mother's pillow and tuck the blanket around her shoulders.

As they stepped out of the room, they heard knocking at the door.

Adnan said, 'That sounds like my father.'

Sure enough it was. '*Khedewy*,' Adnan announced after opening the door and tossing a look towards her. 'Welcome.'

Olive hastily removed the apron she still wore from preparing their supper, and curtsied. She didn't know the proper protocol and hadn't really paid much attention to it when she first met the leader of Egypt in Alexandria, vexed as she was about leaving Rasheed and having to see Lord Whitmore without having found her real father yet.

She'd not really had any other occasion to greet the khedive after her wedding to Adnan. But Olive had the sense she shouldn't embarrass Adnan in front of him.

'Apologies, Your Highness, or is it Your Honour?'

she fumbled. 'I'm afraid my knowledge of English royal etiquette is much more established.'

The khedive didn't answer that for when she rose, she found him staring angrily at his son.

Barely looking at her, the khedive said, 'Lord Whitmore has sent word. He's arrived safely back in London and resumed his duties. I thought his daughter would like to know.'

That sounded ominous to Olive, especially when the khedive followed up with 'Will you give my son and me a moment alone? There are matters we need to discuss.'

'The workday is done,' Adnan countered, shoulders squared.

'It is not work that needs to be discussed.' The khedive met her gaze. 'Kindly, Olive?'

Her own gaze flickered to Adnan, sensing the tension between them and feeling somewhat protective of her husband—which was ridiculous since he could clearly hold his own.

But the khedive noticed and interjected, 'Surely Olive does not need your permission to do as I ask, Adnan?'

She wasn't sure what was going on but she didn't want to make the situation worse. 'It is not a problem, sir, I will leave you to it.'

'Apologies, Olive,' Adnan said tersely, 'whatever the matter, it should not take long.'

She crossed the space to her room feeling more self-conscious with her bare feet over the plush carpet. The men remained quiet until she'd shut the door to her room and though she tried to listen, she only heard muffled voices, cave-like as the private apartment was.

She paced, worried.

What if the khedive had found out about her parentage? What if he was telling Adnan that he needed to immediately separate from her and free their family of an illegitimate connection—or worse, send her back to Lord Whitmore without finding her real father?

But Adnan and I have a bargain.

He promised to take her back to Rasheed, find who she was looking for as soon as he could. And she thought that she fulfilled her part of the agreement with his mother, even if that aspect of it did not feel like an obligation. Plus, from what she knew of her husband, he did not seem the sort to renege on any bargain.

Maybe Olive should have told Adnan the whole truth. Dare she believe he'd even be kind about it, understanding even, given his parents' divorce?

The difference was that Lord Whitmore had sought out another man to be intimate with his wife and she was the result. Olive was not sure that Adnan would understand that. Given that their marriage was one of convenience and that its hastiness would likely be matched by its short duration, there was no purpose to telling him the whole truth.

But what if the khedive was exposing it a few feet away?

The worst of Olive's worries—which came as a surprise then—was that hers and Adnan's marriage would be done before it had a chance to be something more than what it was. What that *something* was exactly, she felt frustrated for not being able to name. She only knew that it was the same feeling of frustration experienced during the nights since returning from the pyramids.

And if she was being very truthful, maybe even that first night when he caught her naked in the bathtub. Olive decided that no matter what was happening outside of her door just then, once it was open and Adnan entered, she'd ask him not to leave.

She'd show him that it might be worth exploring that frustration, despite what he may have learned about her. Or what an annulment needed in order to be granted. It was reckless but wasn't recklessness the essence of her soul? Was it a trait one inherited from a parent?

Olive brushed her hair, let it loose. Slipped out of her clothes, and put on the negligee hanging from that first night. She dabbed her ear lobes with the jasmine blossom perfume she found in the dresser and blotted her lips with the rouge she wore on her wedding day.

Her heart pounded, just thinking about the prospect of what would happen with Adnan.

A shyness overtook her. What was she thinking?

I cannot do it. I will not seduce him.

It wasn't a part of their bargain; it was an explicit condition of it. Even if she wanted him, wanted to have a man hold her, experience lovemaking, it wasn't fair to use Adnan for it. He thought she cared about the opinion of London Society, that she wanted to return there afterwards, but the truth was that she didn't care. She was living in the present, not in an unforeseen future. She might not be able to speak the shameful truth about her real father, but she could tell him that much.

But before she'd decided definitively on what to do, Adnan entered.

A bewildered expression crossed his face when he saw her. He was *rattled.*

'I should have knocked,' he managed. 'My father left and I only wished to let you know. I…um…should leave.'

In getting to know Adnan better, Olive realized that he was quite adept at schooling his face so that he never seemed rattled. But now, he looked more than rattled. He was upset too.

Olive found herself miffed on his behalf. 'What did the khedive say?'

Adnan kept one hand on the knob of the bedroom

door and pushed his head back. She walked to his side and he didn't seem to know where to look. 'Nothing of value.'

'It clearly was not "nothing".' She touched a hand to his chest, wanting him to talk to her. Confide in her. She didn't expect the thrumming. The way his heart pounded and he avoided looking at her. 'Was it about me?'

When he didn't answer, Olive touched his cheek, demanding, waiting until his gaze finally locked on hers. God, the darkness in it simmered, refusing the lightness of the candles in the room.

'I tried to listen, but that door is…thick.'

'You would have heard only ugliness. He berated my behaviour, how I heaved my mother's illness upon you.'

'You have been nothing but good to me. Elham is the mother I have never known.' Just as soon as Olive swallowed with relief that his father hadn't found out the truth about hers, she gulped with the sentiment over Adnan's mother. When all was done, she'd lose her too.

The hand he had attached to the knob came up to her face. His thumb wiped the tears that fell. 'I am glad you did not hear any of it, he spoke crudely. If he were not my father, I'd have boxed him.'

The hitch in Adnan's tone put Olive on alert. 'Crude? How?'

His eyes fell to her lips. 'He reminded me that I am considered by many to be his illegitimate son, that I need to keep you happy, to think of the political implications of our marriage. That in lieu of a proper honeymoon, I sneak you out of the palace in common woman's garb rather than the full covering of women of the harem only because it's easier to unclothe you when we get back. Easier to ravish you. Yet harem word from the maids is that your virginity is intact. He wants me to be conscious of the gossip. He did not come out and ask what the truth was but if I'd given him the opening to, I think he might have.'

'Oh.' It was all Olive could muster but then Adnan leaned in, inhaled the perfume she'd dabbed beneath her ear lobe and it threw her off completely.

She thought briefly of her plan to seduce him. Her rethinking of it. And then she forgot about both, letting her recklessness lead her. 'He does not know about our agreement.'

'I could not tell him about that but joked that I have you cook for us, refuse to let you speak English because I want to tame you into a docile wife to match my uncultured, ungentlemanly status.' There was a sadness in his tone that he seemed to try to lighten. 'My apologies. I did not mean to speak of you so, but he angered me.'

'How long have things been strained between you?'

'Since I learned he was my father. But neither of

us have ever spoken about the lie that was there or the anger that brews now. For me, the conflict was always internal. For him, Saleem's upbringing took precedence. That is when my "illegitimacy", my common-man upbringing, served the khedive. When he thought I would be a good influence on his heir.' He took a deep breath. 'Now my counsel is unneeded, my father looks upon my commonness with disdain and I am unsure how to proceed because it is territory we have not ventured upon together before this.'

He shook his head like he'd made a mistake, not realized that he'd been lost in thought and had confided to her aloud. Olive recognized that look and put a hand to his cheek.

'You are a prince,' she said. 'Noble, gracious. Handsome. And I am not sure that any of that has to do with who your father is.'

Were the words for him or for herself?

Olive did not have time to think of the answer before Adnan's arm came around her waist and pulled her close.

With the movement, she could recognize that he was trying to change the subject. As she might have done when confidences became too vulnerable.

'Not a prince,' he said, his tone heady. 'I am like Edmund in *King Lear*. He is called the illegitimate, the bastard.'

Olive reacted viscerally to the comparison but she

could not tell if it was disdain or personal shame. Or excitement at her proximity to Adnan. 'I dislike that play of Shakespeare's. That word.'

Olive could feel the warmth from his breath. A warmth that, ironically, sent a chill up her arms. The minty tea he liked to brew in the evenings was intoxicating between them. He slid his thumb over the crux of her chin. Olive could not get enough of the movement and he seemed to know the effect for he continued.

Adnan held up the finger before her face, stopping. 'What are your thoughts on that word *bastard*?'

'It is an ugly one,' she heaved, barely conscious at how his mouth quirked thereafter.

He flirted, 'Tell me, Olive, do you think you'd want to be with a bastard?'

'*Be* with one?' She could tease him too.

Olive rose on her tiptoes, then touched her lips ever so gently to his. He groaned, both his hands cupping her face for a kiss. He brushed her lips, at first hesitant. She opened her mouth, welcoming. Wanting more. He deepened the kiss and that curl in her toes was nearly too much to handle for the sensation spread through her body and to every extremity. And when their tongues touched, she was sure she'd burst with pleasure. Staying on her toes was too much to bear, so Olive pushed her fingers through his hair, dragging him downward towards her. Adnan came willingly, kiss after glorious kiss.

Olive did not know how many they shared but when her lips throbbed, she wanted him to take his to other places. Adnan must have sensed it, for his mouth traced her chin, peppered her neck with kisses, slid down the collar of her gown.

He teetered on the crevice between her breasts for too long. Hesitating over whether to sample her there.

Then, finding his strength, he said, 'You are cold. Let me build you a fire.'

'Do not stop,' she demanded. She pressed her body against his until she felt the hard bulge between his legs pressing against her.

He tore himself away. 'We must stop before things get out of hand.'

'Must you always be so bossy?' She unfurled the tie at the top of her gown. She'd force him to carry her to the bed. Get her under the covers.

She dropped the top from her shoulders, wiggled out of it until her breasts were bared. Under Adnan's stare, her nipples grew hard.

He gave a quick shake of his neck, then went in for another kiss. It was rough and glorious. She wanted more.

'We have a pact, Olive.'

'What if I don't want to keep it?'

He stared at her for a long minute. He stressed,

'Making love to me, consummating our marriage, would make an annulment impossible.'

She stubbornly asked, 'What if I don't care?'

He shook his head. 'We are caught up in the moment.'

The shift, she thought. *Things were different between them.* She argued, 'Your father already assumes—'

'What he assumes does not matter. The maids gossiping will be to our advantage. It means an annulment will not be contested. Is that not what you want?'

Olive tried to not take Adnan's refusal as a rejection but seeing he was determined to end what was happening between them made it hard. She stepped back. 'What I wanted was for us to not care about what happens outside of this room for one night. To spend it in each other's arms. To satisfy our human desires—*bastardly* as they may be. I did not think of the consequences one way or the other.'

Which was true enough.

Adnan frowned. 'That story about the woman desperate for the baby you told my mother? You understand that may be a consequence of one reckless night.'

He spoke as if she was a child who did not know right from wrong.

She marched to the closet, put on the heaviest robe she could find. She lifted her hair up, wrapping it in a bun so tight it was sure to give her a headache.

'Goodnight, Adnan,' she dismissed him. 'I will not need a fire tonight.'

When he was gone, she cried over the shift between them that did not change anything.

Chapter Eleven

Adnan

As Adnan stared at Olive's door, thinking about that kiss—*kisses*—early the next morning, and her dismissal of him for not agreeing to take it further, he was reminded of another door.

The one in Rasheed, that first day they met.

He cringed with the memory of how he'd pounded on the cottage door then, angry as he was for her abandonment of Saleem and Elise in Alexandria. It had been early morning, she'd not had long to settle in and when she'd opened the door, confused, frightened in a new city perhaps, he'd railed at her. No wonder she believed him a grump.

Last night when he kissed her, almost let himself go entirely and surrender to his deep desire for Olive, he'd been so angry with his father that he wasn't thinking clearly. Was that the state in which one should ever make a hasty decision? Considering he'd asked for

Olive's hand in marriage that way, it would be more prudent for them to slow down.

When his father had been taking him to task, Adnan had held his tongue over the hypocrisy of him divorcing his mother and then trying to tell him how to behave with Olive.

He had thought to himself, *I am better than the khedive because when she and I separate, she will not be ruined by any pregnancy. Olive will not suffer as my mother did when he divorced her.* On the other hand, as angry as Adnan had been with his father last night, he hated the prospect of disappointing him. He'd been worried about any ensuing scandal his annulment might cause but a divorce would be much worse.

He wasn't sure how to feel after their kisses, how close they had been to going further.

Adnan could knock on her door, 'throw caution to the wind', as the English might say, and make love to Olive like there was no tomorrow. She was his wife today, after all, and that was what mattered.

No.

He'd survived the night on kisses; he could weather the day on his patience.

Adnan turned and took a quick bath, after which he prayed *fajr*. He disliked praying in places when a mosque was near, and would actively avoid praying in the palace, but Olive had turned the apartment corner into a suitable substitute. She'd chosen a beautiful mat and folding Koran stand with a set of *sibha* beads for his remembrances too. His father had rudely pointed out Olive's domestication last night but Adnan hadn't asked her to do any of it. She did what she wanted when she wanted. But after reflecting on their first meeting in Rasheed, Adnan could have counter-argued how he'd observed that she was happier with him, more at ease at least.

She'd wanted him to make love to her last night.

He'd felt her desire for him growing for a while but he'd brushed it off because he thought it was his own for her that clouded his judgement. Since the balloon ride, however, there was no denying it was there.

Adnan had no doubt that them making love would please her.

The sheikh in his mosque would often say that having a wife was completing your faith. He'd preach that just as bedding a woman outside of marriage was a forbidden *haram*, making love to your wife was a good deed, worthy of manifold rewards. The sheikh would say that a couple who felt invigorated and happy were enjoying a natural benefit of love-making in the sanctity of marriage.

What the sheikh wouldn't know was that Adnan and Olive did not plan to stay married. For all intents and purposes, theirs was a bargain, a temporary contract built upon convenience. Once his mother was gone and Olive's mission in Egypt complete, it would fail to be a marriage.

Was it halal to make love to a woman you did not love, one you did not plan to be a husband to for the rest of your life?

As he was pondering that question, the doctor arrived for his inspection of his mother.

'I'd like to take her home today,' Adnan told him. 'She seems to be getting better.'

'The nurses report to me the same. I do not like the idea of moving Elham but if, upon examination, all is well, I will go to the hospital and immediately send the ambulance carriage from there. It comes with orderlies and a stretcher, keep bumps to a minimum. It is the safest path. It is early yet but later on in the day, after the siesta, the roads will be less occupied.'

Adnan nodded and gave them privacy whilst he went to the kitchen to brew a pot of tea. He plated biscuits Olive had baked the day before—which he did not get to sample after…the kisses. He bit into one and was surprised to find it savoury rather than sweet. It was similar to the crunchy *ka'ak* they sold on the street carts but in a smaller form and flavoured with toasted cumin seeds.

Adnan was seized with the sense that he should buy her a gift, a token to express his appreciation for all she'd done. He should ask Nawal's or Saleem's advice about what exactly to gift her since he couldn't think of anything himself. He could practically hear them teasing him mercilessly for it, say his one-time indecisiveness must be due to a 'love' sickness.

He was setting down the tray of tea when the doctor emerged. Adnan didn't like the worry on his face. And then the quick shake of his head. 'I am sorry but Elham cannot move anywhere. Not today.' He put a hand on Adnan's shoulder. 'She is near the end. I suspect in the next few hours, and Allah knows best.'

Adnan's throat constricted. He sputtered, 'How? She was fine yesterday. Laughing.'

The doctor's words came in bits to Adnan's ears. 'I have seen it before, patients, they get better near the end so it seems like they are healing but it is sometimes a sign that…'

Adnan couldn't listen to the rest and he pushed past the doctor to see his mother lying in her bed. By the light of dawn, he could see her pale hue, even from afar.

'When she eats, drinks, she'll be better. There is this breakfast Olive…my wife… It's a porridge. She feeds it to her. I will wake her.'

'Your mother cannot eat anymore, Adnan. Her breathing is compromised. All you can do is stay with her, talk to her.' The doctor pointed to the prayer mat. 'Read her Koran, spend time with her, call all her loved ones to be near. Whatever and whoever eases Elham's passing.'

Adnan rushed to his mother's side. He touched her cheek but she didn't stir. She was cold, hard. He covered her with another blanket, but in the movement, he caught sight of her toes. They were a stone-like hue, curled over.

The fire was roaring now, but had it faltered in the night when he was too lost in the aftermath of kissing Olive?

He pulled off his own socks and worked to slip them onto her feet. They were too big for her; he might as well have been trying to put them on May's feet, small as his mother's were. He sat beside her, taking her right hand in both of his, trying to warm it under the covers.

Her eyes flickered, she tried to say something but gave up almost immediately.

He would not leave her side to bring the Koran but he began reciting all he knew by heart.

He told her that he loved her. That he was sorry for the pain he'd caused her. The bouts of silence. The anger. He begged for her forgiveness. Thanked her for all her sacrifices. Assured her that no matter what was written for him in the future that he would do his best to be a good man, give charity in her name. He promised too that he'd do the hajj pilgrimage on her behalf because she'd become sick before she was able to do it herself.

Adnan was not sure his mother had heard him but he sensed she did. And that she too was asking for forgiveness. That she wanted him to know that what she cared about most was his happiness. Contentment with his life.

When their silent communication ended, Adnan too felt the chill in the room. His mother's eyes opened in shock, her pupils trailing to the ceiling as if there was a bee flying overhead.

Then came the final exhale.

Adnan didn't know how long he lay there, his face buried at his mother's side, until he heard his name, became aware of the hand on his shoulder.

Olive.

She was trying to comfort him but his mother was gone and he did not want anyone to see him like this. Half orphaned.

When he looked up, the room was full, his pain there for all to witness.

The doctor had returned with the promised orderlies. Nawal, with her husband. His other sisters too. And behind them all stood his father.

But when he blinked and looked again, the khedive was gone.

In Adnan's mind, irrational as it may have been in that moment of his mother dying, he placed the blame on all present then. He knew it was wrong. His faith taught him it was Allah's decree that Elham Abdel Hameed, mother to Adnan Ahmed Ali, should die on this day and in this place and upon that bed but…she wouldn't have been here if it were not for his marriage festivities. And each of them played a part in those, but rather then rail against them all, he concentrated on Olive.

He shrugged away from under her hand.

'She should have been at home' was what he growled, biting down to not let spill what was on the tip of his tongue.

How Olive had been pathetic, practically forcing him to propose in the first. That she was too beautiful, that she made him feel weak for wanting to make love to her, break their pact. He would have told Olive that her kindness to his mother, her care, gave him false hope, made him believe she'd be with them for longer. The meals Olive made, the stories she coaxed, the hopes she engendered. The laughs they all shared.

What if that activity had expended his mother's limited energy?

It was Nawal's gentle coaxing that finally had Adnan letting go of his mother's hand. He allowed his sister's hug, let her comforting arms console him.

The orderlies covered his mother's body and expelled everyone from the room.

The condolences began in earnest thereafter, and it became easier to ignore Olive.

When the line of those offering condolences formed—how many of them had been those same guests at the wedding?—he wished he could ignore them as well. He wished he could escape, lock himself away to drown his sorrow and regrets alone.

Adnan admonished himself.

His mother was dead. That was the reality. And who faced realities better than him?

And when the khedive returned to be present with the rest, expressing sympathies, it was a reminder that Adnan had been facing realities ever since he learned who his father was.

His lying, hypocritical father.

There'd be no time for pettiness.

'I have a funeral to plan,' Adnan announced.

'You will want to do it near your home in the city, is that correct?'

This diplomatically worded *request* from the khedive told Adnan what he already knew but it disappointed him nonetheless. His father would not want the negative attention that a funeral would bring to whatever political schemes were foremost in his mind at present. They might learn he was also a divorced man. The khedive would not care to honour the mother of his son, not even for the friendship they shared as children.

Adnan suspected that the khedive only agreed to the marriage celebration because of Olive's status as Lord Whitmore's daughter. If he'd married a woman of his choosing, that too probably wouldn't have been allowed in his father's palace! And by the khedive's own admission last night, he was displeased and disgusted with what he thought were uncouth changes in Olive due to his son's 'uncultured' influence.

If Adnan had learned anything about his father since coming to the palace, it was that the khedive was a leader with a tentative grip on power in times that were ever changing. He should've led by integrity, rather than use it as a tool only when it served his current goals.

Had not the khedive's initial acknowledgement of Adnan as his son only emerged from wanting his heir to learn about the common Egyptian man? As much as he was grateful for Saleem's brotherhood, Adnan did not have need of the khedive. He did not need a father.

His mother, his neighbourhood, all his experiences, those had made Adnan who he was. They had made him learn to be self-sufficient. He didn't need a father when he was a boy, and now he was grown, he certainly did not.

As he stared at his father before him, that petulant look, Adnan knew he did not want one who acted as his did in his son's moment of utmost need.

Islamic tradition meant that the deceased must be buried as soon as possible. It would likely be this very afternoon. Adnan needed to talk to the shcikh at the mosque nearest his house to lead the funeral prayer. He needed to purchase his mother a plot, a task he'd been avoiding since she'd become sick. She'd talked to him about it once but then, sensing he'd become upset with the conversation, she'd not mentioned it again. The sheikh would know what to do.

Elham had mentioned the designated woman in their neighbourhood who did the traditional ghusl, the cleaning of the body and the *kafan* shroud for burial. She would gather other women to help.

'It is what my mother would want,' Adnan finally answered.

His father said, 'What else did Elham want?'

Adnan could only recall what she did not want.

My final home shouldn't be near where you make yours. I do not want you to feel the need to visit me so often because I want you to have your own life, joy with your family.

'Do not trouble yourself.' Adnan stepped away from the khedive. 'I will handle her funeral arrangements on my own.'

Chapter Twelve

Olive

Olive tried to be understanding, to tell herself that Adnan was grieving and not in his normal state of mind. Was it normal for him to ignore her? Perhaps. Save for the night before, when they'd shared passionate kisses, the stoic man before her *was* typical Adnan.

I am grieving for his mother too, she thought dejectedly. Olive only had Elham in her life for a short while and though she'd known her death was imminent, it was heartbreaking.

Olive did not have much time to dwell on the matter, however, as the whirlwind of activity in preparation for the funeral surrounded them.

After Adnan had led the doctor out of the apartment with his mother's body, the maids opened all the curtains, flooding the rooms with blinding sunlight. They proceeded to begin cleaning.

Given the tension between him and his father, she

doubted Adnan would come back here. She knew he'd want to return to his own home but she was not sure of her own place there.

There were so many questions in Olive's life, but today of all days, she wouldn't try to answer them. She'd simply prepare for any inevitabilities. She moved to pack her bags in the empty apartment, colder now that all the fires Adnan would stoke had been extinguished.

When she was done, Nawal came to her wearing a black cloak that covered her body, the one Olive had learned was worn by women of the harem whenever they left the palace.

Nawal saw the suitcases but did not comment on them, instead explaining, 'Adnan left me the key to his house. He asked that none of the palace maids accompany me but I will take my personal one to ensure all is well for guests should they arrive to pay their condolences. I will see that coffee is brewed. Would you like to come with us? Adnan needs the comfort only a wife can offer.'

Olive thought of his kisses last night, how they burned through her, enflaming a passion she had not thought she possessed. And how she'd tried to get him to spend the night with her—but he'd refused in the end. Rejected her pleas. Adnan had wanted things to remain above board between them so that he could have his annulment. Now his mother was gone, there wasn't any reason for him to keep up the pretences of a proper marriage, save for maintaining his part of their bargain in Rasheed.

She looked at Nawal, and felt jealous of her bond with Adnan. 'He should have asked me himself.'

'Adnan keeps too much contained, but he will get better at realizing you are his wife, his life's companion. If only you knew how bitterly he and I butted heads when he first came into our lives. It's why we call him the goat. I understood why my father brought him on to spend time with Saleem, but I was afraid he'd hurt my younger brother's big heart. What I came to realize and what surprised me the most was that Adnan has the biggest heart of us all. Once he opens it up to let you in, there is no greater joy than being in his life. His loyalty, the way he will be in your service, honour any perceived debts on your behalf, put your security and contentment above his own, it is remarkable...' Nawal's voice broke as she spoke of her brother. When she'd gathered herself, she continued, 'He would never say it but I fear it is my fault for first inviting his mother to the wedding.'

'No.' Olive felt moved to console her. 'Elham told me many times how pleased she'd been to attend. I think she liked being in the palace too since she'd spent her childhood here. It brought up memories that surprised Adnan. There were a few she told me and made me promise not to tell him.'

Nawal sniffled. 'It will be hard for me to help him through the heavy loss if he is not here in the palace. I can tell that he is upset with my father, who is in fact the literal father of stubbornness. The khedive will not even admit to himself there is any rift between them.'

Olive thought about their fight last night. 'I think I am the cause of that.'

'It could be any other number of things—do not trouble yourself with that thought, Olive. I only mention it because I would be there for my brother but cannot leave here unless under protection from the khedive's guard. The area in which Adnan lives...it is not accustomed to women of the harem visiting. I myself have only been there two times and our other sisters have never been.' Nawal leaned forward and squeezed Olive's hands in her own. 'I need to know that you are going to support him.'

Olive was not sure Adnan would accept support from her but she nodded, 'My luggage is ready.'

It was not a difficult task to slip out of the palace, so different it was to when she'd first come here to experience the pomp and circumstance of wedding preparations. Had the place changed or were the changes in her? Stripped of the red carpets they'd laid down and the scores of staff in service then, the palace's magnificence shone more brightly, prouder. The columned marble pillars, the sconces on the walls that looked like they might have been entire chandeliers in and of themselves, the artwork and urns that celebrated ancient Egyptian culture whilst grounded in cosmopolitan or perhaps Ottoman sensibilities…

It seemed to Olive that the palace had been made more noble because of Elham, and that it was bracing itself to suffer her loss with dignity.

When she stood beneath the rotunda ceiling, elaborately tiled with intricate geometric patterns of aqua and gold, Olive felt like she were on the wrong side of gravity, skimming the sky whilst staring down at the sea and land below. When Adnan had taken her on the balloon ride, she'd felt free and happy. Now she mostly felt sad to think she'd likely never return here.

Once our marriage ends, I will not have cause to visit the khedive's palace in Cairo again.

Nawal had procured one of the simpler carriages and two men from her father's guard who she ensured were not dressed in any official manner. 'Adnan would not want us to announce where we'd come from,' she explained.

She offered Olive a cloak as well and though it felt odd to don it, its black colour felt right for the occasion.

Nawal agreed. 'Common women in towns and villages across the country wear a version of the abaya and I believe it appropriate for periods of mourning.' She spoke about how funerals differed in Egyptian custom with regards to prayers on the deceased. Women were not recommended to be present in the burial ground, and afterward the men headed to a large, oftentimes outdoor venue with lots of chairs to sit and listen to Koranic recitation and offer their condolences to the deceased's family.

When Adnan had pointed out the tent the day they were on the rooftop of the citadel, Olive recalled him mentioning that it was used for weddings and funerals.

Nawal continued, 'Not many in his neighbourhood would know that Adnan got married and because he never wanted them to know he was the son of the khedive, the security is less. Most just think of him as successful in business, which is true. I would caution that if there are mourners who visit, we be cognizant of not exposing his role here.'

It was quite a long ride to Adnan's home, or at least it seemed like it to Olive. When they finally arrived, the street in front of his building was nearly abandoned. It was the nicest home on the road but still humble. The only external indication that a wealthier man lived there was the iron gate and the guard manning it. When they were allowed inside, Olive saw it had once been an apartment building with different units on multiple levels. The first-level apartments were closed, save for one.

Nawal instructed her maid to clean it up but then shut it as well. 'Adnan will not need a reminder of where his mother was forced to live when the stairs proved too much.'

'There is a live-in butler,' she explained to Olive, 'but he is likely to be with the men at the funeral and whilst Adnan did employ nurses to ensure his mother's needs were handled, my brother is quite conservative and as a single man did not want to incite rumours of anything untoward happening under his roof, so they would do their work during the day and then leave when it was done. This means too that he does not have any female live-in housekeepers or cooks. Now that you are his wife, you'll be a safeguard against anything untoward. If you need help choosing maids and other domestic aid, send word and I will help you choose suitable ones. Until then, it might be a bit of a hassle to do the cooking and cleaning.'

'It should not be a problem,' Olive said. 'I was able to handle the apartment in the palace.'

Nawal led her up the staircase to what was the top floor of the building. Unlike the lower levels with multiple apartments, the upper level only had one. As she slipped the key in its locked door, Nawal said, 'When Adnan's business began to flourish, he bought the leases on all the apartments and added this floor, a "penthouse", the architect called it. My brother could have lived anywhere, certainly a wealthier area of Cairo or its outskirts, but he once told me that he thought it important to honour your roots, to build on what was there already.'

When Olive stepped inside, she saw how vividly

Adnan's apartment embodied that very dictum. There was a solid feel to the space, a utility to it even as it exhibited a classic sort of charm. It was not as masculine as a smoking room might be, despite its oriental carpets and abundance of round ottoman cushion seats. The walls were adorned with decorative urns and plates rather than artwork.

It was the sheer number of books that softened the hard lines and most surprised Olive. They were everywhere: stacked on the dining table, piled onto a window sill, overflowing on a series of shelves. English, Arabic, Turkish, even French. They were not the books of a man who was uncultured, as his father seemed to think. When she spotted a leather-bound set of Shakespeare's works, she flushed to remember how Adnan had referenced *King Lear*.

When the guard brought up Olive's luggage, Nawal ordered him to put it at the door of Adnan's bedroom, one that neither of them felt comfortable opening.

Nawal directed the maid to brew the coffee strong. 'For any who may come and pay their respects or for Adnan when he returns.'

The apartment was large but spaced out evenly enough that everything was accessible. The kitchen was wide and beautiful with a large window. The appliances were the latest innovations, including an icebox. Pots and pans were plenty and the cupboards held a full-service tea set.

'Oh, would you look at that,' Nawal commented when she opened one of the drawers, expecting it to be cutlery. Instead, it was a display case being put together with all manner of seashells. Adnan had been working on an art project?

'They were collected by my daughter, Maysoon. Her father said we couldn't keep them because her younger siblings might get into them, and could choke on them. When she cried, Adnan said he'd take care of them for her. I thought he'd tossed them, but...' Nawal started crying then, 'He doesn't deserve the hurt he is suffering today.'

Olive hugged her but felt a bit awkward when she did. Clearly she did not know the same side of Adnan his sister did. Everything about this apartment and all it contained pointed to the complexity of Adnan, and all the parts of himself that he kept hidden felt like an insult to her. He'd insulted her this morning when she reached out to comfort him about his mother.

In many ways it was his mother who had been the bond between them and now it was broken, the gulf between Olive and Adnan would widen.

Although she didn't know exactly when the addition to this building had been made, she felt sure his mother had never lived here. This was a bachelor's apartment and the truth was that Olive did not feel welcome in it.

He might not like to hear it, but the little apartment they'd had at the palace felt much more like a home to Olive. Although it was a hassle with the intrusions from his family and the shameful history of her parentage that she was compelled to hide, at least it was a space originally intended for her.

And even more so was the *ezzbah* cottage she had rented in Rasheed. It certainly was much simpler and she'd only been there for a short time, but she loved it. She loved that she could be herself there and not feel like she had to live up to the expectations of being a lord's daughter. She appreciated not having to hide the lie.

The smell of Turkish coffee filled the space. Women of the neighbourhood trickled in tentatively, unsure that there would be anyone present. Adnan's guard seemed to know who to let in, who wouldn't ask questions about who they were. Olive and Nawal felt able to sit quietly amid the tear-soaked condolences and fond memories shared about Elham.

'She was the funniest person. If you threw her jokes into the Nile, the fish would have laughed.'

'Elham loaned me an amount of money when I had need, despite her not having much herself. This was while her son was still a boy.'

'Tell Adnan that he should drill a well on Elham's behalf. Anytime people drink from it, she will get the reward from Allah, even in her grave.'

Although Olive nodded politely, she muttered to

herself, 'As if anyone can tell Adnan what to do! He'd not listen.'

It was night when he finally returned to the apartment. Whatever anger Olive had accumulated towards him melted when she saw him. He was dusty, haggard. *Sad.*

Nawal ran to him first. He patted her on the back when she hugged him. Comforting came more naturally to him than accepting comfort.

'You are still here?' he asked.

'I needed to see you before I left, show you I brought your wife.'

Olive watched him nod.

He said, 'I was informed. Thank you. Go home to your husband and children now. I will see you soon.'

'I can leave my maid to handle—'

'No need. My butler will return with whatever I need.'

'One of the neighbours brought a dish.' Olive stood behind Nawal. 'It is covered but she mentioned it would be dinner.'

Adnan's gaze locked on hers for an instant, as if he was surprised to find she was there. 'It is probably *koshary*, a neighborhood tradition.'

There was a mighty attempt on Nawal's part to make her farewells casual. She kissed her brother on either cheek and then hugged Olive. 'Come see us at the palace soon. Send word if you need anything in the meantime.'

'Thank you for everything.' Olive nearly started crying once again. Why did she fear the finality of the moment? Nawal had been good to her, lovely in her efforts to ensure she felt welcome and a part of their family. The wedding dress she'd gifted her, the party she'd put together. The visits to her apartment in the palace. It had been for Adnan's sake, she knew, but that didn't take away from the feeling of being in the midst of such deep familial love.

'Never mind all that, we are sisters and that is what sisters do,' Nawal whispered with one lest peck on the cheek. Then she was gone.

Olive and Adnan were finally alone.

He said, 'Allow me to clean up and then I shall come and eat that *koshary.* I forgot to eat anything all day.'

She went to the kitchen to plate the meal but it was only a few minutes later that Adnan returned. His eyes were bloodshot still but his hair was slicked back, the water still dripping onto the towel casually left around his neck.

'That was quick.'

'It is a shower cabin, a stand-up bath.'

'I've heard of them. Yes.'

She'd made two plates, held out one for him, but he took both, digging up spoons from one of the drawers and setting dual places at a small kitchen table.

They ate in silence. The pasta of the *koshary* was rubbery, the rice mushy with the lentil sauce, and the browned onions too greasy. Or maybe the taste was an expression of what they were feeling.

She wondered, 'How are you feeling?'

Adnan set down his spoon, rubbed his temple. 'I am all right.'

'If you want someone to talk to about it—'

'My brother is here. In one of the apartments downstairs. I'll stay with him and you can have this one to yourself.'

'Saleem is here from Alexandria? So quickly. Did Nawal know?'

'Royal trains can clear the tracks when there is… *cause*. If she didn't, she would have seen him on her way out.'

He looked tired, confused at the question, but Olive felt like he'd only ever turn to his siblings for support. Never her. And that was a sobering thought. 'Did Elise accompany him?'

He shook his head then pulled an envelope from his pocket. 'I forgot to give you this.'

It was Elise's writing. Olive read her news and her apologies. She was not feeling up to snuff but sent her love. She said she had been feeling a bit under the weather and there was more: 'I haven't seen the doctor yet but I have a feeling I will be a mother soon.'

'Oh!' Olive gasped with joy for her best friend. Even

when they were girls, she knew that Elise would be the best of mothers someday.

'Is all well?'

The letter said that Saleem hadn't yet told Adnan anything. He'd not want to give his older brother such potentially wonderful news on such a horrid day. And she would follow suit.

'Yes. Elise sends her condolences. I suppose the short notice made travelling difficult.'

When the butler knocked on the door, Adnan ushered him in to deliver fresh fruit and snacks. He tasked him with taking Olive's luggage inside the previously closed room and setting her up with whatever she needed, but to do it quickly because he should not keep Saleem waiting.

'You'll be safe here for the night,' he told her. Then Adnan said, 'Now that your part of our pact is…*completed*, it is time for me to fulfill mine. I will wire Yasser, tell him we will come to Rasheed in a few days in order to find the man you're looking for. Would you want me to share any information about him in the wire? A name perhaps?'

'I would rather wait until I am there, speaking to Yasser face-to-face.'

So that was it then? Adnan still wanted to end their marriage, but even amid his grief, when he was forgetting things, even to eat, he'd not lost sight of their agreement. Olive couldn't help but be sadder than she already was, which, she told herself, was silly since what he was proposing now was what she wanted too. She wanted to find her father, find out who she would be if she were no longer the daughter of a lord. And she couldn't do that as the wife of a prince.

And then, perhaps because she wasn't thinking so clearly either, she added, 'Tal'at is the name.'

Adnan frowned. 'Yasser's name?'

Now it was her turn to throw him a confused look.

'Are you referring to Yasser Tal'at?' he prompted.

Olive took a steadying breath while her mind ran rampant. Yasser was named Yasser Tal'at? Egyptians took their father's names as their last ones—what were the odds of Yasser being her brother? That his father and hers were both named Tal'at?

Her head pounded at the thought of it, the possibility.

'I suppose, yes, that is what I was referring to.'

Chapter Thirteen

Adnan

Adnan's sleep was disturbed with dreams of his mother. In the most vivid of them, she and Olive were in a field together, sitting on a blanket with yarn all around them. When he asked if a cat had made the mess, his mother laughed at him and said they didn't have a cat. 'I am teaching my daughter how to knit. Why are you here?' But when Adnan looked at Olive for confirmation, she disappeared before his very eyes.

His mother reprimanded, 'It is your fault she is gone.'

'But *Ummi*,' he countered, 'you are the one who is gone.'

He'd cried, the tears racking his body, until his mother wiped them away.

She'd asked, 'Do I look gone?'

In the dream he'd decided he'd been wrong, that there'd been some terrible mistake and she was alive and well. 'Thank Allah, you are not dead. I can still be your son, be a better one, less angry.'

And then Adnan awoke to Saleem's gentle shaking and it all came back to him.

They'd buried his mother the day before. Prayed upon her soul. He'd lowered her into the earth himself. She'd been sick for a long time, but there was always life in her body, the energy of someone trying to hold on for as long as she could. Yet when Adnan saw her wrapped in that shroud, he knew it was but a shell and that her spirit had already moved from it.

Saleem's look of concern made Adnan sit up, prove to him that he was fine. 'It must be nearly noon if you're awake.'

His brother grinned as Adnan looked around, noted the pillows and blanket. It was a two-bedroom apartment but rather than take a room, he'd collapsed on the sofa. 'You covered me?'

'I was not about to carry you to the bed.'

It was Adnan's turn to smile. 'And I was surprised that your guard wasn't at the foot of your bed, that he'd taken the other room.'

'Mustafa's learned to relax around me, because he trusts Elise.' His brother's expression turned serious. 'You should have been in your bed last night, with your wife. There is comfort to be found in a woman's arms.'

Adnan would say nothing on that. 'I am used to sleeping in here. It was closer to my mother.'

'Nawal told me she closed the other apartment. She was upset also about…'

'About?' Adnan prompted with a frown. He disliked it when his siblings kept things from him.

'It was wrong what our father did, not having a state funeral. You're a Prince of Egypt. Elham was the khedive's wife, secret as it may have been. He's been wrong about many things lately, but this one is unforgivable.'

Saleem rarely got frustrated, so to see it on his behalf now touched Adnan. Still, he was the older brother and didn't want him to worry. 'Nawal should not have said anything.'

'She is afraid the khedive has made such a mess of things with you that she'll never see you in the palace again. Coming here yesterday after such a long period , she was impressed by what she saw. She remembers what this building used to look like and has seen the improvements you've made. She told me that she knew about your successes in the sugar cane industry but didn't realize how rich you'd become on your own. Now she knows that you don't need employment with our father, and because I rarely visit… Well, she's concerned that now you have escaped the palace as I have done that you won't return.'

'You should have reassured her.'

To be honest, Nawal was likely right about him

never wanting to go to the palace again. Yet Adnan would never cut his siblings from his life.

Saleem leaned forward. 'I did, of course, but there is more you are not telling me.' His brother had a way of getting people to confide in him. Adnan had the fleeting thought that if he'd been the same, Olive would have told him more about the man she was looking for in Rasheed.

Who was he and why did her demeanor change whenever the subject of the search for him arose? *It wasn't because of their impending annulment, was it?*

Adnan told his brother, 'Since you made the Lodge in Alexandria your home after marrying Elise, the khedive has been *difficult* towards me. Insulting and petty, pointing out my faults or assuming them. The truth is that I never took any favours from him beyond my salary, which was fair but not exorbitant. I never wanted to ask for more. Indeed, anticipating that a day would come when he didn't need me anymore is what contributed to my business success, so none of his behavior is entirely unexpected. Yet all this time I hoped to be able to regard him as more a loving father and less an employer.'

Saleem's understanding nod prompted Adnan to continue, 'You were as affected by the khedive's lie about his secret son as I was. The difference is that I was called on only when he needed me to be there for you. He was using me from the start.'

'He loves you, Adnan, is proud of you. Often he made me feel like the most disappointing son he could have had. Certainly that he wished you were the heir rather than me.'

He'd known Saleem felt that way but Adnan never really believed it to be true. Maybe it was because of his history *before* he knew his father. He closed his eyes for a minute, let the bad memories claw their way from the pit of his stomach and rise through his chest. 'Mine was an unpleasant childhood. My mother kept the secret of who her husband had been so we had to weather the storm of neighbourhood gossip. The boys at school called her terrible names to my face, suggesting she made money to support me while I was there through haram means.' He fixated on the far wall, a place that marked his extensive renovations to the apartment. 'I hated this building, feared to come home lest I run into something unexpected.' It was hard for Adnan to admit aloud that he'd let the maliciousness affect him.

'I have stubbornly believed I needed to prove this house was not a brothel, make it a better building than those schoolboys or the neighbourhood could have ever dreamed would be here someday.'

When he looked back at Saleem, he saw the horror of it all reflected in his brother's face.

'You have not said any of this to me before.'

Olive had wanted to talk yesterday but Adnan wasn't

the sort to share his deepest hurts. Maybe he needed to do so today, the first in a world without his mother.

'I was angry for too long and even though deep down I knew she was an honourable woman, that gossip—coupled with our father's lie—it wreaked havoc on our relationship. My mother and I were not as close as a mother and son should be. I did not tell her anything and she did not explain anything to me.' Adnan laughed bitterly. 'Would you believe Olive got more out of my mother in the last few weeks than I did in years?'

'Oh? That is surprising.'

Adnan did not want to talk about Olive either.

'My point is that the khedive being the way he is now is precisely what I anticipated when I invested any money I made. Do you know he mocked my sugar cane investments at the start, saying it wasn't worth the little I paid at the time? Now he wants to nationalize it, like cotton was done before. He will latch onto anything that turns a profit.'

'He worries over Egypt's khedival legacy. Times are changing. I am not the heir he envisioned and his anger with me over that likely transferred to you. That can be the only explanation for his behaviour. I apologize.'

'It is not your fault, Saleem.'

They quieted when the butler came in with a tray of mint tea and sandwiches. Adnan asked whether he knew if Olive was awake. If all was well there.

'I believe so, sir. I took up a breakfast tray earlier and the madam seemed well when she accepted it.'

'Good.'

When they were alone again, Saleem smiled and asked, 'I know it is counter-intuitive, but would you consider taking advice from your younger brother?'

Adnan could find barely enough energy to nod. He did not mention that it had only been yesterday when he wanted to ask him and Nawal what kind of gift to buy Olive. He'd been short with her after his mother's death—focusing blame on her—but it was not fair of him to do so. Last night he'd begun by telling her they'd go to Rasheed, that he'd fulfill his part of the bargain, but dealing with an annulment now, explaining that to his father... Adnan needed more time to figure out how he'd do that with the least possible damage.

Surely Olive would understand.

Saleem said, 'Get out of Cairo, out of this building. Take your wife and go on a proper honeymoon.'

Adnan shook his head. 'The one that's supposed to "culture" me enough for an honourable English lady, or so said the khedive? No, I will not do that.'

He nearly told Saleem about the agreement he and Olive had around their marriage, the annulment they'd planned if it wasn't consummated. But that would mean he'd have to tell him about the kisses they shared that night. The truth was that the longer he and Olive were alone in each other's company, the greater the danger of breaking that agreement.

She wanted to be free of him to do what she'd come to Egypt to do, and didn't Adnan want the same now his mother wasn't around to please? Allah knew he needn't care about pleasing his father.

'It does not have to be Aswan,' Saleem said, 'You and Olive could come to the Lodge. It will do wonders to strengthen your relationship, to get to know each other better, for the both of you to spend time in a place entirely of your own.'

Soon that wouldn't matter anymore but Adnan mulled over his brother's advice. 'Perhaps you are right. Olive has been wanting to return to Rasheed to find an old family friend. I promised to take her after—' he couldn't bring himself to say *after my mother died* '—but there is also my investment there.'

'The one Yasser Tal'at helped settle?'

'Yes. There is a house there, on the land I purchased to begin the sugar company expansion. It is old and abandoned, used to belong to the *ezzbah* owner. I can renovate it. Olive stayed in a cottage there when she ran from— Well, I saw it and thought it had potential. Now the cottage belongs to me, and the house… I can do whatever I want with both.' Adnan was getting excited. He stood, walked around the apartment. 'Did you know my mother said that she didn't want me to live close to her grave? Rasheed is far enough, do you not think? What if I built up my own Lodge there?'

Saleem held up both hands. 'That is not the advice I am giving. Nawal would kill me if she knew I pushed you even further from the palace!'

'It does not mean that I will not return to Cairo but…'

Adnan didn't say that it would be his gift to Olive. But he decided that it was perfect. If they were going to be separated, she'd need a place to live that was hers. A sanctuary, rather than a bad neighbourhood, like his father had done with his mother.

'But?' Saleem prompted.

'But it will be a project that will occupy me while I heal from my mother's death.'

Saleem stood to face his brother and put two hands on his shoulders. 'Rasheed it is then, but so long as you prioritize being with your wife. *Enjoying* each other's company. You're new to it but there is nothing like love-making to make a body forget all of their pains. Unlike sleeping on back-breaking sofas.'

Adnan arched his brow. 'Now is when the younger brotherly advice stops.'

Saleem chuckled and stepped back. 'Fine. When do you want to leave?'

'I would have to inform the khedive. He'd insist Olive must travel as a lady should in the royal train.'

The thought of talking to his father so soon after his mother's death, however, seemed impossible.

Saleem said, 'Never mind that. Mustafa and I are masters of conducting covert missions. And this is very low stakes, no danger at all. As you know, we have done worse.'

'And do you recall the bullet your guard was devastated to not have taken for you?'

Saleem waved a dismissive hand. 'We will have you in Rasheed by tomorrow morning.'

When his brother's guard entered, the three devised a plan and Adnan was sent to inform Olive. Before he did, he asked his own guard to open the apartment that had been his mother's. Nawal had closed it, likely thinking it would be easier for him to not be reminded of her, but that wasn't how Adnan found solace.

It was in witnessing that he found healing. In facing the truth.

And indeed he had of a moment of pride standing on the apartment's threshold, seeing all he had done to try to make her comfortable.

His father had access to fancy doctors, but Adnan had spared no expense in seeing that she was taken care of daily. His faith, his time in the mosque and heeding the lessons imparted there, meant that Adnan could understand that her death had been the will of Allah. If she'd been holed up here, never having attended his wedding, it would have been worse. His mother had a time willed for her to die, as everyone living in the world did.

Adnan was fortunate to be able to pay for her treatments, to prioritize her happiness, even making a deal with his wife so his mother would die thinking he was settled. He had done the best he could.

One part of his life had ended. This next part, without his mother, would be difficult but a fresh start would ease the transition for him.

He found Olive in the kitchen, rifling through the books on his shelves. He watched her for a minute. She was wearing a kaftan, a blue one he'd not seen before. Its sleeves capped short and it fell above her knees. It fit snugly and the curve of her hips and bottom made Adnan yearn for her in a way…*he shouldn't.*

He cleared his throat gently so as to not startle her. 'Olive.'

She turned, startled anyway. Her face was swollen, her eyes red.

His heart clenched to see she'd been crying. He stepped closer and took her hands in both of his. 'Hello.'

She responded by tearing up again. 'You've no right to speak to me kindly,' she admonished.

Adnan nearly laughed, and was inspired to kiss the top of her head, the mess of sunny blonde curls. He held himself back at the last possible second. 'I should only ever speak to you like a mean grump then?'

'I was mourning Elham as well. You left me in this apartment, alone. Alone, Adnan.'

'I thought you'd be more comfortable. There is only one bed.'

'We could have shared it.' She flushed. 'I meant sleeping. Only sleeping. You are grieving, in mourning…'

'I know what you meant, Olive.' Adnan let go of her hands and stepped back.

She gave him a terse nod. 'You're here for the wire message to Yasser Tal'at?'

'Actually, I was talking to my brother and thinking we could go to Rasheed ourselves. You remember the cottage there, yes? We will stay in it while I ready the *ezzbah* for my business there and the main house.' Adnan did not say the house would be his gift to her once their annulment was finalized. It made sense that Olive should decorate it to her taste. 'I could use your help with that.'

She nodded absent-mindedly and he was glad that she'd not guessed at his intention. He wanted it to be a surprise. She asked, 'You mean to keep your initial promise, fulfilling the pact we made about our marriage?'

'Yes,' he confirmed, but the word sounded too formal to him. 'As I said that I would.'

'You have been saying that, yes.'

Was she questioning his motivation on the matter, thinking he wouldn't live up their bargain? It was, after all, an easy task. She wanted to find a man that knew her parents. Unless it was something more.

The recollection of her in the balloon, soaring, happy, made Adnan venture a guess as to what she wanted most. 'You will have your freedom, Olive.'

She sucked in a breath of air, her lips puckering so prettily before releasing it. 'All right.'

'You recall Mustafa, my brother's personal guard? He will take us to the train car covertly. My own guard tells him that you came in wearing an abaya, in the tradition of the harem women.'

'Yes, Nawal gave it to me and it felt right, the colour of grief.'

Adnan nodded brusquely. He did not want to talk about grief anymore. 'He asks that you wear it. He'll be waiting downstairs, whenever you're ready. I'll leave here separately but meet you on Saleem's private car in a short while. Do you need some time to pack your luggage?'

'I never unpacked it,' she said, walking towards his bedroom, and beckoning him to follow. Adnan tried not to focus too hard on her bottom in that dress, the swinging movements that made him want to stop her and press his body into hers. Kiss her as he had that night.

Three days, he thought, recalling the sheikh's typical speech at his mother's burial site yesterday, *that is what we mourn officially. And though the pain and sense of loss may last longer, the lives of the living with their obligations should proceed as they had been, after three days.*

What would happen between them when his mourning period was over?

Chapter Fourteen

Olive

It took a further three days for Olive to feel like she could begin to unpack her bags after they'd arrived in Rasheed. The place she'd stayed at initially, it turned out, was one of a few cottages dotted around the ezzbah, a large parcel of land Adnan explained he was cultivating for the expansion of his sugar cane company. He said that sugar cane would grow well considering that it had once produced cotton and that areas along the Nile were always going to be good for agriculture of almost any kind.

He told her that the main house would be a project to occupy them for the next while. The previous owner had never completed the construction when the price of cotton fell and the *ezzbah* was abandoned.

Adnan wanted Olive's help in turning it into a glorious home. 'It will not be my father's palace, but one worthy of a man who thinks he can manage a sugar company efficiently.'

She'd made a comment about how lucky that manager would be. 'Not like the manager of the one in Sohag whose sister had to go looking for her own business venture.'

Adnan laughed. 'What do you have against entrepreneurial women like Dalia?'

'Nothing,' she grunted, not wanting him to think she was jealous.

He'd looked at her so intently then, she thought he'd kiss her again like he had that night. Instead, he shook his head and said, 'You made that apartment in my father's palace a home, Olive, and did it with limited space. Now, consider this larger place your canvas. What magic will you work here?'

Olive devoted herself to the task during the days alongside him, and by nightfall, both were so tired that they barely managed the walk to the cottage for some sleep. Adnan kept his distance for the most part, careful to ensure that the single bedroom there was hers alone. Since the weather was warmer now, summer nearly nigh, there was no need for any fire stoking.

No need for Adnan to enter the bedroom at all.

Yasser, it turned out, was away, visiting a nearby village, and unreachable. Olive was almost grateful for it. She couldn't quite remember exactly what he looked like and was frightened that she would gasp at the similarities and determine that he was indeed her brother when she came face-to-face with him. Or would she be disappointed to learn that Tal'at was a very common name in Rasheed and there were multiple possible travellers to England twenty years ago? Olive hadn't changed her mind; she still wanted to find her real father and sensed that when she did, she'd have a better understanding of who she was and could move forward with her life. In the meantime, however, it was nice to delay for a bit longer.

And it was *really* nice to be with Adnan, work by his side. He was more relaxed; the heaviness in his demeanour since his mother died lessened as the days passed. They shared laughs, even a few stolen glances that were...heated.

For the smaller items that the new home required, he took Olive shopping in the marketplaces of Rasheed and nearby villages. Stalls were not as abundant with items nor as crowded as Cairo, but the service was certainly attentive. Merchants did not know he was a prince for he'd been careful from the start to ensure that Yasser would tell no one else, but they recognized that Adnan had money to spend and had discerning taste.

He commissioned a draper to make curtains, letting Olive pick the colours and materials she preferred. He ordered oriental carpets for every room and marble flooring to be put in as well. Saleem sent a team from

Alexandria to work on the bathrooms, installing the latest in water closets, tubs and even a shower cabin, which Adnan said he preferred best in his Cairo house. 'It is nice after runs. A quick way to get clean.'

That was when Olive suspected that the house was actually for Adnan, not the manager he intended to hire for the company. And when he took out a wall to expand the kitchen and make space for the installation of the most current cooking implements, her suspicions turned to jealousy. A well had been dug nearby and, because the kitchen opened onto the garden, he brought in the sort of clay oven one might find in bread bakeries.

'That will be a dream for the wife of your sugar company manager.'

'You think so?' Adnan seemed pleased by the comment but Olive was the very opposite.

Would he be so thoughtless as to think that once their marriage was over, he could bring a new wife here to this city of all places, where they had first met? And, if things worked out with her real father, the city where Olive might stay or at the very least visit often?

Of course, she could say nothing on the matter. Not yet. But at times it bothered Olive to not feel like she could tell him the whole truth. He was curious about it, venturing to ask about the man she was looking for, but there would be interruptions before she could answer. Or her own fears stilled her tongue. That was an odd sensation to be sure. Where once Olive feared she'd blurt out the truth, reservation and stoicism now made her wearier. It was Adnan's effect on her, perhaps.

And maybe she was affecting him too for she hadn't seen Adnan as excited about anything as he was when he finally found the right gardener to hire. 'He is not as talented as Raaouf, the fellow who works in the pal-ace—remember, he sent the apricots that first day? We wanted to add them to my mother's porridge because she was mad about them.'

Olive smiled, glad he was able to mention Elham without sorrow. 'I remember.'

'Beyond the heavily used tomatoes, cucumbers and arugula for salads and cooking, we can put in a guava tree. It might take some time to grow but…the fra-grance will be heavenly. My mother used to make juice from ripe ones but had a hard time straining out the seeds. It did not matter, however, because the taste was incredible.'

'I have never eaten guava.'

'A little more time, and it will flood the marketplace. You shall have your fill.'

Olive dared not ask how much, for the more time that passed, the closer they'd be to parting ways.

Adnan had stained-glass lanterns put along the porch, bright pink flowering shrubs along the walkway and large clay-potted ferns. And there was a grapevine plant along one wall that would, the gardener stressed, produce the 'sweetest green baubles'.

When the house was practically ready for living and they were finished winding the last of the vine's branches through the latticed trellis, Adnan stood at the foot of the pathway that led to it and beckoned for her to join him.

'Come admire our handiwork.'

'It was not *just* us. It was an entire team.' Olive twinged with sadness. They were done and there would be no long busy days. No purpose to be in each other's company.

Adnan took her hands in his, sensing her melancholy. 'Do you think it is fit for a princess?'

Did he already have one in mind? Dalia perhaps? No, Adnan would choose a dignified woman, someone composed, regal.

'What would I know about that?'

'You are the daughter of a lord and likely used to places that are much more cultured and aesthetically fine. Your opinion matters.'

Olive was disturbed by the lie of being the daughter of a lord and felt guilty for still not having told Adnan the truth about her real father. *Guilt* was the right word to describe the feeling, rather than the one she was more used to: *shame*. He had been straightforward with her, kind and trusting. Bringing her to Rasheed so soon after his mother's death had proven that he wanted to honour their bargain. Giving her the opportunity to help revitalize an abandoned home into one of the most spectacular mansions she'd ever seen had truly been a gift.

Why then did she quip 'Now you sound like your father'?

He must have changed, for rather than be insulted, Adnan smiled and lifted his broad chest to the bright sun. 'That is a fair assessment.'

In his working *galabaya*, with his sleeves rolled up nearly to his elbows, he was a fine specimen of a man. His hair had grown a bit longer, peeking from under the keffiyeh scarf wrapped around his head. And his beard was fuller. Olive was overcome with a desire to delve her fingers in it, touch the skin beneath.

She offered, 'It is perfect for a princess or any girl who dreams of being one.'

He smiled and threw her another one of those heated looks.

When she finally tore her gaze away, she said, 'I should head back to the cottage. Are you coming?'

Adnan hesitated. 'There is a surveyor coming in to assess the grounds behind the house. The town's mayor, the *eumda*, sent word that it is necessary for governmental permits. Which is funny considering that those will be sent on to the khedive's office. Were I in Cairo now, I might have even seen them myself.'

The *eumda*, she also recalled, was Yasser's grandfather. Was he Olive's too? She suddenly felt uncomfortable. She tried to seem like she was stifling a yawn. 'Then I will to the cottage myself. A nap is in order.'

'Why don't you go upstairs, rest in the main bedroom? It is the only one that has been entirely completed and the housekeeper I am looking to hire insisted on readying it last night. She said I could test her efficiency through the work but I haven't had a chance to see it myself. Go rest there and let me know if she succeeded. After we can walk back to the cottage together if you would like.'

'Very well.'

He led her through the house's large double doors and watched as she climbed the spiral staircase. She slowed because she knew Adnan could not quite pull his gaze from her bottom but even when he'd left her alone, she kept the pace. The marble steps had been newly installed with red velvet runners and the twisting hand railing was polished to perfection. She absorbed the details of each iron spoke, the scalloped edges that caught the glimmer of the chandelier overhead. It had come with the house originally, but Adnan had had it reinforced so that there was no danger of it falling and breaking.

He'd put so much care into the place. There was a real awareness of the future, like he was determined that it would last long after him. *His children and grandchildren.*

When Olive reached the top and found the bed-room, she nearly gasped with how beautiful it was. She'd not noticed the workers bringing in furniture here, but spread before her was a huge four-poster bed with lavender-coloured silk sheets, plump pillows and cushions aplenty. There was a chaise chair by one wall with a matching vanity table and gilded silver mirror. There was a large vase, nearly half of Olive's height, filled with large-stemmed white hydrangea blooms.

The bouquet's perfume melded exquisitely amid the luxury, but there was an authenticity to the space too. It was meant for a couple who were wealthy, clearly, but also she imagined they'd be ones who appreciated beauty for its own sake rather than revelling in material possessions in order to impress others.

Olive's favourite part was the gigantic window that overlooked the western garden and beyond it, a stretch of the farmland that was barren now but that she could imagine would soon be green with sugar cane crops beneath a bright blue sky.

This was no cave apartment. This was living in the open. High and free.

But it isn't my life.

Olive wished it was. She could see herself here. She wouldn't even need it all. Just the kitchen down-stairs during the days. This room and view during the nights.

Adnan sharing that bed with her.

She sighed, trying to hold back a wave of melancholy.

There'd be no nap for her.

She'd go and report to Adnan that the housekeeper had done fantastic work and that she should indeed be hired.

But it was time for Olive to return to the humble cottage. That was where she belonged, neither a princess nor the daughter of a lord.

She marched to the bedroom door but then heard a flurry of activity that made her suspect it was not just a single surveyor. Perhaps the *eumda* had come himself?

Was her grandfather downstairs? She needn't wait for Yasser to return to Rasheed; she could ask the *eumda* if he had a son named Tal'at who travelled to England twenty years ago.

No, she couldn't do that in front of Adnan!

Focus on something else, Olive.

What else was there to focus on now that the house was all but done? She could not depend on Adnan to distract her with a new project. Heaven help her, for if he was eager to dissolve their marriage now he'd brought her to Rasheed, Olive may not know how to be alone with her panicked thoughts about meeting her father or the shame that she may never be free of.

She looked through the closet and surprisingly found a ladies lounging robe and pant set for men. The housekeeper must really want the position. She'd gone to the trouble and expense to have the owners imagining having their own garments filling the wardrobe shelves. Olive was not sure the robe would fit but it looked right enough.

She stepped into the adjoining bathroom, which housed the shower cabin Adnan was so proud of. The water was warm and refreshing on her bare skin so she reached for the two bars of soap from a holder shelf amid the metal arms of the contraption. The first she recognized as Adnan's—perhaps he'd put it there himself after the installation!—so Olive used the other. It was a soft peony citrus that was lovely smelling and invigorating. As the water fell over her body, she couldn't help but remember the bath in Cairo, Adnan walking in on her that first night.

She'd wanted him to make love to her even then. Now, as she touched herself in the places she wished him to touch, she thought she'd die with want of him.

Olive lingered before reaching for the large towel, hoping he'd find her naked again, but Adnan didn't barge in on her this time.

The lounging gown was a perfect fit. It was a fine material, something between cotton and silk, and it draped smoothly over her belly and hips, making Olive's legs look long. She left the top buttons open, exposing her bare cleavage and she rather liked the look as she spun before the vanity mirror. In its drawer she located a proper hairbrush, a tube of rouge and even some kohl. She made use of all of them and was rather pleased with the result.

She decided that it wouldn't hurt to make it hard for Adnan to resist her just as she had a hard time resisting him. She stared at the bedroom door, willing him to come in, find her there.

But again, nothing.

It was late in the afternoon; surely the surveyors had left. If Olive had learned anything about life in Egypt, it was that people took their *ghada*, or late lunch, seriously. It was the largest meal of the day, and often times, after a siesta, they might leave their homes to go back to a second shift in their workplaces. Or if they didn't work, they'd go out and spend time with friends and family.

As for their main meal of the day being altered because of their work on the house, she and Adnan had taken to having an early supper that she'd whip up at the cottage, falling into a similar pattern in Rasheed as they'd had in Cairo when his mother was alive.

But when Olive opened the bedroom door, the mealtime smells coming from the kitchen below indicated that supper was already afoot. Fresh parsley and lime filled the air.

Perhaps the proposed housekeeper was demonstrating her cooking skills too. For those, Olive would be warier of doling out compliments. She rather liked cooking for Adnan and would miss that task when their marriage bargain was fulfilled.

She descended the stairs and walked past the two living rooms, not entirely furnished yet, but one of which would be large enough for grand parties, and to the back where the expansive kitchen was. 'Adnan,' she called.

He peeked his head from the doorway and when he caught sight of her, his eyes widened appreciatively. *Good*.

'I used your precious shower. The room is wonderful. The housekeeper knows what she is doing.'

He strode towards her, still in that *galabaya*, but his hair was mussed up from the scarf he'd removed. When he stood over her, she lifted a hand to his curls, fixing them. 'I could brush that for you.'

Adnan took a deep breath. She was making it hard. He said, 'You are ruining my surprise.'

'What surprise?'

He turned her around, gently guiding her to a side table far from the kitchen. Then he bent his head low so that she could feel his breath next to her ear.

He lifted his free arm above her head, kept one barely touching her waist. Slowly he inched his chest forward until it was pressing against her breast. She stared at him throughout the movements and it was thrilling for he knew that she was watching him as he was watching her.

'The gown or night dress or whatever it is called,' he whispered, 'was made for you.'

'There is an outfit upstairs for you too.' She held his gaze. 'Not that I am complaining, but what are you doing, Adnan?'

He went in for the kiss so suddenly, it shocked her— but only for a second. Every inch of her wanted him. She gripped his hair to prevent him from stopping.

Adnan shook his head, had to practically tear himself away.

She would have damned him for it, but then he said, 'Happy birthday, Olive. It is today.'

She gaped, unsure how to react to that news, remembering how he admitted knowing it that day on the roof in the citadel. He'd read the details of their marriage contract, one that would be torn up soon.

'I had forgotten.' She didn't even know what day it was, could barely name the month.

Olive had been happily occupied; now reality was setting in.

None of this life with Adnan would last.

And it made her sad.

Adnan must have sensed it. He cupped her cheek, his thumb rubbed it gently. 'I need a minute to finish my surprise. Go back to the room? No, actually, I think I need to take that shower. The colder the water, the better. Don't go there or the kitchen. Can you wait here? I will be quick with both.'

Adnan had spoken in such a matter-of-fact manner that she might have even called it 'bossy', but Olive didn't know if she could, in fact, wait.

He was getting more appealing by the minute. And she was getting more desperate.

'Did you cook for me on my birthday?' she called as he slipped inside the kitchen.

'No, and no peeking.'

'The housekeeper?'

'It was catered. She will be hired for housekeeping purposes only,' he called back.

Well, that was good news.

A beat later, he shouted, 'Why are you so quiet? Do I have to cover your eyes with a blindfold?'

'I will be good,' she said, her voice thick.

The sound of his laugh was music to her ears. He'd heard the suggestion in her voice despite the distance. 'You are naughty, Olive.'

'But you like me the way I am?'

'I like you the way you are.'

Knowing Adnan had remembered her birthday and had planned a surprise for her made Olive feel loved. She knew he was grateful for her presence in his mother's life. And everything Nawal had said about how her brother opened up his heart…? She was starting to feel that too.

Olive was safe with him. Adnan wouldn't reject or purposely hurt her ever again.

And, pending annulment be damned, that would be enough for Olive today.

She watched as he dashed out of the kitchen and to the stairs, wagging his fingers so that he'd not resume the position he'd taken over her moments before. 'Stay here.'

'Hurry then.'

He did, his hair still dripping from whatever quick washing he'd given it. The shirt he'd changed into had a few buttons undone at the top, and the trousers he wore, she noticed, looked like the sort that might easily be slipped off.

He made for the kitchen but she caught his hand as he passed her, wanting him to resume that position he'd taken before he rushed off.

Adnan tilted his head to one side, looked younger than she'd ever seen him and let out a groan. 'Please, Olive, let me do this for you.'

'Are you begging?' she asked, feeling bold, playing the seductress.

She ran a finger down the center line of his chest.

Adnan grasped her hand when she got close to the top of his trousers, stopping her. His willpower was strong but did she imagine that he held her hand a bit too weakly?

She pushed off the wall and into his arms. 'Did you get me a birthday gift?'

He didn't let go of her hand but held it back and took her by the elbow too so that he could walk her through to the veranda.

Beyond the new birdbath that adorned it, there were two chairs and a small table. The closer they got, the clearer she saw what it was.

'It's a *tawla* set!'

'We'll fill the bath with water and the birds will come to sing as I teach you how to play the game.' Adnan smiled hesitantly, 'You told me you wanted to learn to play, that you thought it less confusing than chess. That first day at the marketplace?'

She teared up because he remembered and because he said 'we'.

Dare Olive believe what she thought might be happening between them?

From inside the empty birdbath, he pulled out a jewelry box.

Inside were bracelets, three gold bangles. Delicate and etched beautifully. He slipped them on her wrists.

'They are exquisite,' she said, admiring them on her wrists.

'Exquisite,' he agreed, but he wasn't looking at her wrists. Then Adnan cleared his throat. 'I could only find them by way of jewelers in the city. I was told that Rasheedi women are most enamored by bracelets but we can get them changed or a complete set in Cairo if you don't like them. Nawal would have better recommendations.'

'I must be a Rasheedi woman then because I love these and will never take them off.'

The bracelets she could understand as a gift. The *tawla* set even. Those could be moved. But the bird bath, the things he'd said? Dare she read too much into it?

'This house, Adnan. My understanding is that you renovated it for the company head. Is that really who it is for?'

Chapter Fifteen

Adnan

Why did her question make him feel sheepish? 'I am the company head but this house is for you, Olive. I didn't box the keys because there is still furniture that needs to come, but all of it is yours. To live in for as long as you would like. To lock up and have for whenever you decide to come back to it, if that is what you want. It is a lifelong lease for you. This entire house is my gift to you.'

A look of disbelief crossed her face. 'For what?'

'For what?' Adnan said. 'For everything, Olive. It is a birthday gift, a "thank you for being good to my mother" gift. A wedding dowry gift. And, when we end our marriage, it can be considered a compensation gift, what we call *muakhar* for the bride from the groom. You'll never need to feel like you're abandoned in the world. You will always have this house. If you have a child or children in future, this will be their sanctuary too. No uncouth neighbourhoods for them, only a beautiful countryside that is quiet enough for them to decide who they want to be.'

He was comparing her future children to himself, giving them what he wished he had, but Adnan wasn't sure if she understood and it pained him to try to clarify it more. The thought of Olive with children that were not his? It was not an image he wished to dwell upon.

He forced a smile. 'We should eat now. I catered a meal and there is cake after, so long as you eat enough of supper first.'

He ushered her from the veranda back into the small dining room that was off the kitchen, where a family was expected to dine when they did not have guests. The table was laden with their feast for two. Adnan had found a small balloon and figure of a camel—to represent their time in the pyramids. He wanted to show her how much of an impact she'd had on his and his mother's life, that his gift was given with gratitude for every moment she'd spent in their presence, every bit of kindness she'd gifted them.

Olive had followed him but she barely looked at the food. He held out the chair for her and she sat, but she didn't take her eyes off him. The confusion in them as clear as the sky on a cloudless day. She asked, 'Where will you be when I am here?'

'Where do you want me to be?'

He stared at the pout of her lips, could almost make out what she would say before she said it: 'Right now? I want you in my bed, Adnan.'

He wanted to make love to Olive. She wanted it.

And yet to make love to Olive whilst both were planning on an annulment would make theirs a divorce. And he had to think about that because he didn't want to put them in a position of divorce, nor did he want to compromise his values.

He was a principled man and he needed to remain one. He cleared his mind, decided that now wasn't the time for thinking. He cleared his throat and edged his seat closer to hers: 'Will you eat first? *Mahshee.*' He picked up the fork, cut into a piece and held it up to her mouth.

She bit into the tangy baby zucchini filled with tomato, rice and beef. He sampled the next bite. Then, using his fingers, Adnan ripped into the tiny roasted bird and brought that to her lips. 'Pigeon with country butter.'

She nipped at his finger, wet with meat juices. 'Delicious.'

Because of the desire he was barely keeping at bay, it was difficult to watch her chewing—difficult to watch her doing anything, really. He poured them each a glass of the hibiscus tea. It was lemony and likely not sweet enough for Olive. And though ice cold, it did nothing to temper the heat rising in his core.

Her smell, her nearness, the curl of hair that had escaped its confines that he wanted to push behind her ear.

'You did not have to do all this,' she said, sounding almost like she didn't believe she deserved it.

'It is the least I can do, Olive. Even the best of cooks needs a rest,' he said, trying to make light of her mood.

'I meant…everything. The home, the gifts. I am sorry Elham never visited, did not see it.'

When she started crying, Adnan thought his heart had come up to his throat. He put down his fork and turned her chair to his, so that they were facing each other, their knees squared. He leaned forward and rubbed her tears away. 'Listen to me, Olive. All my mother wanted was my happiness. She wouldn't have wanted to see this place—she would have wanted it to be a new beginning, free from sadness over her loss.'

Olive sniffled, tried to stem her tears. Be stronger. That was nearly as hard to watch for Adnan as her crying.

He asked, 'Do you think you can be happy here?'

She met his gaze, nodded. Then she leaned forward and cupped his face in her hands. She touched her lips to his and it nearly undid him.

'Then I am glad for you.' When he tried to pull away gently, she held him there.

'Why do you do that? Pull away when we get close?

Do you not think that my happiness might be bound to yours?'

He was not sure how to answer that so he told the truth: 'No, I have never thought that.'

She scraped back the chair and stood, paced around him and the table like a rabbit marking its territory. A very cute but frustrated rabbit.

'You are my husband, Adnan. I know we are set for annulment and ours was a hasty marriage to begin with but I thought things were changing between us. I thought *we* were changed. The kisses, the looks. All of this! If you are trying to give me it all today only to leave me tomorrow, then be clear with me. Tell me too so that I can try to figure out what my life will be after I...'

'After you what?' he prompted, waiting for her to say more but she pressed her lips together. What was she keeping from him?

Seeing he wouldn't go on until she answered, she said, 'Forget what I said. Who cares about "after"? Has death not taught us to carpe diem?'

He needed her to slow down, to be sure that she wanted a future with him. 'I haven't fulfilled my part of our pact yet, not helped you find the man you are looking for.'

Olive, however, threw him an exasperated look, 'As soon as Yasser is back in Rasheed, one conversation should solve whether or not he knows the man. Consider your duty fulfilled!'

Adnan stood in her path, blocked her body with his own so she'd stop her pacing. 'And what if he doesn't know who this man is? What will you do then?'

'It does not matter!' She folded both hands at the top of her head. 'I cannot be near you, Adnan, thinking you would rather not be here. You kiss me and then pull away. You gift me all this and say it is for a future without you. I do not care about what is to come tomorrow! First your mother's care took up our time, then the house took up our time, but now it is just you and me, not any others, no project to occupy us. I will no longer bide my time when I know you are marking the days until we are done.'

He gently untangled her fingers from her hair. Lifted her chin so that she'd witness his sincerity. 'I want to be with you, Olive. I do. Every time you are near, it takes every ounce of me to resist the desire to make love to you, to be reckless and unencumbered. Damn it, I don't even have to be near you. A whiff of your perfume, the lightness of a cloudless sky just before sunset when the blue of it matches the shade of your eyes.' He inhaled, deep and long. The confession was dangerous. A jailed entity, shaking at its bars, calling for help, hoping that release was nigh.

'But one of us has to think carefully about tomorrow. The consequences. I am a man, and Society—whether

Egyptian or English—allows me to take your body for my pleasure and then divorce you. You would then be regarded by them as tarnished—or worse, ruined—if you were to become pregnant, whilst I could hide even if had a child, barely acknowledge them when they came of age and still not suffer consequences.'

Adnan hated the emotion in his voice, the pain on one hand and fighting off his attraction for her on the other. He was on the precipice of surrendering to it.

And Olive, she must have sensed it, for she pushed. 'You are not your father, Adnan.'

'Precisely that. I want to be honourable and not make the same mistakes he did. If I make love to you now then you may pay the price in the future. Are you sure about this carpe diem, Olive?'

She closed her eyes when he finished his little speech and Adnan held his breath, wondering what she would say. Wondering what exactly he was asking. The future wasn't clear enough to him; was it to her?

'You're a grump,' she said when she opened them. 'A stoic, hard and utterly annoying man.'

He clenched his jaw, resigned to hear the rest of what she had to say. What he assumed she believed: that they were not compatible.

'I was in a bind when you offered to marry me and I know that you did it out of pity.'

'No, not pity.' *That* he could refute. 'You were in

need, Olive, desperate even, but a woman as full of life and spirit? No, you could never be pitiful.'

She swallowed. Adnan watched every muscle of her face. He'd believed he knew her after all these weeks but right then it was like he'd never known her at all.

'But you are my very handsome, very good-hearted husband and I have not regretted our marriage. I will not lie to you and say that I know what the future holds but I'm sure of what I want today. Is that enough for you?'

He kissed the top of her head, sighed there with a sense of relief that he'd not known for a long time.

This house. Olive. She was his wife today, as she'd been yesterday. And right then, it felt like Adnan's whole world.

He was ready to embrace it, *her*, and they'd weather with any consequences that tomorrow might bring.

Chapter Sixteen

Olive

Adnan had kissed her before, but never like this. With hope and acceptance. Devotion and fervor. He lifted her to one of the tables near the dining room, spread her legs so he fit his tight body between. She hugged his slim waist to bring him nearer, needing them to be closer. Why was it not close enough? He let his fingers roam freely as his mouth explored her face and head, his lips nibbling at her ears, chin, neck.

He called her *'marati,'* my wife, *'amari,'* my moon, *'hayati,'* my life.

And for someone who usually erred on the side of silence, Adnan was quite a chatty lover.

'Do you like this?' he asked as he cupped her right breast.

'I like that,' he groaned when she grasped the left cheek of his bottom.

'In the cottage, we slept in separate bedrooms,' he

said, 'but here there is only one bed. Shall we go back there or would you like to share the one here?'

'The bed here, it…is…large…enough…for…two,' she managed as his lips met hers. 'Unless you are a snorer.'

He laughed while kissing her and Olive revelled in the tickling sensation.

'I am a runner, you recall? We are generally healthier. *Harder.*'

Everywhere she touched was proof of that fact. There wasn't a bit of Adnan that was less than firm. The muscles of his upper arms, the breadth of his shoulders, the sharp cut of his chest and tautness of his stomach. The spread of his back and upper thighs.

Those were the places Olive could touch from her position, but it was not enough.

She arched her body with want, in the hopes he'd tear off her gown, demonstrate that brute strength of his, for the material stood preventatively between her flesh and his.

'Adnan, make love to me. Now.'

'If I am a grumpy, then you are demanding,' he protested as he swept her up into his arms.

She wrapped hers around his neck. Being carried by him was better than being aloft in a balloon. The anticipation was meshed with a desperation so strong, she felt like he would have had to carry her regardless.

He watched her as he ascended the stairs. He didn't

kiss her again, focusing instead on ensuring he didn't misstep, that she was safe, but he repeated the earlier endearments.

Then when they reached the bed, he set her down gently, looked at her so intently, she melted beneath his gaze. It was late afternoon by then, and dusk outside meant that the brightness in the room was dimming. But rather than turn on the lamps, he stepped back and went to the curtains, drawing them open further.

'People make love in the dark, silly man.'

'The bathtub in my father's palace, that first night? Much too dim.' Adnan smiled and it was a look that smoldered in Olive's core. 'I wanted to revel in your perfection but was forced to be a gentleman, get you a towel. Do you understand what that took?'

'No.'

He spoke matter-of-factly. 'Any common bastard would not have.'

'And you are a noble one, are you?'

'Hmmmm.' He clung to the curtain rod as his chest heaved, his arousal impossible to hide. 'I am a good, patient bastard.'

She rose from her place on the bed, neared him, but not near enough that he could touch her. Rather, Olive found the angle with the most light and she slipped off her gown. Slowly, so that it pooled at her feet and she stood naked before him. 'Then you should get your fill.'

He looked at her like she'd never been looked at before. Any imperfection Olive might have been conscious of before that look would forever be forgotten with the memory of the desire in his eyes.

'Perfection.'

And then she spun, gave him a view of the bottom he seemed smitten with. She looked over her shoulder and saw how he closed his eyes just a tad as if the view of her bottom was too arousing without the covering of the clothing he was more accustomed to.

'Perfection,' he repeated.

'My turn to examine,' she said, facing him again and gesturing with a slight up-down movement of her pointer finger to indicate his trousers. 'Will you take them off, or do you need my help?'

He bent obediently to slip them off and the angle of his body, every muscle rippling as he did, the way he held her gaze as he straightened again, made Olive throb with want.

She'd seen sculptures of men in museums or art collections of people in London Society. She was familiar with the male anatomy, but nothing could have prepared her for Adnan naked, in his bare bronzed glory. Her eyes roamed the line of dark hair from his chest to his navel to his manhood.

'What do you think?' He was almost bashful when he asked it.

She wanted to say something witty like 'decidedly

not ugly' or 'the running should be kept up', but an approving moan emerged instead. In response to it, Adnan closed the distance between them and pressed his body against hers. He wrapped one arm around her waist to hold her close, but not before slipping one hand between her legs. That moan transformed into tiny tremors, her chest heaving as he peppered her breasts with kisses.

And when the fingers between her legs stroked her womanhood, gently, hesitantly, she felt herself get wet.

Adnan didn't seem to mind; his two fingers continued their exploration and she felt like she might drown, shaking with pleasure and moaning his name. Gasping when he pressed deeper.

His fingers stilled suddenly, and he stared at her with concern. 'Did I hurt you?'

She shook her head, pressed her fingers into the small of his back. 'Do. Not. Stop.'

'We need to go gently the first time.' He kissed her neck, traced his lips along her collarbone and finally resumed stroking her womanhood.

Somehow, this time though, it wasn't enough anymore. 'Not. Gentle.'

Using his body, not letting her go, he guided her back to the bed. In one deft movement, he lay her on it, pulled her arms above her head and held them flush against the headboard. He pressed his mouth to hers, long and deep, and because she wasn't able to move her hands, she writhed with the near inability to catch her breath.

'Oh. God.'

His hardness pressed near her core, teasing at the gate of her desire. She wanted him inside.

He'd made moving her hands difficult but Olive could push up the lower half of her body, move to a rhythm, a little dance. And the more she did it, the weaker he became, loosening his grip on her hands.

'I said gentle.' He sounded like he was trying to convince himself.

'Rough.' She sounded raspy. Perhaps it was her desperation, for, hands now loose, Olive lowered them so that she was cupping his manhood.

Now it was his turn to gasp. Eyes shut as he enjoyed her stroking. And when she brought him near to release, leading him to press into her, his eyes shot open. His hands delved into her hair.

Turned rougher.

'*Aywah*,' she moaned the Egyptian way of saying 'yes' and that was what finally threw him over the edge. He lost control, pressing deeper into her, piercing her finally. Olive bit down the initial shock of it and he mumbled apologies, something about the blood, but she didn't care. She wanted him to take her and he was too far gone to control himself anymore.

He thrust again with a pressure that was quickly becoming more pleasurable than painful. Olive could tell he was waiting for her to say something by the way he was watching her, arms anchoring him above her chest so that he could get a good view of her expressions.

For her part, she rather wanted the sensation to go on, even though beads of sweat slicked her entire body and had gathered on his brow. She stuck out her tongue, playfully panting, but he took it in his mouth and sucked. Thrusting faster as he did.

Olive couldn't hold back anymore; she fell off the edge, pulsating beneath him.

And then so did he.

'We are not virgins anymore,' he announced, then he started laughing.

'As I live and breathe, Adnan, this is the first I have ever heard you laughing!'

Which caused him to laugh more and the sound of it ignited hope and contentment in Olive's core.

'I am happy,' he said, bringing her into his arms. 'Bathe with me?'

It was probably a mistake to do so together. The shower cabin was made for one. But they squeezed inside thinking that they'd succeeded, until the water turned cold, forcing them to slip out.

'Hungry?'

'You promised me cake.'

'Did I?'

Adnan closed the curtains and lit up the lights in the house. It was stunning by night and as they descended the stairs, she could imagine how it would become a 'forever' home, even if she still could not think about the future.

'Although I rather like watching my wife walking around naked, I think we need to hire that housekeeper,' Adnan said. 'And probably a few other staff. A maid for you.'

'You held off on a cook.'

'I did not think you would want one but we can get the finest. My butler in Cairo would move out here, I believe, if we can hire his wife full-time. She cooks and did so often for my mother and I. Not as good as you but...'

'As long as she is married, that would be all right. A single woman might...' Olive thought about Dalia at the pyramids, how jealous she'd been. How unpleasant the feeling was that Adnan might want a different wife than her. Still, she wasn't ready for talk of the future, could not be until she found Tal'at and the truth about her father was resolved. 'The maid with the red hair in the palace? I caught her ogling you.'

'Here I thought I was the jealous one between the two of us.' Adnan teased. 'I never gave any indication that I was interested.'

She sidled up to him, cupped his face and then kissed him. 'It does not mean other women will not want to find a good man, seduce him.'

'There is only one woman I have ever wanted to be

seduced by.' He raised a brow and looked up towards the top of the stairs.

'Will you not feed me that cake first?' she laughed.

He grabbed her hand and ran her to the kitchen, pulling out the cake from the icebox, a plate and knife.

'You cut it like you did our wedding one.'

He made it difficult, putting his arms around her from behind as she did, his breath in her ear, his chin in the crux of her collarbone.

It was a pink cake with strawberries and sweetened cream.

He sighed with a depth of feeling. 'Happy birthday, Olive. I hope this one will be a happy memory for you.'

'I don't know. Lord Whitmore could certainly throw a party,' she said to tease Adnan, but then she was lost in the pleasant memory. 'Elise was there for my fourteenth. I was fixated with the novels of Jane Austen at the time, so he took us to Bath. We saw all the sights that inspired her, some of the spots where dramatic events in her novels occurred. We even ate foods that she'd described. It was gloriously fun.'

A faraway look crossed Adnan's face. 'I read *Mansfield Park* when one of my father's diplomatic connections mentioned it. I was newly hired, anxious to prove myself but felt wholly unsuited to his world.'

'Is that why you have all those books?'

'I read to know, to not be accused of uncultured-ness.' He shook his head. 'I enjoy the works but do not read them for pleasure, as you. But where did it get me? He still accused me of being uncultured.'

'Your father is wrong, Adnan.'

Why was the topic always going back to fathers with them? Maybe it was a sign that it was time to tell him about hers?

He nodded. 'Now that I think about it, *Mansfield Park* might be what inspired me to invest in sugar in the first place.'

'So, we all owe much to Jane Austen.'

She slid a piece of the cake onto the plate, licking her fingers, which were covered with jam and cream. Then she dipped them back in to give him a taste. When he grabbed her hand and nibbled at it, she feared they'd not get any food in.

And he was not done talking about fathers. 'You have a good father, Olive. I should like to be the same to a daughter or son of mine one day.'

She looked away before he could see how the sentiment confused her. But when he cupped her chin, lifted her face until their eyes were locked upon each other, she could not hide it.

'What's wrong,' he asked.

'Nothing.'

He looked like he wanted to ask more but then he smiled. 'You do not wish to talk of the future.'

'I wish to eat cake.'

He fed her a bite as he had at their wedding, but then

when it was her turn to do the same, she had a better idea, a way to guarantee that they would talk no more of fathers or futures. Olive made a show of smearing the cake on her nipples. 'Bite.'

He groaned. 'I don't even like sweets, yet you make me work for it.'

She threw him a mischievous grin, grabbed the plate of cake and bent to her knees to paint it onto his member.

'What are you doing?' He couldn't hide the eagerness from his tone.

He was moaning even before she took her lips to him and when she did, the quaking of his thighs that she'd anchored herself to was enough to pleasure her as much as the sweetness of the cake.

He tried to pull himself back, to avoid losing control. Olive forced him to stay there, inching forward as far as she could take him.

He swore obscenities in English and Arabic and the more unfettered he became, the harder she pushed.

When he finally let go, he pulled her up to stand, gave her such a look of appreciation that Olive wanted to do it again.

'Why does it feel like my birthday?' he said.

Later, after he took his turn in making her lose control, they found their way up to their new bed.

She lay, spent, warmed by his embrace. 'You are very *knowledgeable* for a virgin.'

It was dark now and Olive couldn't quite see his face when he said 'A man learns a thing or two about how to please a woman in a neighbourhood like mine. Putting the knowledge into practice, however, has been surprisingly...fun.'

He gently pushed back her hair and then he asked, 'And what of you? You were not raised like the women in my neighbourhood but you seemed to not want me to hold back like a lady might.'

Only a short while ago, Olive might have been torn or saddened by such a comment. Now she understood why he was asking. His concern for her. His gentleness with her.

He added, 'Only, I do not want to treat you in any way that might *hurt* you, Olive.'

'You were a proper gentleman, only doing what I asked.' She admitted with a laugh, 'I suppose I am learning new things about myself.'

She loved making love to Adnan. It didn't matter that they were bastard or prince, daughter of a lord or born to a man who'd been paid to father her.

It was the pure carnal pleasure of two bodies who were husband and wife.

And there was no shame in that.

Chapter Seventeen

Adnan

The persistent knocking on the house door pulled Adnan away from staring at the beautiful naked woman in his arms. His *wife*.

Olive's curly dark blonde hair sprawled over her shoulder, catching the morning light through the slit in the window curtain. The smoothness of her body, the soft and gentle parts that accommodated his hard ones. The dark peaks of her breasts against the ivory of her skin, the rounded curve of her hips, the sweet valley between her legs.

He sighed with the memory of the night before.

Adnan wondered why any sensation of happiness was foreign to him. Why did he not trust the feeling? Complete joy had rarely come into his life, if ever. When he wasn't frustrated or in mourning, he was content enough, certainly; but having made love to

Olive, in a way that had him releasing his inhibitions, was an incredible feeling.

He remembered enjoying watching her in the balloon, how free she looked as they flew over the pyramids. But watching Olive climax whilst he was inside of her?

That was something else entirely.

He feared he'd never want to stop making love to her, that the control he'd honed for so long was now destroyed. There was a nagging voice in his mind that all was not right with Olive. She was holding something back. And she could be reckless, foolish. Had any of that changed? She'd left Elise in Alexandria; who was to say that she'd not do the same to him?

He pushed aside the voice of doubt, and kissed her forehead gently. Her eyelashes fluttered and she smiled with recognition.

He said, 'There is someone insistent at the door. Remind me to add a guard to the team of people to hire. I would stare at you all day, uninterrupted, until I can ravish you at night, uninterrupted.'

Olive stretched as a cat might. Adnan wondered if she were ticklish. He'd have to test that later when there was no one at the door.

'Or you can make love to me all day and night. Not just stare.' She purred suggestively, 'We could start now.'

An enticing offer but he said, 'Go back to sleep—it is early yet. And I have errands to run in the city.'

She nodded, turned to her side and was breathing steadily the next minute.

She was a late riser even without a night of…activity.

He slipped out of bed and put on the clothes he wore yesterday. Another order of business was to get their things from the cottage. He was happy that Olive would be able to settle, finally start living out of a closet and drawers instead of from the cases she'd lugged around since arriving from England.

When he opened the door, it was the team come from Alexandria with furnishings for the living room. He asked them to work quietly as they arranged the sitting area. 'Ensure the large couch is placed there.' He pointed to where he'd like it. They'd need the support of the back wall if he were going to make love to Olive there.

The rest of the morning was a whirlwind as Adnan got to work negotiating hours with the housekeeper. She mentioned that her son who would normally walk her to the house was a strong youth—'he would yoke the oxen himself as a boy'—and would be an excellent guard once the gates were put up around the house.

'Can he move our things from the cottage now? Make sure you're with him the whole time. No young man should be alone with my wife when I am not present.'

There was no way that Olive would be more protective or jealous than him.

'*Hather, sayedi.*' The housekeeper nodded. 'He will not enter the house.'

Assured, Adnan then walked into the city to arrange with local farmers and merchants the delivery of typical items. Milk. Eggs. Bread. Fresh chicken and meat. Fruits and vegetables.

He happened upon Yasser, who'd returned from his trip outside Rasheed. After offering his condolences on Adnan's mother, he'd said that all of Rasheed was talking about how quickly he'd renovated the main house.

'I was coming to see it myself and give you this,' he said, holding up a telegram that had arrived from Saleem.

Our father is looking for you.

'Can you send back to tell him I am finally taking that wedding trip?'

'I will do it now.'

Only later, when they'd separated, did Adnan wonder why he did not ask Yasser to come to the house. Why he did not tell him that Olive wanted his help finding a man who knew her parents in England. Was it because he was afraid that once that part of their marriage deal was complete, whatever they were doing now would crumble? They'd agreed to an annulment but now they'd made love, it would be a divorce.

She'd said she did not want to think about the future. And maybe Adnan was having too much fun with her in the present.

It was odd how things which seemed pressing one day could be forgotten the next. In consummating their marriage, the reasons for why they had a pact in the first nearly became moot.

What became pressing was going home to his wife and making love to her again.

They were enjoying an afternoon cup of tea the next day on the veranda because they really did *need* to get out of bed, when someone was insistently knocking on their door again.

'You should put a mechanical doorbell on your list of things to get for the house. It sounds like that will be used more than your shower cabin.'

'I doubt that.' He cocked an eyebrow and then said, 'Wait here, try to learn the moves.'

'Moves?' she repeated but with a suggestive tone.

The housekeeper gone for the day, Olive had slipped into a pink negligee that barely covered the top of her thighs and was held up by two thin straps that exposed the flesh of her arms and a generous amount of cleavage.

He pointed to the backgammon set. 'I meant the *tawla* maneuvers.'

But then he changed his mind. 'Actually, come inside. It's getting cold and you are practically naked.'

'Still giving orders, are we?' But she picked up her tea and walked in front of him, sashaying and purposely lifting the already short dress so that the outline of her bottom was visible.

As soon as he'd closed the veranda door, he pounced on those cheeks and she screeched. He squeezed, turning her around as he did so. He kissed her deep, and she melted into him.

The visitor, however, did not cease knocking. Olive ignored it, standing on her toes to kiss his neck and the lobe of his ear.

She admonished, 'You are a bad *tawla* teacher.'

'You are a lousy student.'

'I have a hard time concentrating.' She slipped her hand into his trousers. 'I want to go riding instead.'

Whoever was at the door had finally surrendered . And so did he. Maybe this was what it was like to be newlyweds.

They didn't make it up the stairs or to the couch they'd yet to sit upon. Rather, it was the plush carpet in the hallway that he dropped down onto as she straddled him. They made love achingly slow at first, and he let his fingers explore the nub of her womanhood as he thrust into her. It was wet and tender and he took his time, patiently rubbing there even as Olive's movements turned frantic and she began to call his name.

He waited for her to climax before letting himself go too. They might not be good at playing games together, but he and Olive were becoming particularly adept at making love.

Perhaps this was their way to get to know each other, to build their marriage into something that would last beyond the now and into the future.

Maybe through love-making, they would learn to trust one another.

And maybe he would fall in love with his wife.

She kissed him deeply and then stood. 'I am hungry.'

As she made for the kitchen, Adnan checked the door and found an invitation from the *eumda*.

He waved it in explanation as he returned to her. 'The mayor is hosting a dinner in our honour tonight. The messenger was probably insistent because he needed an answer.'

'Mayor?' Olive stopped what she was making and gulped at a mug of the tea Adnan had made. Her face changed with distaste. She clearly didn't like it, even though he'd sweetened it for her benefit.

'It's not nice when it is cold.'

'It was not nice when it was hot,' she snapped, dumping what was left in the sink.

'What's wrong with my tea?'

'Too strong, cooked for too long, it becomes bitter. No amount of sugar can hide that aftertaste.'

He tried not to question the shift he'd noted in her tone. 'Why bother pretending you were happy with it earlier?'

'Papa…er, Lord Whitmore…taught me to never look a gift horse in the mouth.'

'You English and your sayings.'

He watched her struggle to smile. She said, 'The mayor invited us to dinner?'

'I saw Yasser yesterday,' Adnan explained. 'Since his grandfather is the *eumda* that is probably why we have the invitation.'

Olive frowned now she was watching him. 'Strange you should not mention Yasser being back, considering speaking to him was the main purpose of this trip.'

Adnan schooled his reaction to that. Had he been foolish to think the reasons for their marriage pact didn't seem to matter as much after their love-making? Maybe he'd been right to doubt Olive's commitment to him. That once she met who she came for, she would leave.

He soured. 'If you want, we can go tonight, I am sure Yasser will be there. You can ask him about the man you're looking for then.'

'Yes, we will go. Of course I want that.' She nodded distractedly. 'Do you think other members of the *eumda*'s family will be there as well? Have you ever met him or them? What is he like?'

Adnan hadn't planned on accepting the invitation,

would have made some excuse about not having received it on time. 'What is going on, Olive? I think it is time you tell me more about who it is you want to ask Yasser about.'

She huffed in frustration. 'All I am asking about the *eumda* is because I wish to know what I should wear to meet him. How I should greet him. Is he comparable to your father, for example?'

He held back his tongue from reprimanding her that she sounded too much like the Olive he'd barely known before their marriage. Or maybe in getting to know her body he had willfully ignored this side of her.

'I have never met the *eumda* myself, but he would be older, having served for my grandfather. There have been calls to appoint a new mayor in Rasheed, but no elections have occurred precisely because of his lack of organization. Or maybe it is because the city has suffered outside influence for so long that they are keen to not attract further problems. An election would do that and they might want the status quo to remain as is.'

'What do you mean, outside influence?'

Adnan examined Olive, but as far as he could tell, she was sincerely interested in the politics.

'The Ottomans were the first to recognize the value of Rasheed, building it up in the late 1500s and turning it into one of the foremost trading ports in the country. Not only is it rich in soil as part of the Nile Delta, but it's also a strategic gateway to Europe and even the rest of Africa beyond Egypt and through the Nile. In the wake of the Ottoman collapse, the French and English have fought for control in different parts of Egypt, but what few realize is that many of their battles began here in this city. Locals feel excluded, robbed even. A prime example of this is Napoleon's Rosetta Stone discovery in the late 1700s. Though it now sits in the British Museum, it was the French who deciphered it and still claim ownership.'

'It was stolen from here.' Olive nodded. 'I can understand why they would be upset, but surely such outside influence is in the past now?'

'For people in power like the *eumda*, my father and the khedives that preceded him, outside influence is welcomed, seen to be a boon. The cotton industry, for example. It is English demand which kept their pockets lined. All prime planting land in the delta was used to grow cotton, and the benefit to labourers was minimal. Cotton cannot be eaten. Then, when the price fell because of the end of the American Civil War or cheaper routes from India, landowners took the hit with the khedive because it had been nationalized. Better to plant grain or sugar, beets and cane. Crops that can be eaten even if they cannot be sold.'

'That's what you did in Upper Egypt. Where you get your money.'

Olive had switched from politics to business? But she seemed distracted, like she was trying to make out something. If only she would share with him what it was.

He remained silent for she'd ceased asking questions.

'Nawal mentioned how you invested your earnings into something that would separate you from the khedive.'

It didn't sound like something his sister would say or at least not in such a way. Olive had added her own interpretation and now she looked at him expectantly.

He chose his words carefully, sensing the start of an argument. 'It was never my intent to challenge my father.'

'Why not? Why don't you toss all you've done to improve yourself in the khedive's face more, flaunt all you've acquired without his aid? The monies, the culture he thinks you do not possess? For goodness sakes, Adnan. You should show him how much better you are than he is!'

'Where is this coming from, Olive?'

Olive cried, 'Nowhere. It is nothing. All I am saying is that maybe you're more like the khedive than you care to admit. Maybe you're afraid that the things you value are the things he values as well. And that is why you stay quiet on just how cultured you are.'

Adnan clenched his jaw. Their love-making had had him forgetting how contrary and stubborn Olive could

be. Besides, she was wrong on this. She wasn't interested, however, in hearing his rebuttal.

'I shall go and find something to wear to the *eumda*'s party on my own.'

Their conversation was over.

He didn't quite understand what their fight had been
about or even if it was one to begin with. But beyond
asking him if her sky-blue-coloured gown with its
long sleeves and high neckline was appropriate for
their invitation—it was, but Adnan thought he'd have
much rather stayed home and freed her from it so that
they could do decidedly *inappropriate* things together
because that was where it seemed they connected—
Olive didn't speak during the carriage ride to the *eumda*'s house.

No, not house. *It was a politician's mansion.*

It wasn't as open as his and Olive's *ezzbah* house but
sprawled wider. Nor was it as grand as even the smallest of the khedive's various palaces, but there was a
regality to what was before them that felt similar. The
eumda's mansion looked like it had stood there since
Ottoman times, and the guards at the gate reminded
Adnan that it probably had.

There were five guards in total and though they had
the right stance, they seemed much too unprofessional
to have worked for his father. In fact, he guessed that
they attained their positions by virtue of a relation to

the *eumda*. The guards kept peeking at Olive. One of them was outright ogling her like she was a piece of meat he was about to feed upon. Such behaviour would have been immediate cause for dismissal if it had happened anywhere near the harem.

Could Adnan blame them entirely, however? Olive's beauty was that of a shining star, one that was transformed as soon as she stepped past the threshold of the gate and shook the *eumda*'s outstretched hand. All of a sudden, she wasn't the passionate wife who'd asserted herself atop him a short while ago; rather she was the perfectly poised political wife.

Indeed, she reminded him of his stepmother, Ulfat Hanem, who was, after all, a Turkish Princess. And that realization in turn made Adnan feel ashamed as he recalled a time when he was angry at his own mother for a long-forgotten reason. He'd said he knew why his father hadn't stayed married to her: 'It is because you're not as beautiful nor as graceful as Ulfat Hanem.'

Adnan felt haunted by it now. Maybe Olive was right; maybe he was more like his father than he could admit, because Allah help him but he was proud knowing that he was the husband of a great beauty.

Being pleased that other men would be jealous of him over it was a realization about himself that both angered and shamed him.

'Nawartu Rasheed,' the *eumda* declared, then translated in English for Olive, 'You have lit up Rosetta! The city is made bright by your presence.'

'My wife speaks and understands Arabic,' Adnan corrected but Olive nudged him.

She said sweetly, 'The sentiment is appreciated nevertheless. Thank you. Rasheed is *munawara bi woggodkum*.'

It was a seasoned response, a remonstration that Adnan should mind his manners.

The *eumda* led them through to the *istiraha* living room and pointed to his wife, an older woman surrounded by a handful of other ones, lolling about on the couches.

'Then you will not need me to translate for you, my dear. Please join the other women, while I introduce your husband to the city's most important people.'

He and Olive were not in a competition for who could make the better impression, but Adnan wondered if *she* thought that after the annoyed look she tossed him over her shoulder. As he was introduced to the men, his gaze kept seeking her out. The men riddled him with questions, not taking the hint that his blunt answers were meant to be a deterrent, whilst Olive chatted away, too far from his hearing.

'What happens to sugar cane crops when the season is done?' asked a man named Gamal who, Adnan was told, was a local doctor and owned a number of pharmacies in the region. 'Or when your position with the khedive's office has you moving back to Cairo?'

Adnan bristled at the directness or lack thereof. Did the men here know he was a Prince of Egypt? Who had told them if yes?

He could walk away, but this wasn't his house and the *eumda* clearly did nothing to reprimand Gamal for overstepping. Besides, he'd never lie about who he was. He just didn't lead with it if he could avoid it.

This was why Saleem was the prince who'd always been the one to attend such parties.

Adnan said, 'I have another company.' He didn't mention the Sohag name because the manager there did keep his status a secret. 'The workers there live in a compound with subsidized rent, very much like the traditions of the *ezzbah*, but it is year-round. When it is not harvest season there is other work to do. The families get to know each other, and the company pays for their medicine or other life expenses. We even finance the hajj pilgrimage as a bonus for the eldest ones. Perhaps you are looking for a job, Ostaz Gamal?'

The fellow was not bothered. 'There is talk the khedive would nationalize any crop, like they did cotton.'

Who would have spread that rumour?

Seeing Adnan's face heat, the *eumda* finally held up his hands and came between them. 'Gamal speaks in the voice of those discontented. It is not his nor my opinion, you must know.'

Adnan didn't want to say anything bad about the khedive. If rumours were spreading in Rasheed, he didn't want to contribute to them. Hurting his father was hurting Saleem. And Nawal. Their whole family. And now his own. Olive would need protecting.

He'd turn to Saleem and Mustafa to find him guards for his house, commission that gate immediately. For now, Adnan put on his most serious face, the one he'd seen his father use to intimidate others.

'I should hope not.'

Chapter Eighteen

Olive

The *eumda*'s wife was a gentle lady, meek and quiet, her eyes a watery greyish brown, her skin pale by Egyptian standards, and to be completely honest, Olive found her to be utterly underwhelming. After getting to know Elham and witnessing her vitality even in the face of certain death, Olive hoped that her own Egyptian side of the family might be the same. The *eumda* had been gracious enough, but his near-immediate dismissal of her to the ladies' side of the gathering absolutely proved what Adnan had been saying from the start. In a village this small, a woman needed a father or husband to hold any sway.

The first day she'd arrived in the city, having abandoned Elise, she'd found Yasser's Rosetta Carriage Company, and he'd proven helpful with her plan to lease a place rather than stay at a hotel meant for foreigners. He didn't question her because she'd had a bit of money to spend but what she'd tried to impart upon him then was that she did not want to be found. A hotel would be the easiest place to find her. Because he spoke English and knew the city well, Olive felt reassured.

It turned out that Yasser knew Saleem and he immediately put Adnan onto where she was staying. Maybe he'd been scared, what with Saleem and Adnan being princes but it underscored how men held the power here. And if Yasser did end up being her brother, he might be as weak-minded as his grandmother.

It was a frustrating realization.

The women were relegated to the kitchen area for dinner. The table itself was set up nicely enough, the servers moving from the main room, where the men were eating, to the women. And the food was certainly the same, but Olive couldn't help but feel disappointed.

Adnan was out of her sight.

His glances had burned a hole through her earlier with their intensity but she couldn't exactly tell what he was thinking. Their love-making had been voracious earlier, but the news about this evening threw her. Reminded her that she still had not found her father. Made her ask herself what she was doing being intimate with her husband if he didn't know the truth about her.

Once he did know, he'd reject her; she was sure. She needed to prepare for that inevitability. She needed to be prepared for the future that she'd avoided thinking about.

'Are the spices on the lamb good?' The *eumda*'s wife was not necessarily addressing her, just the table in general. 'I told the chef not to put too much.'

The lamb was gamey, in fact, and would have benefitted from spices to cover that unfortunate taste.

'Did you request it so for the Englishwoman?' said one of the other women gathered. 'They say that is how they like their meat.'

Olive plastered on a forced smile. They all knew by now that she understood and spoke Arabic but they still acted as if she weren't in the room at all.

'My palate has been introduced to many wonderful flavours since my arrival.' Olive reached over and squeezed the hand of the woman who might be her grandmother. 'Thank your chef for me.' She then proceeded to pick at the tomato salad and rice on her plate, which weren't too bad in relation to the lamb.

The conversation at the table turned so mundane that Olive began to tune out. Only when talk turned to grandchildren—one of the women mentioned that her latest had terrible wind and she forced her daughter to give him water boiled with fennel seeds and honey—did Olive realize that it was an opening she may not get again.

'Do you have children?' she asked the *eumda*'s wife. 'Or grandchildren, perhaps?'

The woman gulped her water, looked to the others at the table as if begging one of them to change the subject.

One of the women, whom Olive had been introduced to only as the doctor's wife, said, 'She does have a couple of children, yes, though they are no longer small. Two grandchildren as well.'

Could the *eumda*'s wife not speak for herself?

'What are their names?' Olive asked but rather than get an answer, she got a different question from another one of the women:

'Have you ever been to Paris? I tell my husband that he needs to take me shopping for fashions in France. That is how he will keep his wife happy.'

'And why would a man care to keep his wife happy? If she's not, he'll tell her to drink from the Nile.'

It must be an Egyptian joke for they all laughed heartily, save, however, for the *eumda*'s wife, who barely cracked a smile.

Olive was frustrated. She wriggled in her seat. The wooden chair was covered with a brocaded velvet too thick to sit in, so it felt more like a carpet. And her gown? It was supposed to be summery but she'd had to put the corset on herself and she probably did it wrong because she wanted to rip it off. Or get Adnan to do it for her.

Had Olive turned into one of those people who needed love-making to feel calmer and more relaxed? Had her father been the same, selling his seed for money or had he enjoyed the times he was with her mother? How many times had it been before the pregnancy took?

It was a terrible way to think about your parents and Olive shook her head, disgusted with herself. She gulped down the water in her glass before trying again with the *eumda*'s wife: 'Is it daughters you have or sons?'

She answered but it was a whisper, 'I have one daughter and one son.'

The other woman asked, 'Is that gown you're wearing from Paris?'

'I have no clue where it is from,' Olive snapped. 'It was a present from my father.' Except Lord Whitmore wasn't really her father, was he?

Olive looked around the room, the smooth marbled floors, the fine cherry-wood hutch and serving closet. Had her father grown up here? If he was surrounded by wealth and prosperity, why go to England in the first place, why work on the docks? Why agree to an illicit affair with a married woman? Why abandon whoever Yasser's mother was to do it? And then, why leave her—leave the child he might have known was coming?

She had so many questions now she was here and she wasn't getting any answers!

She needed to get this night over with! She turned

back to the *eumda*'s wife. 'What are your children's names?'

The *eumda*'s wife abruptly pushed back her seat, both hands gripping her temples. 'I hear my husband calling. One moment, please.'

When she was gone, the woman who'd asked about Paris admonished Olive: 'Her children have been a disappointment and only one of her grandchildren has somewhat salvaged the family name. His name is Yasser. He owns a carriage company. Perhaps you have heard of it?'

Olive nodded abruptly. Maybe she'd only get information from him. But Yasser hadn't deigned to show up tonight and that further infuriated her.

Olive stared into the faces of those around the table and the servers now cleaning up their mostly filled dishes. She heard the chuckle of the men gathered in the main dining room. It was as if they were all laughing at her.

What did they know that she did not?

The more she thought about it, the more questions Olive had. She'd come to Egypt to get answers and even now she was close to getting them, it all felt out of reach.

Her heart raced. She'd not been this flustered, this erratic since Adnan had proposed to her.

She hated that she wanted to be in his arms right then. In the absence of being Lord Whitmore's daughter, she'd become Prince Adnan's wife—but now that his mother was gone and his promise to her soon fulfilled, even that role might end soon.

They were having fun now, playing house, but if the khedive learned she wasn't a lady, then there would definitely be conflict for Adnan. He was more like his father than he cared to admit; the things he'd said earlier were proof. That must have been why she'd pushed him into an argument. Although she didn't think her husband would go against her, would Adnan go against the khedive?

This was what she got and deserved for her lack of foresight!

She kept on looking to where the *eumda*'s wife had walked out but she did not return. As for the other women at the table, they resumed their gossip, ignoring her.

To keep from screaming, when the servants came around serving a warm drink they called *boza*, Olive downed a cup. Then, she stood and called them back for another.

It was warming, both sour and sweet. The drink proved to be the most stimulating part of the evening, gifting her an odd energy.

A third cup of it would be too much, very unladylike, but she did not care.

Olive was not exactly a lady, was she? If she'd learned anything about herself after she'd overheard her father and Elise talking, it was that there was no nobility about her whatsoever.

She'd turned on the man who'd raised her, abandoned her friend in Egypt, used a man for marriage, threw her body at him at the first chance she got—the night before his mother died, in fact. He'd rejected her then but couldn't afterwards. He had wanted her not to become a divorced woman, but she broke their agreement, uncaring.

Olive was a terrible person! Why had Adnan stopped telling her that much?

The doctor's wife put a hand on the cup to stop the servant from pouring a fourth cup of the *boza*. 'We do not want to require the use of my husband's knowledge.'

Olive wasn't sure what she meant but she said, 'Do you think your husband would have answers to the questions I had about the *eumda*'s family? Why did none of you answer?'

The doctor's wife's smile was one of pity. 'They do not like to talk about their children. Their son, Tal'at, ran off to England when he was newly married, his wife pregnant with Yasser. Leaving her like that did something to the poor girl's mind. And then there was a tragedy. There are rumors that Tal'at drowned his wife upon his return from England, but none are allowed to talk about that.'

Tal'at.

The doctor's wife had said the name so casually.
England.
Where he bedded her mother and she was conceived.

Olive's heart raced, her body flushed like it had been tossed in a fire and she was flailing, trying to escape the flames. *What is wrong with me?*

At some point, she caught sight of her husband at the grand door of the room they were in. Which was it? The kitchen? The study?

Adnan would rescue her.

He looked devilishly handsome as he walked towards her, the sort of dark and mysterious rake debutantes would whisper about. She reached for him, but he caught her hand, kept it at her side.

'We will go now.'

Olive had the sense that she would very much like to have him carry her to their bed or take her right there. *I would have been a great debutante.* Olive had got better than a rake. She had landed a prince.

'You want to make love to me, to continue our lessons.' The words felt heavy on Olive's tongue; the English after an evening of Arabic was an odd sensation but maybe she'd spoken in Arabic. She forgot.

Adnan got so close that she thought he was going to kiss her. Instead, he sniffed her breath. He hissed, 'Did you drink a glass of *boza*?'

'Three. Or four.'

The disappointment she read in his face, the judgement, made him look formidable.

'Why are you angry at me? I am the one who is angry at you.'

He took her shoulder, whispered in her ear, 'Let us leave graciously. We will talk about it at home. Sober you.'

Olive elbowed him, pulled herself away by pushing on his abdomen. It was hard and flat and oh, but...no. Her father may be a murderer on top of a louse and Olive was *angry* at Adnan. 'You said Yasser would be here.'

He hissed, 'I was not privy to the guest list.'

'I want Yasser now.'

'Tomorrow.'

'Now.'

'Yasser?' This was from the *eumda*, who interrupted them. 'You inquire about my grandson?'

Olive looked around, saw that they somehow were already outside on the patio. Her father's house patio. If he was the right Tal'at. Which he must be.

She was confused and there were so many guards. And one of them was watching her intently. Adnan was trying to shield her but she had things to say.

'Yasser is not *just* your grandson, Mr *Eumda*, Honour. Sir.' Olive was speaking in English. Did he understand it? She could not remember if he did. She hiccuped and the effort of it nearly made her lose her balance.

She thought she heard Adnan mumbling something about her not being in her right mind. *Wasn't that the truth*. Olive was sick. Sick to her stomach. She was sick of the lies, the silences.

She covered her ears from the loud chirping of the crickets.

Olive was angry.

At Adnan and the *eumda*. At both of her fathers. At her dead mother. At losing Adnan's mother. Elham was lovely and kind and answered all her questions and told her stories and oh, how Olive missed her! Her mother-in-law had been nothing like the *eumda*'s wife and her friends. But she still lost her too and if Olive started crying over that fact now, she'd not be able to stop.

The *eumda* was a small man, easy to grab by the lapel of his jacket. 'Do, you, *Eumda*, have a son named Tal'at?' she blurted. 'One who travelled to England twenty years ago?'

The timing, that was the important thing here. She did not know the date.

The *eumda* stiffened. Adnan pulled her off the man and right after he said, 'I do.'

'Then you should know that Tal'at is my real father. He impregnated my mother and they bore me. Which makes Yasser my half-brother. And you and your wife are my grandparents.'

Chapter Nineteen

Adnan

Adnan had been the one to handle Saleem's 'experiments' on his brother's path to becoming a responsible heir, but he'd never been tempted even for a minute to join him. It was for a few reasons. Firstly, he believed, like the sheikh at his neighbourhood mosque preached, that alcohol and drugs were haram, *forbidden* by Allah, and that reason alone should be enough for people not to question it. Secondly, Adnan had wanted to be a good older brother, and had desperately wanted to fulfill, to the best of his ability, the task his father had set for him.

Still, taking Olive into the house, forcing her to eat a portion of bread after she'd been sick and expelled the *eumda*'s dinner, he nearly regretted never having experimented with his brother. Maybe if he had, he'd know how she was feeling. Know what would best help her.

'Thank you, Adnan. You're being kind. Very kind. Sweet.' She wrapped her arms around his neck, kissed his cheeks. 'I should not have said I am angry at you.'

In the next breath, she'd dropped her hands and shouted, 'Do I disgust you?'

Why would anyone ever want to lose their heads and act out of their norm?

He'd first known Olive as reckless and without a filter, blurting the first thing that came to her mind. Constantly 'putting her foot in her mouth,' as the English might say. He recalled Olive meeting his mother at the wedding, the insulting things she'd said to her. That memory wasn't as buried as he'd like to think. Then there was the time in Alexandria when she'd practically begged Saleem to marry her, completely unaware that his brother was in love with her best friend. And hadn't she been rude to him, right outside the cottage door near here, after he'd come to retrieve her?

What kind of useless prince are you that you have time to track me down?

Adnan had held his tongue then. It was their first meeting after all. He'd not told Olive that he had the work he did for his father and his own business to run. Nor did he mention that his mother was ill, dying, in fact.

Adnan had stifled what he'd wanted to say: That he was the sort of man who loved his 'more useful' prince of a brother, and would drop everything to be there for him. To help him find his happiness because that was what he deserved.

Maybe Olive wasn't drunk now.

Maybe it was Adnan who had lost his senses to her—in their bedroom and every other place they'd made love in the last few days—and he who'd brushed this reckless side of her from his mind. Pretended it wasn't there or told himself that he was man enough to handle all sides of her.

Her doe-like eyes and luscious lips, her sensual bottom and soft curves had seduced him, dulled his senses.

'Adnan,' she moaned, her mood turning again. She lifted her dress, baring her thighs and wrapping them around his midsection. She slurred, 'I am wearing a corset and need a bastard prince to undo me.'

'Did you forget what you said to the *eumda*? The embarrassment we have been through! Not to mention the insult to your father, a true gentleman. Is that why you were blatantly unkind to Lord Whitmore? Because of some ridiculous belief you have in your mind?'

She scoffed, 'He's not my father, that's the point. It is not a lie. Tal'at is my father. He ravished my mother in England. I don't know how many times until she became pregnant with me. You can say it. I see it in your face. My mother must have been a trollop, my father a cheat.' She spread her arms wide and then met his gaze. 'And I am a product of them both.'

Adnan looked away. She was saying ugly things and he didn't want to give her fodder for them. But it couldn't be true, that Lord Whitmore wasn't her father, surely? Adnan tried to believe that her outburst at the *eumda*'s was merely a drunken mistake but of course he knew it wasn't. He'd known Olive was keeping a secret.

Tal'at was the man she was looking for, the one she called a family friend that only Yasser could help her with. The resemblance was obvious to Adnan now. Yasser was quite pale, his hair only slightly darker than Olive's. And the *eumda*'s wife today, certainly.

'I wanted you to trust me. To tell me yourself about the man you were looking for.'

Adnan hadn't wanted to push the matter in their initial agreement, sure that Olive would tell him when she was at ease with him. But clearly that had never come. They'd had numerous conversations about their childhoods, and she'd stayed quiet. They'd made love and were the most vulnerable in ways that two humans could be. He'd told her about his struggles with his father; she'd lambasted him for it earlier tonight.

But the fact remained: Olive had not told him the truth. She had not trusted him, did not want to think of a future with him. He'd always been the man she married in haste just so she could stay in the country.

'You're thinking it is shameful,' she said, watching him.

He shook his head, protesting, but she was not listening. 'It is more shameful than you know. It wasn't just an affair between my mother and Tal'at, it was a transaction.' Her eyes locked on his before she shouted, 'Lord Whitmore paid him to sleep with his wife.'

'I cannot believe that.'

'Does it disgust you, Adnan? Are we so different? Hmm? You offered me a marriage of convenience and we made a transactional deal—but I've been sharing your bed, begging you to take me again and again. Do you think my mother was the same, enjoying an Egyptian steed whilst my father watched?'

Olive started crying.

Adnan wasn't sure what to do or say. 'Do not say such a thing about your mother.'

'What would you know about mothers and their past relationships? You barely spoke to yours about hers.'

Adnan tried to remain calm, to not hold Olive's comments against her. 'Go to sleep, it's late. You're reckless at the best of times but tonight…tonight was a disaster and you're going to regret it in the morning when you remember it all.'

She slipped off the counter, jabbed at his chest, pushing him back. 'Regret the truth? Never! You are a hypocritical snob. Admit it. You, the bastard son, judging me? Did you want a wife like those men at the *eumda*'s today? One you can keep out of the way, cooking for you in the kitchen. A pretty English rose who likes to get dirty when no one is around.'

With that last one, she grabbed him by the trousers and touched him there. Allah help him but his body reacted to it. He did want her. He would never stop wanting her. But not like this. He pressed her hands away. 'Stop, Olive.'

She let out a bitter chuckle, sounding angrier than she did drunk. 'Is that it? Are you disappointed in who you married? Your cousin in the harem, she said it first, shocked that you'd marry someone non-Egyptian. I overheard her talking to your sister, saying the only reason you married me was to please the khedive after Saleem disappointed him. But then at the apartment, when you kept on about how much your father had insulted you, all that nonsense about you influencing me to be uncultured—I was sure they were wrong. Yet now you're away from him, Adnan, and still you want to please him. Where is the lie, Adnan?'

It took all his might not to rail at her, to tell her she knew nothing about him or his relationship with the khedive.

'Maybe,' she answered her own question, ''tis you lying to yourself. Maybe you only married me to please the khedive. You're afraid he's going to find out about this, yes? Admit it.'

Adnan was done. He was angry and he'd say things he'd regret if he continued to listen to her. He would not have regrets. That much about him hadn't changed. 'I'm going to put you to bed, Olive. We'll talk when we're calmer in the morning. A night's rest will clear our minds.'

'Stop treating me like a baby!' she shouted. 'I can put myself to bed.'

'Fine, go.'

But he followed her up the stairs, not wanting her to fall and get hurt.

She managed them by herself. When she got to the room, she tugged at her gown.

Adnan was afraid he'd have to help her with that. He didn't think he'd have the physical wherewithal to deny her if she touched him again. Thankfully, she managed it on her own too.

It was the corset that gave her the trouble. Olive tugged at it, babbling about how she'd not known how to put it on herself and it nearly choked her all evening.

He should have hired a maid.

'Get out,' she shouted, sitting on the edge of the bed in defeat.

Adnan would have but she looked pathetic and what if the corset suffocated her at night?

'Lie down and turn over,' he said approaching.

She did as she was told. He tried to work quickly before his desire got the better of him but she really had made a mess of it. The lacy strings were knotted and the boning was digging into her flesh.

He worked on loosening it but her writhing made it hard.

'Stay still,' he demanded.

'Make me,' she countered.

He came onto the bed, covered her legs with his own but even as he did it, she arched her body to his manhood.

'Why would anyone wear such a restrictive thing?' He tugged harder on the string, lowered his teeth to it when his fingers got stuck.

'Do not tear it,' she warned.

'Keep quiet, Olive.'

'Or what?' she challenged, writhing harder.

He angled himself so that his hands were underneath the ribcage of the corset and then he tugged hard enough to tear not just the string but the whole thing. Her breasts spilled into his hands.

'You ruined it,' Olive said. 'I demand compensation.'

'What do you want?' He breathed into her ear, his voice husky, out of his control.

She began touching herself. 'Take me.'

Though his desire for her demanded to be satiated, this wasn't right. He pulled away, stood over her. 'No, Olive.'

Adnan wasn't sure what she wanted him to see in her face and it was too dark now to see much of anything anyway, but the accusation in her words, the hurt even, would linger in his mind long after he'd left her for the night.

'Remember the crude thing your father said to you about us in Cairo? About how it was easier to take me whilst I was wearing Egyptian clothing? Now you reject me when the clothes are not so easy to remove. Am I too tainted for you? Am I that easy to reject?'

At first light, Adnan walked into the city. Yasser had pointed out an apartment over the Rosetta Carriage Company on his first visit. Adnan was sure he did not live there but only stayed when things were busy at work. As he passed the stairs behind the stables, it looked as if they'd not had much work in a while. There were hansom cabs aplenty in the city and the company's horses had been halved in number. Those that remained seemed annoyed that they had to be in stalls that hadn't been mucked out enough to mask the smell.

Why had Yasser been out of the city for so long? Where had he been?

Adnan had time in the night to recall all that his father had said about why he didn't like Yasser's friendship with Saleem. Most of those reasons linked back to Yasser's father, Tal'at.

Apparently, Olive's father as well.

If it were true, her father was a wanted man, a rebel against the khedive's government who enticed unrest in the Egyptian countryside. Although that fact alone would not hurt Olive—Yasser was allowed to run his business and Tal'at's father was still the *eumda* of Rasheed—it meant that associating with him in any capacity would put her in harm's way. When Adnan promised to help her find who she was looking for in the city, he did not think it would compromise the duty he had to his father. To his own brother and family legacy.

Olive was his wife, in every way possible. He believed he'd got to know her better, seen the hidden inside of her that was more beautiful than what was on the outside. But her behaviour yesterday, the things she said, shook Adnan. Of course he understood why she'd kept such a secret, the shame she had internalized, but she was an innocent babe, caught in the middle of her parents' decisions, ill-informed as they were. He certainly had experience with that too. If Olive would listen to him, he'd tell them both that neither one of them could be held accountable for that. Their parents' choices were not their fault.

They could define for themselves what they would hold fast to, their own principles. Adnan had made Olive a deal after their marriage and would have given her the annulment, but she wanted them to make love and damn any consequences. He tried to warn her about the future, the commitment that it would entail, but the truth was that he let himself go. Lost his senses.

Adnan used to tell Saleem that one must always stick to their principles when negotiating in the marketplace or in life. *Always be willing to walk away.*

Was he willing to walk away from Olive?

It was a question he didn't want to answer last night, and this morning, he still didn't know the answer to it. If she'd only talked to him earlier, trusted him, he'd have proceeded with more caution.

Now things were out of Adnan's control and he hated that feeling.

The *eumda* and his guests hinted that they knew exactly who he was at the dinner, rather than just a businessman who bought land to plant sugar cane. That meant that somebody was talking and it could only be Yasser.

He would get to the bottom of that at least.

He knocked on the wooden door of the loft. There'd been voices coming from within right before it but they went silent.

'Yasser,' Adnan called, knocking again. 'Is Yasser Tal'at at home?' he shouted, louder. 'It is Adnan.'

A minute later, Yasser was unbolting the door. He stuck out his head, seemed nervous to see him. Had he already heard about Olive's revelation yesterday?

No one else was there when she was talking to the *eumda*, and guessing by the look that crossed the older man's face, Adnan thought for sure he'd not repeat it so quickly.

'Adnan? It is early for the post office to open. Did you want to send a telegram or… Is everything all right?'

Yasser always referred to him as 'Prince'; why was he doing away with honorifics?

Adnan made a point of looking over Yasser's shoulder as a kind of hint. It wasn't very hospitable as an Egyptian to not invite someone into your home when they stood at your door—even if was just a customary invitation. Yasser had been welcoming ever since he'd met him.

'I am sorry. I would invite you inside but the place is embarrassingly unclean,' he said, understanding the faux pas. 'If you go down to the office, I will join you. We can call for chai from the cafe.'

Yasser was trying to hide whoever was inside with him. Why?

'We were at the *eumda*'s house yesterday,' Adnan said, not making a move to go down to the office. 'I assumed you would be there for his dinner party.'

Yasser rubbed the back of his neck and offered him an uneasy smile. 'My grandfather's events are not for family, typically.'

Adnan sensed that whoever was inside was getting closer so he raised his voice, 'I wanted to speak to you on behalf of my wife. She's looking for a man who visited England some twenty years ago. One who knew her parents, Lord and Lady Whitmore. She thought with your knowledge of the city you would know its people but then we learned that the name of the man is question is Tal'at. Like your father's name.'

Yasser frowned. 'My father was in England but I don't know if he met a Lord or Lady Whitmore.'

And then came the person who was inside. He wasn't much older than Yasser; they looked nearly like they could be brothers. He was shorter and stockier, his curly hair a light brown to match his moustache.

Now that Adnan was searching for—or dreading— a resemblance, he found it.

The man before him *was* Olive's father. And he confirmed, 'My name is Tal'at and I knew the Whitmores very well.'

Chapter Twenty

Olive

Olive woke with a raging headache. It was late morning but she had hardly slept, wishing it was all some terrible nightmare but then being glad that it was all out in the open. There was a relief that came with the release of her shame. Now Adnan knew everything, things could be more honest between them. She could deal with whatever came next.

And he could decide if he was willing to stay with her.

She sighed, stretching her arms to his side of the bed, left undisturbed. She'd hoped he'd return. Tell her that he would be there for her because that was what husbands did. Lord Whitmore had done it with his wife, had he not? To reach out to another man to give his wife what he could not, that…well, that must derive from a deep and nuanced sort of love. The sort of love that defied ego.

Adnan had made love to her in every which way, given her so much, but he had never said he loved her. And last night, he had rejected her. Walked away.

She could understand why but she would be lying if she claimed it did not sting. And Olive Whitmore-Tal'at never wanted to lie to herself again.

She needed coffee, breakfast, lunch. Anything to calm the pounding in her head.

First she collected the remnants of the night before, unable to look at the torn corset or reflect on what it represented. Adnan's rejection.

Then when she was bathed and suitably dressed, she made her way to the living room, saw that everything was clean. No indication that Adnan had even slept there. A breakfast was on a tray on the table in the kitchen but none of his signature tea. Olive had a moment of panic, wondering if he'd left for good, gone back to Cairo. She frantically searched everywhere for a note he might have written, but remembered that his closet still held his clothing.

She rushed to the foyer when she heard a bustle at the door. A plump middle-aged woman was there, dressed in a long black dress and white apron. She smiled when she saw Olive and rushed to her side. She shook her hand gingerly and then bowed, introducing herself as the new housekeeper. She slowed her Arabic so that it almost sounded patronizing.

'Per Mr Adnan's direction, my son is outside guarding the house. He will not enter and he is a good boy. Big. I was giving him a sandwich because he needs to eat often but I will heat your coffee now. Your husband says you like it with milk and lots of sugar?'

Olive felt unmoored. She'd hoped to see Adnan, talk to him. She didn't mind the woman standing before her but shouldn't she have a say in the matter? Shouldn't Adnan have consulted with her that he'd hire a full-time housekeeper, breakfast maker and guard apparently?

'Did Mr Adnan say when he would be back?'

The woman shook her head, then proceeded to ask if she'd like the coffee and breakfast tray brought up to her room.

'The dining room will be fine, *shukran*.'

A short while later, Olive nibbled at the cold food, and sipped the hot, overly sweet—even for her—coffee alone at the table. She felt lonely and sad and wondered if this was her future. Rasheed was a small city, the *ezzbah* located on its periphery. It occurred to her that even when she'd been here that first time, unmarried and in the cottage, it was Adnan's pestering visits urging her to return to Alexandria with him that had kept her company, gave her something to depend upon.

She laughed with the irony of it all.

She needed to stop feeling sorry for herself. After she met her father, she would visit with Elise. Her friend might very well be pregnant and need her help, and Olive would benefit from the inspiration she would offer her. Yes, Elise was married to a prince but she had always been a woman who did what she pleased. A talented painter and musician, even a mobster father hadn't held her back when he was alive, and after he was killed, Elise had found her mother's cousin here in Egypt, a family with roots in Alexandria. Even if she'd not fallen in love with Saleem, Elise would have made her own way. Olive needed her advice so that she could do the same.

Here she sat waiting for Adnan, sad he'd left her in the care of a housekeeper and her 'big' boy who wasn't allowed to enter the house while she was there. It was all so ridiculous. Maybe it suited him to have her trapped in a big house, keep her confined lest she cause another scandal.

She didn't need him. She knew her way into the city. Knew where to find Yasser. He would have answers for her. Maybe his grandfather had already told him what she'd said, but unlike the *eumda*, whose reaction was decidedly subdued as far as she could recall—she wasn't that intoxicated, was she?—if Yasser was her brother, surely he would not deny it. He'd tell her everything he knew. About both his parents. Unless… it was their father's sin in England that ruined his relationship with Yasser's mother. What if Olive's existence was the reason why the woman was now dead?

Olive would lose her own mind with this manner of thinking. She'd wasted so much time doing nothing.

She would walk to the city on her own!

The housekeeper startled at Olive's sudden jump, which had caused the remainder of her coffee to spill in the process. As the woman rushed to clean it, Olive ran from the kitchen.

She was halfway up the stairs to ready herself when Adnan opened the house door. He locked eyes with her but before she could decipher what she read on his face or grasp what she herself was feeling—relief that he was still here or anger that he'd made her doubt him—she saw he wasn't alone.

He'd brought Yasser with him and another man.

He was a middle-aged man with a thick moustache and curly hair. He proudly wore a plain navy blue suit with a burgundy fez cap, tattered as they were. The latter he slipped off his head when he, following Adnan's gaze or drawn to her staring, saw her.

'Jane,' he said, chest heaving.

Jane had been her mother's name and it felt unsettling to hear it.

'Olive,' Adnan said. 'There is someone for you to meet.'

She ran down the stairs, nearly stumbled at the end but righted herself before Adnan could lend her a hand.

'Meet Tal'at, the *man* you were looking for when you first arrived in Rasheed.'

'Olive,' Tal'at corrected himself, gaping as she neared, 'you look exactly like her, your mother, Jane. What a wonder that you should seek me out after all these years.' He spoke in a charming English accent, his smile transforming his face, his whole demeanour, into a man that looked like he would be the most dynamic of fathers.

He gripped her shoulders. 'That I should have a daughter! I dreamed of it, a son or daughter who would find me someday.'

Olive had waited for this moment, dreamt of it herself. Now it was here, it was more than she might have imagined. It felt like a side of her was about to be revealed, a knowledge of herself, a past aspect of her identity, a history that she would appreciate getting to know. If yesterday's confession to the *eumda*, and by extension, Adnan, had been a difficult release, this felt like the sun at the end of a dark tunnel.

She hugged Tal'at, tears in her eyes. Nothing about him was familiar, but she'd loved Lord Whitmore as her father and this gesture felt like coming home to him.

'And to think that your brother was the first person you met upon landing. Do the English not say that God moves in mysterious ways?'

He reached for Yasser, brought him into the hug. 'My children.'

Olive turned to look at Adnan. She wanted to express her gratitude for bringing her this moment even though they'd fought and he probably did not want to. But when she did, she saw his frown.

Surely he must be relieved that his part of their original bargain was done?

'Come into the house,' she invited. 'There is a new cook. Shall we get her to make you tea? You must stay for lunch. We have much to talk about. I have lots of questions.'

'*Itfadaloo*,' Adnan welcomed them in Arabic and led them to the plush couches of the living room, waiting until they had taken their seats. 'I will ask for that chai, from the *housekeeper*.'

That last bit was emphasized for her benefit, Olive sensed, but she did not care to argue with him. There were more important matters, and they were sitting right across from her.

'I cannot believe you are here,' she said as she settled into the spot between her father and brother. 'I grew up as a single daughter but to have you now. Both of you. A father and a brother! And grandparents. Tell me, is there more?'

Tal'at grinned but it was Yasser who spoke: 'I cannot believe you are my sister. May I call you Olive?'

She nodded enthusiastically. 'Remember when you came to the wedding and weren't sure what to call me! I wanted to ask you then if you had heard of anyone in Rasheed who'd travelled to England twenty years ago. To think if I had, this reunion might have come much quicker.'

'You attended their wedding?' Tal'at asked Yasser. 'You did not mention that.'

Her brother's face reddened. 'It was months ago.'

'In Cairo?'

'The khedive hosted it for us,' Olive supplied, trying to take the pressure off of Yasser, for she felt like he was nervous. 'A very hasty wedding, it was good fortune that Yasser happened to be in the city, delivering some papers I think for Adnan's purchase of the *ezzbah* lands.'

Tal'at looked confused for a minute and then it dawned on him. 'I thought he was only a businessman but your husband is Adnan Ali Ahmed, the Prince? Not the heir, but the other son, from an Egyptian woman? A poor country maid, no?'

Olive bristled at the reference to Elham and was afraid Adnan would return and take offense.

Tal'at did not wait for an answer to it, calculating on his own what he knew of the royal family. 'Prince Adnan is elusive, does not appear with the khedive in any official capacity, but they say he is the brains behind him. That the other son, the heir, Saleem, is too soft, that once he is in power, Egypt is sure to *change*.'

Olive could understand Yasser's hesitancy to speak but Adnan had told her that he and Saleem were friends even before she'd come to Egypt. *Why did their father not know that?*

'Adnan runs his own businesses, has investments, and his mother, Elham, was a wonderful woman, a mother to me. She passed away recently. It was heart-breaking to lose her.'

As Adnan re-entered the room and took the seat opposite, all three of them had the good sense to change the subject.

Yasser explained to their father, 'I took Olive to one of the cottages on the outskirts of the *ezzbah* when she first arrived. At first, I thought, oh there is a customer finally, but she did not have very much money to pay even for the hotel.'

'A brave girl, though, travelling on her own,' Tal'at said proudly, but he seemed to be addressing only Adnan when he said 'She is my blood, *akeed*.'

Adnan transformed the Arabic word into a question that sounded rude, 'For certain?' Olive tossed him a look but he ignored it. 'Did you know that there was a child before you left England or was the news this morning a complete surprise?'

Before her father could answer him, the housekeeper came and Adnan rose to take the tray from her. Olive had the feeling it was because he didn't want her to see their guests. Was he ashamed of her father and brother? *Was he ashamed of her?*

She watched Adnan as he himself poured the tea for all of them, and avoided her gaze.

He was upset but she didn't think it was over their conflict; there was more. Was he dreading telling the khedive the truth or was he readying himself to reject her?

She could not very well ask him right then, in front of their guests, but later she would get to the bottom of matters. She would stress they needed to be honest with one another from now on, that it was the only way they could move past their strife. *If he still wanted to.*

Yasser said, 'I was telling my father how it was a wonder Olive went from a travelling girl who did have enough to pay for the local hotel to living in this *ezzbah* house that you transformed into a beautiful mansion.'

He'd spoken it innocently enough but Tal'at turned the comment back to Adnan. 'It must be nice to be a royal. You see a pretty girl, you marry her. You see a piece of land with potential, you buy it at a ridiculously low price.'

Adnan's eyes widened. It was a slight change, but Olive had learned to recognize his turns of stoicism, the things he'd do to maintain control of his emotions. If they were making love, she would have enjoyed getting him to lose control—but now? In front of the father that had just come into her life? Accepted her so easily?

Olive did not want Adnan driving him away.

She jumped in: 'Adnan perceived my desperation and was gentleman enough to propose marriage so that I might stay and find you, *Father*.' She wasn't sure what to call him, exactly. *Papa* was Lord Whitmore and well…even she could fathom that it was too soon for that. 'Egypt is not very kind to women on their own.' Olive added, 'Not that England doesn't have its own rules.'

Tal'at didn't let up entirely though. 'Then the *ezzbah* land is what interested you first? Was it your idea, Prince Adnan, or your father's?'

'*Abu'ya*,' Yasser began, using the Arabic possessive of *father*, 'we should not talk about business now. It is a time to get to know Olive better.'

Adnan, however, spoke on his own behalf. 'I came to Rasheed to fetch Lord Whitmore's daughter as a favour to another and happened upon a land that needed investment, a neglected *ezzbah* that was all but rundown.'

'Smarter people, those who know the history of cotton, would say that better let it go to ruin than be used by the khedive to fill his coffers at the expense of our people's labour.'

Adnan countered, 'Seems that was the sentiment among some of the men at your father's dinner last night. It is false, however. I assured them and would assure you of that.'

Tal'at scoffed.

Yasser repeated, 'Let us not talk of business.'

'Politics,' Adnan amended.

He finally looked at her pointedly. Adnan had looked at her in many ways before. She could name the emotions on his face over the weeks as a kind of trajectory of their relationship's growth:

Annoyance. Anger. Pity. Surprise. Warmth. Gratitude. Desire. Maybe even, a little bit and very rarely, a sentiment close to *love*.

But right then?

Adnan's look was outright animosity.

Chapter Twenty-One

Adnan

It took every ounce of Adnan's patience not to argue with Olive's father. He was a lousy excuse of a man—filled with justifications rather than any sort of apologies for what he'd done. He complained about all manner of things, among them that he'd had to leave England, to abandon his daughter and Jane to Lord Whitmore.

'I didn't know then the damage that nobles and *royals* could do to those of us who wanted to make an honest living for ourselves.' When Tal'at spoke the word *royals*, he looked pointedly at Adnan.

Adnan would not be cowered. 'How long has your father been the *eumda* of Rasheed? Surely that is a noble's title.'

Tal'at smirked. 'It's a title by virtue of who the government thinks will best serve them. Your father and his father before him believed that was mine. Most of

Rasheed have been asleep, however, and are just now realizing that the bargain they made with the nobles who work for the royals can break a man's back.'

He was talking like a revolutionary, the sort of fiery speech that would get him thrown in jail. Yasser nudged his father but Tal'at threw him a reprimanding look. 'You failed to mention you are enough of a friend with a Prince of Egypt that you were invited to his wedding.'

Yasser flushed, properly schooled. Yasser was Saleem's age, accomplished in his own right, and the dynamic between the two and their respective fathers was markedly similar. In that moment Adnan could see why he and his younger brother had become friends. And thankfully and smartly, he said nothing now to compromise Saleem. He mumbled a quick excuse to appease his father: 'You were out of Rasheed when Adnan and I met.'

Adnan added, 'I do not walk around in my regalia, do not tout my family in regular settings.' The warning was mostly for Olive but since he'd poured the tea, she'd become quieter.

Good.

He didn't want her freely offering her heart to this man who, even if he were her father, would exploit it. Adnan would talk to her later. Tell her why he didn't trust Tal'at, make her see that even the *eumda* must have had reason to ban him from his house. He'd impress upon Olive that as her husband, it was his duty to protect her. And he couldn't do that if her father was allowed complete access into her life.

Adnan spoke of Yasser. 'Your son was a help to me when I arrived here. My mother was ill in Cairo and he used his resources to help me keep abreast of her health while I was here. I will always appreciate that.'

Yasser nodded humbly.

Adnan recalled the conversation between them about his mother's sickness that first day after Olive refused to leave Rasheed. He'd mentioned that he did not want to bother the khedive. In response, Yasser had taken the address and said he would wire his friends in Cairo to check in on her, but then said something that had given Adnan pause at the time: *One can never depend upon a father to treat a mother better than her son. It's why mine is buried now, too early for her time.*

He'd not inquired further then but now Adnan wondered what had happened to Yasser's mother. He'd assumed that Tal'at was exiled for his political views against the khedive, but what if it was something else?

'You will stay for lunch,' Olive said. 'I can roast a chicken with potatoes and carrots. Would you like that?'

'Your husband, the Prince and wealthy business-man, does not ask the housekeeper to cook?' Tal'at smirked. Was the man unable to read the cues Adnan was giving him? Perhaps he felt confident that Adnan wouldn't insult a guest by kicking him out of his home. And though every instinct told him to do exactly that, Adnan tried to keep his composure. *For Olive's sake.*

'I quite enjoy being in the kitchen. My best friend, she paints magnificently, and I was always jealous of her talent,' Olive said, her tone a bit too cheery. 'Only recently did I realize that cooking is my canvas. Even living at the palace in Cairo, I disliked the maids coming in, felt stifled by them.'

Adnan thought that Olive might be trying to quell his dislike of Tal'at's statement, but it was true. He'd seen that she was most free without people milling about her. He was the same, but he had brought on the housekeeper and her son after what happened at the *eumda*'s the previous evening. They were out here in the open and though he was not sure how, since it was clear that Yasser had not given him or Saleem up, word was spreading that he was a Prince of Egypt. Discontented people, like Tal'at, could target them. Adnan needed to build a gate, have trained guards. It was the only way to keep his wife safe.

Adnan said, 'It is not a palace here, but I am in the midst of bringing on a *full* staff.'

He'd meant it as a warning to be passed along but Olive frowned.

'Best to ensure whoever you hire are locals,' Tal'at instructed. 'People need the monies.'

'We cannot tell the Prince who to employ.' Yasser

sipped at his tea after he said it, avoiding his father's reprimanding look.

'Maybe not a Prince, but now he is my son-in-law too,' said Tal'at.

'If you knew me,' Adnan said, 'you would know I am the kind of man who decides on all his businesses and life matters on his own terms. Even the khedive knows that if Allah had not made listening to parents obligatory, I would disregard his opinions. And I would certainly not care to listen to a wife's father.'

Tal'at nodded but Adnan saw it wasn't in agreement. He turned to Olive. 'So you will have to make a choice, daughter. Do you take the side of your husband or your father?'

Yasser chuckled nervously, 'What choice is there to make right now, *Abu'ya*?'

'I am speaking *mathalaan*, how you say in English—*philosophically*? Most will say a woman is on the side of her husband but what if the duties to a father are compromised?'

'Is it not presumptuous to put your daughter to a *mathalaan* question on the first day you meet her?' Adnan asked, turning to Arabic. 'She does not yet know if you're worthy of more than a cup of tea.'

'Adnan!'

The shock on Olive's face was frustrating. Surely she could see that the man was trying to challenge his authority?

Tal'at held up both hands in a gesture of surrender. 'You catch me at a difficult time. I cannot seem to separate myself from my political stance, the dislike I have for the government.' He looked back at his son before continuing, 'Yasser will not have told you but I was exiled from Rasheed a while back for, among other things, my politics. Now I've returned by the will of some people who are finally realizing that what I was saying before I left here was right. They've called me back because change is coming to the city and I anticipate there may be a fight between right and wrong, the will of the people to take what is theirs. To loosen the yokes of royalty and nobles obsessed with foreigners and embrace the Egyptian in us.'

Adnan had gone through security reports for his father. He understood the language of rebellion and nationalist movements and while he didn't disagree with the entirety of their sentiments, he knew the movements simplified complexities, didn't mind the chaos it caused in the country or the masses of people who would lose their lives as a result.

He asked him, 'Was this propensity towards your political stance gained before or after travelling to England and leaving behind your infant daughter?'

'Like other Egyptians of my generation, I thought that travelling to the West would furnish me with opportunities. Give me an edge. I was young, uneducated. I wanted to support my wife and son. Make my own way in the world, free from my father's plans for me.' Tal'at reached over Olive to cup Yasser's knee and give it a shake.

'Uneducated?' Adnan questioned, 'Surely that cannot be right, an *eumda*'s son? You could have gone anywhere in the country, the finest schools.' He didn't mention that even in his neighbourhood before he knew who his father was, there were two decent schools—one for boys and another for girls. No one in Egypt could argue that the government had not done well in that regard. Over the last decades, opening schools in even the most remote of areas had been a priority. Only those who did not want to go to school did not go. In fact, there had been talk of mandating it for all citizens up until a certain age.

'I'm interested about your time in England. What parts of it did you enjoy most?' Olive tried to steer the conversation away from a topic that was spiraling out of control.

Her father, however, wasn't moved. He wagged two fingers as if pointing them in accusation. 'The professors in the schools had it out for me. I didn't understand my failures then but now I know that they must have disliked the *eumda*. He'd hurt them in some way and so they wanted to hurt me. Get their revenge on a boy because they could not on his father.'

'All of them?'

'All of them!' Tal'at shouted. He was hot-headed and foolish—along with any number of other things.

Olive stood and said, 'Please make yourselves at home. Adnan, will you join me on the veranda, I would like to consider how that new oven might be utilized for our lunch.'

She beckoned him to follow. He didn't want to fight with her now but he knew it could not be avoided.

She didn't even make it to the veranda before shutting the door of the kitchen as soon as he'd stepped past it.

'What is wrong with you, Adnan? Why are you looking for problems? Being rude to my father? It is supposed to be a happy day.'

'I brought him here.'

'I would have gone to Yasser's myself.'

'That's why I did it.'

'To prevent my recklessness?'

He could not deny it. He crossed his arms, trying to avoid saying something he'd regret but she saw it on his face.

'You think I inherited it from him. That Tal'at and I are the same? You would reject that side of me.'

Adnan tried to change course, or stay on track. 'We need guards, more professional ones, fielded by my family's resources. I have sent word to Saleem now, asking Mustafa to consult on the matter. The men at the *eumda*'s? They know I am the khedive's son and that you are my wife, the beautiful Englishwoman. I cannot leave you alone here. It is not safe.'

'Not entirely English, no? Not entirely the wife you wanted or thought you wanted, no? And so you wish to leave me here alone. Leave my bed as you did last night when I needed you.'

'You were drunk, Olive.' He took a deep breath, knowing she'd not see reason and that their argument was getting out of control. 'I will not always be here. I have other duties. A home in Cairo. A company on the other side of Egypt. A brother and sisters, and a father, a family that I need to visit often. I cannot always be sleeping in your bed.'

'So I am the lowest on your list of your priorities,' she shouted. 'What about my brother and father? Will you go and see yours whenever you like and not afford me the same courtesy?'

Adnan was near to shouting now too. 'They're here, are they not? You are about to make them lunch on the veranda, are you not? I entertain them, though it goes against my better judgement.'

She took a deep breath. 'You do not like my father.'

'I do not.'

'Why? Save for your disagreement with his politics, he seems the perfect gentleman.'

Adnan scoffed. 'Lord Whitmore was a perfect gentleman and you treated him like rubbish.'

She smarted at the accusation but he didn't back down because it was true.

'Papa lied to me! For twenty years, he pretended to be the doting father, never remarrying, making me believe that love was unconditional and lasted beyond the grave! You want to know how I found out? I overheard him laughing casually about how he couldn't be bribed since I looked so English, none would believe my father was an Egyptian! I do not know what he would have done were that not the case. Would I have brought doubt on the memory of my mother? Ruined his career with the gossip that would follow?'

She clutched a fist to her chest. 'I kept my secret because I was afraid people would react like you are doing now. My own husband is eager to leave me, rejecting me. You said this was my house, my gift. Are you upset that we cannot have an annulment? That we will need to get a divorce now, Adnan? I do not mind, would give it. My father is here. And a brother to boot. I have two men instead of one.'

'You are overwrought,' he said.

She pushed him in response, and perhaps would have slapped him too if he hadn't grabbed her wrist and held her back.

He stared at her intently and she didn't break his gaze.

There was a passion between them that wasn't easily extinguished; when their skin touched it lighted a fire in him. Adnan would always struggle not to want her but the fact that Olive could so easily mention divorce, nearly taunt him with it? It reminded him that she'd never promised him a future. They started their marriage with a deal and now it was fulfilled, there was only the present and it was turning out to be a bitter, unsavory one.

Be willing to walk away.

Adnan's own words haunted him.

He dropped her wrist and took on the voice of command inherited from his own father:

'I have matters to attend to in the city. Make lunch for your family now, have your day, the three of you, but know it cannot happen like this again. I am a Prince of Egypt and there are rules for this house, even if it is my gift to you. As for me and you, we will talk about our marriage when they are gone and I have returned.'

He gave her no room for a rebuttal but the look on Olive's face made him question whether or not she'd even be there when he returned.

Chapter Twenty-Two

Olive

Adnan had done the same thing when his mother died. He'd shut her out of his mourning heart to turn to his siblings and lean on them for whatever support he needed. Nawal and Saleem, that smile he reserved for them. The one she'd never see.

She was his wife, but he had not truly accepted it. He'd been compelled into a hasty marriage for whatever weakness he had around women in need, but she'd never been the kind of companion he pictured himself marrying. At the first opportunity, he'd negotiated a deal with her. *Ever the businessman.* Yes, he'd been kind and noble towards her and yes, she had got more out of their pact, getting to spend time with Elham and now meeting her father, but she'd hoped she'd gained a husband as well. That they had finally come to an understanding that could carry them past that initial deal and into a future together.

The way he'd brought up her recklessness? Would he always throw it in her face? She knew it was wrong and that she'd made mistakes but why did Adnan not understand she had been acting out of shame?

Now her father was here, she might find a way to reconcile that feeling. Envision a future.

If she learned to accept herself, then Adnan should too, completely and without conditions.

Olive determined to forget about him for now and deal with whatever his 'rules' were later. Lay down a few of her own.

She took a deep breath and returned to the living room to lead her brother and father to the veranda. 'Keep me company as I make you that lunch.'

Yasser took a minute to inspect the still-empty birdbath before making himself comfortable on the cushioned bench.

Her father sat on one of the chairs next to the backgammon set but then said, '*Tawla* is a drug to keep the masses stuck in chairs all day by the cafe corners, playing games.'

Olive pricked with a touch of disappointment as she chopped onion for their supper.

Adnan had gifted her the set after remembering her staring at one in the marketplace. What he hadn't known then, and what she might have even forgotten about that moment in Cairo, was that she'd been looking at it because she'd seen older men playing the game here in Rasheed when she first arrived. And any she passed she'd wondered if he might be her father.

Clearly not.

Yasser, it turned out, had a surprising ability to tell fascinating stories. He pointed out how when Olive first arrived, he was reading an historical account of one whom people in Rasheed called El Naddaha. '*Nymph of the Nile*, it was titled in English. I was not sure if it was a translation or the author knew someone in the city who'd narrated it, but it was talking about how the Naddaha could possess human bodies and tempt men into complete demise. That she could be cruel and bitter, even murderous, but when she came into the body of someone with a sister, then she would be the complete opposite. Loving and kind, willing to sacrifice everything, including her life for that sister.'

'The fantasies made up by those who are superstitious are utter nonsense,' Tal'at said.

'Yet also serendipitous that I should walk in, *your sister*, at that moment,' Olive countered. She'd washed her hands of the chicken and the spices she'd rubbed into it along with the potatoes. The new wood-burning stove Adnan had installed would do the rest of the cooking.

Yasser focused on what she said instead of their father's rebuke. 'The book did inspire me to go out of my way and try to get you the cottage. I don't normally ask my grandfather for anything but he is the one who had the keys to the *ezzbah* properties.'

'His grandfather—yours too, I suppose now—all but washed his hands of me and my son. He might be good to you because of your husband, however, but you'll know soon enough that he isn't the most caring of men.'

Olive took the chair opposite him at the *tawla* set. She recalled her interactions with her grandparents the night before. 'You have a sister too.'

'How do you know that?' her father asked.

'I met your mother—my grandmother—last night at the dinner at the mayoral house. She grew…*agitated*… with my questioning around her children. One of the other guests said she had two but didn't like to talk about them. She suggested that you may be…' Olive looked at Yasser. Surely their father could not have been responsible for his mother's death. They'd surely not have a relationship if that were the case. Yasser's face, however, gave nothing away.

Tal'at said, 'The gossips will make up lies. As for my mother, she is a woman with a weak constitution, a personality that likes to fade. I think the English would call her a wallflower.'

Olive nodded; she'd seen it herself.

'She's managed by my father, defers to him for the littlest thing—even her meals, her clothing, the friends she keeps, must be approved by the *eumda*. I love her but even growing up it was frustrating when she said "ask your father" or "do what he tells you" to me and my sister. Only when we married another pair of siblings—my father's choice, of course—and left the house did we understand what the world outside it could be. It meant that both our marriages were not successful. We didn't love our spouses. That is why my mother doesn't like to talk about me or me and my sister. She failed us both by being silent then, so why start talking now?'

Tal'at chuckled. 'I suspect too that your question took her by surprise. If she'd known it was coming, she'd have prepared by asking my father how best to respond beforehand.'

While that sounded about right, Olive's gaze flickered to Yasser, who writhed uncomfortably with the casual mention of how his mother was not loved by his father. Lord Whitmore had only ever spoken in the most devoted of terms on anything relating to 'his Jane.'

'I have an aunt too?' There was so much she did not know about their family. *Her* family.

Tal'at said, 'No need for the ugly bits first.'

'Tell us about your upbringing,' Yasser said. 'What was it like in England?'

The afternoon breeze was faint around them. The sun was at its peak at this time of day but Adnan had said the veranda's elevation and the trees they'd planted near it would keep it temperate all year long. It was a beautiful day but Olive couldn't help wondering if she and Adnan would have another one here together. Or if they would ever be together as husband and wife again. Adnan had been raised in a broken marriage and apparently, it was in her blood as well. Maybe theirs was doomed from the start.

She started talking in order to avoid dreading. 'I cannot complain. Lord Whitmore left me wanting for nothing. I went to the finest finishing school in London, shopped at the best boutiques for clothing, food—anything really. I would have been content enough but something did seem to be missing. I did not know Lord Whitmore was not my father until one awful night when I overheard him talking to a friend. It was devastating, the lie, the hurt.' She shook away the memory of that night and wondered why she'd waited to talk about it to Adnan, and in the heat of anger, no less. Maybe if she'd done it earlier, he'd have listened to her, understood her perspective better.

'People are adopted all the time in England, fathers take on the children of their wives and remain hush about their origins but for so long it was just me and my *papa*…er… Lord Whitmore. We'd been thick as thieves, good friends, you know? I would have never dreamed such a huge secret could exist between us. But it did.'

She watched Tal'at, trying to gauge any hurt he

might feel, but he seemed lost in his own thoughts, it was as if he'd not been listening to her at all.

Yasser gave her a sheepish smile in understanding.

While they waited for the chicken and potatoes to finish cooking, they spoke of mundane topics, ones that were safer, unlike politics or the country's prosperity.

When the food was ready, she served it with the bread delivered earlier that morning. Adnan must have had it delivered. The men ate heartily and she was pleased the food had turned out well, caught herself wishing that Adnan were there to sample it too. She admonished herself on that thought.

When they were done, Yasser stood. 'Perhaps we should leave before the Prince returns.'

Tal'at ushered him to sit back down. 'This is my first meeting with my daughter after twenty years. What if he does not let me back in the next time I come knocking?'

Olive said, 'Adnan is not ungenerous. He would not turn anyone away at his door.' But had he not made clear that there would be a gate and guards outside? That a meeting like this with her father could not happen again?

Before she could say more, there came a noise from behind the trees at the end of the veranda. A whistle, then a bird call, or bad imitation thereof.

Now Tal'at rose. 'Only those close to me know my whereabouts.'

At the puzzlement in Olive's expression, her father explained: 'I am in exile. Your husband found me in Yasser's apartment above his stables today, and that means that place was compromised. I had to inform one of my...*associates* that I would not be there when they came searching for me.'

'Wait for me here,' he spoke to Yasser before moving in the direction of the trees.

Olive said, 'Wait, I can lead you through to the front door. There is no need to hide.'

Tal'at shook his head, 'There is a guard there. It was enough he saw me once. I cannot have him see me again.'

The housekeeper's 'big boy'? Olive would have thought he'd likely gone home with his mother when Adnan dismissed her for the day but maybe not.

Then she spied the man waiting for her father behind the tree.

Why did he look familiar?

Olive frowned and turned to see Yasser had noticed him as well.

She recalled, 'Isn't he one of the *eumda*'s guards? I saw him at the mansion at dinner.'

'Yes,' Yasser said, clearly surprised to see him there too. 'His name is Belal.'

Olive remembered him because he'd been ogling her

when they'd arrived for the dinner party. Adnan had managed to put a quick end to it with his own hard look of reprimand.

'What kind of danger is our father in?'

'Nothing immediate, do not worry.' It sounded like Yasser was trying to alleviate his own worry, 'He took on additional responsibilities with a nationalist movement that operates out of villages around the delta, small ones. I believe they are too inconsequential to be considered a threat to Cairo.'

'And are you involved in this movement?'

Yasser shook his head. 'He asks me for things, but not everything I agree to because I will not risk my future. Yet it is hard to say no to a father.'

Olive nodded, feeling bad for how many no's she'd doled out to Lord Whitmore, and how Adnan's strength of character meant that he could absolutely say no to his if he needed to. Adnan knew the difference between duty and principle. She was proud of him for that, even if she was furious with him.

Before they could say more, Tal'at returned. 'My associate tells me that Rasheed is under siege. Police have come from Alexandria or Cairo, he is not sure which but he thinks they are looking for me.'

Olive sensed the nerves in his words, the defiance rooted in anger. It was a feeling she'd known well over the last few months. 'Then you are safe here. Adnan is a Prince, he will say you are under his protection.'

'I would not be surprised if it is your husband who has reported me.' Tal'at's voice rose and he turned to Yasser for confirmation. 'Recall he went to the post office before we came here?'

'Because you said you had to do something first.' Yasser gestured to Belal, out of earshot but watching them from his position in the trees, presumably waiting for Tal'at. 'You did not tell us you were going to inform *him* where we'd be?'

Their father grew more irate, 'Never mind Belal, his loyalty is to me. Adnan's loyalty, however, would be to the khedive.'

Yasser put a hand on their father's arm to calm him. 'Adnan would not turn you in. He brought you here to meet Olive—that was his intent. And he could not call the authorities to come so quickly from Cairo or Alexandria. I run the telegram service. I cannot tell you his business, but I assure you he did not summon his father's guard.'

'I will go with Belal now. He will hide me until the siege of the city is over.' Again it was as if their father was not listening. Watching him made Olive introspective. Was that how Adnan saw her?

'*Abu'ya*, that man isn't trustworthy,' Yasser insisted. 'We do not know if Rasheed is besieged. Come back with me and we will check for ourselves. Or stay here, wait for Adnan, see what he has to say.'

'Please,' Olive pleaded, feeling compelled to add

her voice. 'I just met you and do not want you to go into hiding again.'

Tal'at closed his eyes, but when he opened them, his mind hadn't changed. He cupped a hand to her cheek. 'It is sad that this is our first meeting, daughter of Jane, and perhaps our last. There was much I wanted to tell you still. I fought with your husband because I feared he'd steal from our time together in much the same way as Lord Whitmore arranged it so that I'd not be able to see Jane and you, my daughter, anymore. Now none of it will matter if I am arrested.'

'*Abu'ya*, let me speak to Belal, get him off your trail. I'll maneuver it so that he and I will walk back to the city, buy you time to make your escape,' Yasser insisted. 'Please listen to me in this.'

Their father nodded. 'Very well. I know a place to go that no one knows of. I'll be safe.'

He hugged him goodbye and Yasser threw her a smile. 'I'll see you soon, sister.'

'I will look forward to it, brother.'

As they watched, Yasser marched to where Belal was and drew him away. Her father waved both goodbye as if nothing was amiss.

When they'd disappeared, she turned to him, sure he was going to bid her a final farewell next. 'This cannot be the end,' she said. 'Adnan has power. I will talk to him, beg him to do this for me.'

Tal'at gave her a bitter smile. 'You said yourself, women do not have many rights here. Even if he wanted to serve you, his father wouldn't allow it. My existence, my beliefs about the country's sovereignty, they challenge the khedive's livelihood. But this needn't be goodbye, Olive. Come with me? I know a hiding spot. We would have to rough it for a short while, but can spend time together. When you are bored of your father, you can return to your husband. What do you say?'

What could she say? She'd come to Rasheed, abandoned her best friend, hastily married a Prince who did not love her all in the effort to meet her real father and now he was here before her...she'd no other recourse.

'I say let me pack a bag.'

Chapter Twenty-Three

Adnan

He'd nothing to do in the city but walked around its emptier parts, trying to blow off steam. Adnan would have much preferred a run, but did not want to draw attention to himself. Doing so may put Olive in danger and no matter what happened between them, that was the last thing he would ever want.

They needed to talk. He needed to be forthcoming with Olive about all his doubts and feelings. He headed back to the house, determined. Adnan did not want a divorce but at the same time, he wondered if it were even possible to stay together. If she even wanted to. He would force her hand on that, not leave it ambiguous as he had the night he presented her with the house. The night they made love. That had been his mistake. But now he'd do the honourable thing, let her decide if or when she wanted the divorce.

Adnan thought about how reckless and frustrating

she'd been since that first day when he met her. But over the course of their hasty marriage, he came to believe he was wrong about her. That Olive wasn't foolish, that she was endearing. Sometimes she said the wrong things but that didn't take away from the fact that she was eager to be understood.

Olive had been keeping a secret and Adnan wished she'd have trusted him enough to tell him from the start, but maybe that was on him too. After he discovered his own mother had kept the secret of who his father was from him, how had he reacted? With anger. He'd had enough secrets to last a lifetime, so he hadn't cared to push Olive to tell him hers. Having seen her reckless behaviour over the Elise and Saleem situation, he'd not trusted *her* enough to think she could be his wife with her heart. And so to protect himself from more hurt he had never given her his. Not fully, at least.

If their marriage could find solid ground, become one where he saw a future, then Adnan could finally let go of the past. Let himself fall in love with Olive.

But when he opened the door to the empty house, he knew it was too late. Olive was gone. She'd packed a bag, chosen Tal'at.

Adnan noted the remnants of their lunch on the veranda, the blanket she liked to warm her legs with when they were sitting out there. He remembered how beautiful she would look watching the green of the *ezzbah* beyond the house. She'd learned to tie back her hair with a bandanna and sip on the limeade she'd make that was much too sugary.

'Limes are sour by nature,' he complained of their cloyingness.

'And thereby necessitating they meet a sweet match! It will bring out the best in them. Do you not think the limes are happy to know they can have such a noble purpose? What other function is there for sour? The limes were useless before I squeezed them into this sugar syrup.'

Seeing Olive laughing had brought Adnan pure joy. The joy his mother wanted for him.

But he consistently pushed aside that feeling, because he thought it could not last. That whatever secret Olive was keeping would eventually come between them.

Smartly, as it turned out, for he'd been right.

A strong rapping at the front door stirred him from his thoughts, and Adnan ran to it, hopeful she'd returned. But when he opened the door, it was his father!

'*Khedewy*,' Adnan said, stumbling back. Seeing him far from any of his palaces was surprising. 'What are you doing here?'

The khedive lifted a brow. 'Can a father not visit his son in his marital home?'

'Yes. Yes. Come in.' Adnan composed himself and

thought, *How many fathers were to be entertained at the* ezzbah *on this day?*

The khedive entered, his efficient and disparaging eyes quickly appraising the foyer chandelier, the spiral staircase, the marble flooring, the carpets that would lead to the kitchen. That look of his would make other men tremble, but Adnan refused to be intimidated by his father—or any other fathers for that matter.

And, in the wake of how the khedive had behaved when his mother died, over her burial, Adnan thought he'd never again want to please him as much as he once had.

He, however, knew the etiquette. '*Marhaban*,' he welcomed him. 'Come into the living room. The house is not entirely furnished yet but the couches are comfortable.'

'Where is Olive?'

Adnan tried to read his father, to see if he knew anything about what had happened with her. He was not ready to tell him about where 'his good friend Lord Whitmore's daughter' was, or the reason why she had left. Adnan could not deal with the fight he and his father would have if he informed him that their marriage might possibly end in divorce.

He and Olive had to come to an understanding on matters on their own before that would happen.

'She has gone out, having made *friends* in Rasheed. If we knew you were coming, she'd have… And I dismissed the housekeeper early too.' Adnan frowned, turned the questioning onto his father. 'You never go anywhere without planning. You being here, travelling to Rasheed in secret, with a small guard, that unmarked carriage outside? It is unlike you.'

'Does a father need a reason to see his son? I have missed you, Adnan.'

It wasn't the entire truth. Adnan could not recall a time when his father had ever been less than blunt with him. The khedive brushed the hairs of his already impeccably groomed moustache. He was sitting in the seat Tal'at had been in a few hours before and Adnan couldn't help but draw comparisons. The khedive looked much older though they likely didn't have much between them. More tired. His suit was nicer, certainly. His manner, though often challenging, was based on a sense of duty and honour. And though his and Adnan's relationship was strained, the khedive was a man who tried to act with his legacy in mind. He wished to ensure his line, his children were strong, protected.

Tal'at, on the other hand, was willing to compromise Yasser's livelihood by hiding above his stables. Had a daughter out of wedlock and then left her halfway across the world. If Olive hadn't been searching for him, if Adnan hadn't been trying to help her and brought him here, Tal'at would never have sought her out. Of that, Adnan was sure.

'You have nothing to say?' The khedive broke the silence.

'What would you like me to say, *Khedewy*? That I missed you too?'

His father huffed, '*Khalas*, Adnan. Stop giving me this treatment. Your siblings have berated me enough for my lack of empathy to your suffering when Elham died. Nawal even sent Maysoon to call me a "grumpy" old man. The girl said she learned the word from Olive.'

Adnan couldn't help but smile. 'You can always count on May to tell you exactly what is on her mind.'

It was only when his father was talking about Maysoon that you could forget who he was. Not Khedive Ahmed Ali, but simply someone's loving grandfather.

'Maysoon does have a special place in my heart,' his father said, 'because she reminds me in many ways of Elham. That same fire, that same willingness to tell me the truth about the worst parts of me, that was your mother, Adnan. It is silly but one of the reasons I came is because I have been having dreams of her, three in as many nights.'

Adnan's father wasn't a very religious man but he believed in the power of signs from Allah. Maybe because he too had dreamt of her, Adnan asked, 'What did she do or say in the dream.'

'She told me that there is peril in Rasheed and

I needed to check on our children, make sure they are safe.'

'Children' not 'son'?

His mother had become close to Olive. She loved her like the daughter she never had and Olive loved her like the mother she never had. It struck Adnan that were his mother alive and healthy that he might be happier in his marriage. And because they'd been talking about Maysoon, he couldn't help but think of how much she'd have liked to see her own grandchildren.

What if Olive is pregnant?

Adnan did not hold much stock in the prophetic possibilities of dreams but…that would change everything. If he was so preoccupied with protecting Olive even when he was angry with her and thinking they'd not have a future, how much more would he be if she were carrying his child.

He nearly growled with the need to find her now, demand they figure things out.

It was the tears welling in his father's eyes that shocked and subdued him.

'I never told you but Elham and I were good friends before we had you. I loved her since I was a boy, but had to marry for duty.' He scoffed, 'A Turkish Princess just like the khedives before me. My father said he learned about my love for a maid's daughter and sent her and her family away. Only when he died and I became khedive did I seek Elham out. It took years to convince her to marry me, and the truth was that by then, I cared for Ulfat too. Elham knew it and said she'd never be happy in the harem, confined in the palace. She asked for the divorce, telling me that any sons of mine would be able to take care of themselves but that I should grant it for the sake of my daughters. I will never forget her words: "If a girl cannot learn trust from her father, how will she ever fully accept love from her husband?"'

The words immediately made Adnan think of Olive—she seemed not to be far from his mind!—but also of his mother. He was proud of the sacrifices she'd made, the satisfaction she derived from his relationship with Saleem, certainly, but especially the one with his sisters.

The khedive sniffled and squared his shoulders, 'You are angry about your mother's burial. You believe my refusal to hold a state funeral for a wife of mine was *wrong*. That I am ashamed of my past with her.'

The question in his father's eyes, the expectation that Adnan was hurt, the dread…those were things he'd never seen from him before.

His father hadn't properly mourned his mother. He'd come here, opened up his heart, for what? Forgiveness? Understanding?

Adnan sighed. He could give him both. And unburden himself in the process. 'In the end, it was the funeral she wanted.'

The khedive agreed, 'I believe so too.'

It struck Adnan that if he and his wife were going to be honest with one another then he needed to sort his own issues with his father too. He could see now that Olive fighting with him over his ability—or lack thereof—to understand his complicated relationship with the khedive had to do with her own complicated relationship with Lord Whitmore and, as much as he hated it, Tal'at too. If Adnan could find a steadfast balance with the khedive, then maybe he could help Olive find it too. Maybe it would be a way for them to find each other. And he wanted that. He wanted her.

He said, 'What has disappointed me, *Khedwey*, is that you seemed disappointed in me, ashamed of me. All talk about me not being cultured enough for a lady? That my marriage with Olive was a chance to be more "civilized." The anger over the cancelled honeymoon trip.'

'It was all *takhrif*, stupid talk from an old man sad to have lost control of his heir and afraid that this other son, the one most like him, would be lost too. And I suppose that I was a man who was trying to be strong in the face of the death of his first love. Having Elham in the palace was a reminder of everything I did wrong. By her. By you. By my whole family.' He buried his face in his hands for a long minute.

'I did not know it, *Khedewy*.'

'I kept you shut out, like you keep your loved ones

shut out. It is my worst trait, likely yours too. And I don't want those mistakes for you, son. That is why I came here today too, to check on you. See if you are happy. You married Olive so hastily, and my concerns around a honeymoon were because I want you to have a life with her that is based on love. Lord Whitmore is a friend, and her mother was a good woman. I've told you before that is why I wanted her for Saleem. You taking his place? Not being in love with Olive the way he was with Elise? It frightened me.' His father took a deep breath. This conversation was hard for him but he was trying and that made Adnan nearly tear up as well.

'I've no doubt that you will treat Olive honourably. This house you've built is proof of that. You are a fine man, son. Noble, the best of *cultured* Egyptian men. But you must give her your whole heart. Because if you do, that nobility would not feel like only a duty. That desire to keep her content and happy, safe…well, that would come naturally, not a yoke around your neck. You must be honest with yourself, if not me— do you love her?'

Did he?

Later, Adnan and his father drank a cup of tea.

'Men can make it themselves' the khedive mar-velled, and said it was one of the best he'd had. Never-theless he declared they should ensure the housekeeper was live-in, and the house would require a full-staff, at

least a few of which were trained in the style of English noble households!

Just then his guard knocked. He handed the khedive
a file, one that he was apparently expecting.

As his father skimmed it, the guard informed him,
'The train is prepared for you, *Khedewy*, whenever you
are ready to go. We will be waiting in the carriage.'

'Stay for dinner,' Adnan offered.

'I did want to see Olive, be assured that she is all
right, so I can tell Elham if she comes back to my
dream, but it will have to be next time. I only got away
from Maysoon today because she said there were apologies to be made.'

'Give her my best salaams and hugs, tell her there
is a whole *ezzbah* waiting for her to frolic in when she
visits and that a guest room will be reserved for her
seashell collection.'

'Which reminds me, May said to tell you you're
her favourite *khaloo* now. Saleem has lost the title of
best uncle.'

'Why?'

'Because she heard Elise is going to have a baby and
she expects he'll be too busy with him or her.'

'It is confirmed *khalas*?' Adnan was overjoyed for
his brother. He'd had a feeling that it was a possibility
when Elise hadn't accompanied him to his mother's
funeral but Saleem hadn't wanted to mention it.

The khedive nodded.

'*Mabrook.*' He hugged his father, congratulating him. 'Maybe a new heir!'

'I would take another granddaughter too.'

'Do not permit Maysoon to hear you say so.'

The sound of his father's laughter, the lightness in it, even as Adnan knew things were undecided between him and Olive, was the kind of alleviation he needed.

Before he left, the khedive handed him the file brought in by the guard.

'When I had that dream, I wondered what could possibly be the danger in Rasheed and remembered my earlier doubts on my sons' friendship with Yasser Tal'at. I had my people do further investigation on the matter. Inside this file is what they accumulated on him and his father. It turned out you and Saleem were right about the boy. And the father is a small man in the rebel group. His position with them began because of his connection to the *eumda*, but the cold relationship between Tal'at and his father has made him useless to them.'

Adnan tried to school his interest as he skimmed the paper in the file and saw the word *England*. 'What was the reason why he was exiled from the city then?'

'If you think it is important, we can check with the *eumda* here on that for it seems to be a family matter. Tal'at and his sister were married to siblings from a nearby village, smaller than Rasheed, but they were the children of the *eumda* there. When Tal'at left his

wife and young Yasser for a jaunt to England, his wife
grew depressed. She drowned upon his return.'

Adnan was shocked. 'Yasser's mother drowned herself?'

The khedive pointed to a notation 'Her brother,
Belal, who is married to Tal'at's sister, claimed that
Tal'at murdered his wife. He got a note from Tal'at
that day, saying to come and get her because he was
sick of her. Belal thought it was a joke but when his
sister ended up dead, he wanted justice, an investigation. But rather than a trial or proper punishment,
Tal'at was exiled by his father, saved by the *eumda*.
His daughter suffers for it, though. While still alive
in the nearby village, she is said to be little more than
a maid in her husband's house, trapped as a prisoner
might be. They say Belal beats her daily as retribution
for what he believes was done to his sister by Tal'at.'

'What misery.'

'Yes.' The khedive sighed. 'When I learned it, I
pitied Yasser and understood why he is worthy of my
sons' admiration. He has worked to better himself in
spite of his broken family.'

The khedive did not know the extent to which that
family was broken.

Nor did his father know Olive's part in it. Adnan
said, 'I do not understand the *eumda*'s action. How
and why?'

'I think he was trying to avoid something worse

for his city. By exiling Tal'at, he brought peace to Rasheed. He avoided a violent conflict between the villages and saved the lives of innocents here, though none can truly appreciate caution until catastrophe strikes. The *eumda* used an old Al-Tar law around blood feud avoidance more commonly seen in Upper Egypt. We really should look to modernize.' The khedive grinned, 'Maybe you and Saleem can work on that the next time you are in Cairo.'

Adnan frowned. There was a pit of dread growing in his stomach. Olive was not here. Her father was exiled and in hiding not because of his position in a rebel group but because of a feud with his dead wife's family.

If she had gone with him… Adnan shook his head, fearful of the ramifications, where his line of thinking was going. And then there was the fact that already weighed on his mind: 'I met the *eumda*. One of his friends is a doctor. Both seemed to know I was a prince but I am unsure how.'

The concern that passed his father's face matched what he was feeling. 'That knowledge might have come from my office but it is not bad. You know these smaller areas of Egypt from your work with me. Because they are far from the center, they need to see power—it is the only way to assure protection. Let my team organize your security here in this *ezzbah* house.'

'I sent word to Saleem and Mustafa about a gate and

guards earlier today, but I would be grateful for your help in expediting the matter.'

'It will be done by week's end.' His father smiled as if he was finally happy to have something to give Adnan. 'Rest assured, your home, your wife will be protected.'

It was all he'd ever wanted for Olive. It was why he married her when she was desperate. Why he held his breath whenever she was in any perceived danger. But did that sense of needing to protect her come from his love for her?

Lest he doubt the answer to that, the slip of paper he found tucked beneath the pieces of the backgammon set a short while later, after the khedive and his entourage had departed, confirmed it.

It was a ransom note that began with 'If you love your wife…'

It was too late to call back his father but Prince Adnan Ali Ahmed would do anything and everything to rescue the woman he loved.

Chapter Twenty-Four

Olive

They walked through the outskirts of Rasheed so that her father could not be recognized. Olive donned the black milaya Nawal had given her when Elham died and though it was mostly women of the harem who wore it in Cairo, in the countryside it was more commonplace. Her father loosened it around her head, saying, 'This is the way the falaheen women wear it across rural Egypt.'

The material certainly differed: hers was a rich silk, whilst theirs was a thick cloth that looked like it could be hoisted atop a felucca. That reminded her of Adnan, their first excursion as a married couple, the fun they had.

And because she and her father were walking along a tributary of the Nile, it was hard not to think about how much she already missed her husband.

Instead, she turned back to the current surroundings. 'The river here is so different than the one in Cairo, it's hard to believe they are the same Nile.'

He lifted her bag to avoid a patch of dried dirt. 'It is the country's lifeline, singular only.'

Tal'at had taken off his fez hat and his hair shone a dark golden in the sunlight; it was so much like hers. Olive always thought she'd got the colour from her mother but wondered at the curls. Strange to think she'd got both from her father.

She said, 'In Cairo, it is wide and distinctive, but there is so much more around it that it seems more like a conduit, a route to get to the city or to the pyramids. Or to spend a nice day in a boat, eating seeds.'

She swallowed down the sentiment that rose in her, reminded herself that she was supposed to be angry with Adnan. 'Here the Nile is a necessity. The delta isn't wide—some of these banks, I can see full across, but the children bathing? The women washing their clothing? The men fishing? It is their lifeblood.'

Tal'at huffed, 'And when the Prince plants his newly purchased lands, the waters will be diverted to irrigate his sugar cane. Rivers can dry out.'

'Surely not the Nile,' Olive countered.

There was a note in Tal'at's tone and a look he threw her then that made Olive recoil, both because of her high regard for Adnan, despite their argument, and because she'd witnessed how Tal'at was with Yasser.

But the man walking next to her was her father and there were things she yet needed to know.

He said, 'It is a long walk, but if we don't talk, it will be less tiring.'

She nodded.

'A little faster too, as we have to arrive before nightfall.'

Olive didn't tell him that her feet were hurting already. Or that her husband was the sort of man who anticipated her being tired before it happened. And if Adnan were here, he'd probably have carried her the rest of the way. Or told her to sit and wait while he fetched a carriage.

Olive didn't say much of anything else until they'd reached their destination.

The closer they got, the more she realized where they were headed. The windy breeze that twisted her *milaya* around her head, the salty smell in the air.

The Mediterranean Sea.

'This is the port where I first landed from England,' she said.

'That is more to the east. Ships will sometimes stop there on their way to Alexandria but oftentimes, they skip this area entirely. I like to think of this spot as where the river *rendezvous* with the sea.' Her father had used the French word somewhat incorrectly but she didn't think he'd appreciate her correcting him.

Besides, she understood what he meant, for the Nile

soon sputtered until it was little more than a stream and the muddy banks gave way to an expansive beach.

Where they stood was more a cove so the waves came in weaker but she could see how strong they were beyond it, white foam spitting and crashing, seagulls flying overhead.

'There is a nice spot I found as a boy. Follow me.'

She trailed behind him, tiredness and resistance from shifting sands making her progress slower. He waved her over to a hill, a small one with a bare tree, as if it had meant to be an island but never had the courage to leave the mainland. It was strewn with beach grass and seaweed, but Tal'at set down her bag and then himself.

Olive sat beside him, finally able to stretch her tired legs and lie back. They'd not brought water or any other drinks and because they were in what seemed an entirely abandoned area, there wasn't anybody selling anything.

If Adnan had been there, he'd have taken that into consideration. Planned for that possibility.

She recalled the day she'd put on that ridiculous get-up to go side-saddle camel riding, how hot she'd been. How he had immediately bought her a refreshing drink and taken her on the balloon ride. His concern for her comfort had always been a priority.

Now Olive wondered how she'd get back to the *ez-zbah*. She did not have it in her to walk all the way home. She should have waited for him to return before leaving. He'd have insisted on getting her a carriage.

'I would come here,' Tal'at said, arms outstretched, 'look out there to the horizon and imagine the world beyond it. I wanted more than anything to leave Egypt, see it all.'

'It was your dream to travel to England?'

'Not just England, but it is the place that made the most sense. We knew it because of our dealings with cotton and because it was easier to get to. I believed, however, that it would be a starting point. A path to America, for that was where the real opportunity was.'

Olive frowned. He must have meant that was his dream as a boy, surely not as a married man? As a father to Yasser?

'I could not forget that dream but when I finally landed in London, it felt more stifling. I grew bored and ended up taking a job in Manchester. A gangster's shipping company that worked the Egypt line even though this was not the direction I wanted to come back to.'

Thomas Clifton?

Olive dared not say Elise's father's name aloud but she thought it. That night she'd overheard him talking to Lord Whitmore, when she'd overheard their secret: that their unlikely friendship had begun with a bribe over the man from Rosetta.

'I was paid less than I might have been were I here,'

Tal'at continued. 'The dream was already turning into a nightmare but got worse. After a fight with another worker, I was tossed into the jailhouse. English justice isn't as *negotiable* as the Egyptian sort or,' he admitted with an ironic smile, 'maybe it is because I did not know the *eumda* there.'

He pulled his fez hat from his suit pocket, unfolded it to fill it with sand, then dumped it out again. He explained, 'My father helps me here, gets me exile when I might have been locked up in jail. Yet, having been nearly forgotten in an English jail, I could empathize with those in Egypt who had no one like the *eumda* supporting them. It is why I speak as I do to your husband. A prince is the biggest example of privilege.'

Olive would not listen to him saying anything bad about Adnan. 'I want to know where you met my... *parents*.'

He turned to her with a squint. 'Are you sure you want to hear the whole story?'

'I need to,' Olive insisted. 'Papa could not bring himself to tell me.'

Tal'at nodded. 'I met them at a traveller's club. Lord Whitmore and his wife, Jane, were members. Foreigners like to "experience" places even from their homes and I was doing little talks there to make some money but when writers began exploring Egypt more than some of its own people, a product of the khedive's policies, by the way, then my services were no longer needed. I had to take the job in Manchester as a result.'

He'd just told her that he was bored in London but Olive did not want to distract him from what she really wanted to know. 'Did you become friends with my parents?'

'In a manner of speaking. They had a special interest in Egypt, because of friends they had here. Invited me to dinner in their home too, were impressed by me.'

'You charmed them.'

He grinned. 'I grew up in a house just as fine as theirs, knew the customs. And yes, I suppose I was charming.'

He swallowed before continuing, 'I knew they were struggling to conceive and I told them that I had a son that took. I had no problem getting my wife pregnant but she had *trouble* keeping the babies in her womb. She lost many before and after Yasser.'

Olive frowned, recalling that bit of gossip shared with her at the *eumda*'s dinner about Yasser's mother. And perhaps it was some sort of sympathy shared by all women but she couldn't help but feel sorry for her. She clutched her stomach protectively. *Where had that come from?*

'Lord Whitmore said that they'd been to all the doctors, that it was his problem, not Jane's.'

'So it was his suggestion, knowing you were *fertile*.'

'Not immediately, no. I reached out to him when I

was arrested in Manchester, hoping for his help, because I knew his position in the government. I realized I needed to see my family, but didn't have enough monies to pay passage. Lord Whitmore made me a deal—lie with his wife for a month and he would provide the monies no matter if it was successful or not.'

Hearing it said so plainly stabbed at Olive's shame. It was a shocking dumping of salt on a festering wound. She felt the lump in her throat, struggled to push it back down. She heard Adnan's voice in her head telling her that she had nothing to be ashamed of, that she'd been a dream of her parents, and like the Nile River in Cairo, the man next to her was only the conduit. One that had loomed large but that she could let loose finally so that he'd sputter out, just like the tributaries of the Nile before her.

Olive would give Tal'at this time. But that would be it. She would walk home if she had to. To her husband.

She would tell Adnan that she chose him and would hear his conditions.

Maybe too she'd admit the truth she'd known for a very long time.

Olive loved Adnan.

I am in love with my husband.

And it was that realization that gave her strength to ask the next question: 'You call my mother Jane. Did you love her during that time? Did she love you?'

Tal'at felt no shame when he answered. 'A beautiful woman is easy to lie with, certainly. But she was stoic, determined during it, said she wanted a child and her husband was sacrificing his honour for her to have one, so she was determined it would work. At the end of the agreed month, I left England with the monies your father promised, went right back to Manchester and bought passage on the same boat I'd been working on, handed the monies to the owner himself. The fellow was shocked I had the money to pay.'

She did not ask if Tal'at told Thomas Clifton how he'd got the money. She knew the answer to that. But it did not matter, Olive didn't need to hear any more. Relief swept over her, an immense respect for her mother and heartbreak over her loss. She'd been a strong woman.

'Maybe she and Elham are in paradise together, new-found friends,' she mumbled through the quiet tears that slipped out.

Tal'at hadn't heard her. He stood to better see someone who was approaching their spot, riding horseback over the sands. And then came that strange bird call whistle that had come through to the veranda earlier.

Belal, the guard.

Olive thought it might be good if he and Yasser had followed with one of his carriages; at least she'd have a quicker way home.

'Maybe he's here to tell you that we can go back

now that whatever siege was happening in Rasheed is over and you are safe.'

Her father squatted next to her. He put a hand to her cheek but it wasn't a fatherly gesture. 'I'm sorry to do this to you, Olive, and to lie to Yasser. But there was no *siege*. Belal is my nephew, the son of my sister and brother-in-law, also named Belal. Can you imagine the arrogance of a man who names his son after himself?'

'Why should it matter to me?'

Tal'at shrugged. 'Belal Senior made my life miserable and as my daughter your enemies should be mine. No matter. Belal Junior and I have arranged to take money from your husband.'

Olive stared at him, aghast.

'It is for the cause, you see. The rebel group that will free Egypt. The leaders in my group, they need to trust my loyalty. But I would never hurt you—we share blood. Do not be scared.'

He grasped her shoulders as if to stop her from running.

But Olive wasn't a runner. Adnan was.

'You are both mad!'

Then Belal was upon her. His ugly leer, as he tied her hands and feet with the rope he'd brought, his fingers lingering on her bare skin, and Tal'at—her father!—watching without complaint.

'My husband will kill you,' she shouted in Arabic.

Olive knew, more than anything else in her life, that Adnan would do *anything* to protect her.

'He will never find us here, and with the money we've asked for, he'll be too poor to look for us when we're gone.' Belal snorted, 'Serves him right, these nobles looking down their noses at us. Even if my uncle hadn't come to me today with this brilliant plan, I'd have visited you at your house, spied on you when you bathed or loosened your hair. This way I get the money and the girl.'

Her father tugged his arm. 'You will not touch her, you hear. She's my daughter, remember.'

'I forgot, *khaloo*,' Belal said sweetly enough, but when Tal'at wasn't looking he went back to his leering. 'Wait, if she is your daughter, that means she is my cousin. Don't I have first right of marrying her?'

'You are disgusting,' she spat.

'Olive is married already, you donkey,' Tal'at said. 'We're taking money from her husband and then taking her back to him. That is our plan. And that money is not for us, but for the cause.'

'But I get my fee though, yes?'

'Yes, yes.' Tal'at was growing impatient and Olive wriggled with dread.

She could save herself. Her father didn't mean to harm her and would not let Belal hurt her either so there was not immediate danger, but she did not want them to take a single farthing from her husband in such a despicable manner.

'How do you mean to gather the ransom from Adnan?' she asked.

Belal answered with pride in his work, looking between her and Tal'at as he spoke. 'I left him a note, slipped it under the backgammon table with directions. It took a while, because I had to wait for the guard to leave and then to lose Yasser.'

Olive hung her head with regret over her annoyance with the housekeeper and her 'big boy.' Adnan had wanted to employ security, keep her safe, and she'd responded by being petty. She'd been utterly wrong about too much!

'Your son,' Belal spoke to his uncle, 'thinks he is smarter than me.'

'He is,' Tal'at said. 'But no matter, we are done. I will not forgive Yasser for lying about being friends with a Prince of Egypt. I hope this incident breaks them apart and he comes back to me, tail between his legs.'

Yasser is a good man. Olive was grateful at least that one of her bloodline was not an awful human being.

The thought caused her to sob. And when she started crying, she had a hard time stopping.

Tal'at heard her but had nothing to offer save: 'When your husband provides the ransom, you will be released.'

Adnan had not liked him. She should have trusted his instincts but she was so filled with shame, afraid that dislike would extend to her, that she'd been unable to see straight. He'd tried to tell her after her confession at the *eumda*'s house that she'd been a babe, an innocent.

But what of the shame of having a father who'd use his own daughter to extort money from her husband? On the very first day he'd learned of her existence, to boot!

If this ended well, she'd not want anything to do with Tal'at ever again.

When the sun set and Olive started to shiver with the cold, she could not quell the chattering of her teeth.

'I brought a blanket, but we will have to share,' Belal taunted.

This time her father kicked him. 'Do not be uncivilized. I told you she is a married woman.'

Belal scrambled to his feet, shoving his uncle. 'And you don't start acting like my father.'

While they quarrelled, she heard her name in the dark of night, above the din of the crashing waves below. Distant but getting closer. 'Olive, Olive!'

He'd found her.

'Adnan, I'm here!' she managed before Belal slapped a hand over her mouth, silencing her.

'*Abu'ya!* Surrender!' *Yasser's voice.* 'We know what you and Belal have done. And his father, my Uncle

Belal, awaits in the city. He will berate his son for a first offense. But no one can save you or exile you now You have kidnapped a Princess of Egypt. You must surrender!'

The rest happened in a dark rush. Olive could not see properly, the moon was just a sliver and none had time to start a fire or light a lamp.

'Adnan,' Olive screamed when Belal's hand over her mouth loosened. 'Adnan!'

But it seemed like she was in a living nightmare and nobody could hear her.

Beneath the loud angry waves, she heard shouts, a scuffle, horses neighing.

And then a gunshot.

'Adnan!' She panicked. What if he'd been hurt? 'I love you, you stubborn grumpy man, answer me!'

'I am here, here. It is over.' His arms came around her and he peppered her with kisses, asking if she was all right, promising to not leave her alone again, to not put her in harm's way. Only after someone lit an oil lamp did he notice that she had been tied up and couldn't move her hand or legs.

And what a sight for sore eyes Adnan was. The concern in his handsome face, then the relief.

As he worked to free her, she noticed that there were a few men surrounding them. Yasser. The *eumda*. A few of his guards.

Behind them, Belal was tied up and so was Tal'at.

'Throw them in the jail,' the *eumda* declared.

When they were dragged away, the *eumda* turned to her and Adnan. 'You have my apologies. My son is misguided and alas I was unable to get through to him. I tried to help but I am old, tired.' He put an arm around Yasser's shoulder. 'I spent a life focusing my energies on fixing the ones I thought most in need. That is why I hired Belal even though you warned me...'

Yasser, ever gracious, told his grandfather, 'Do not concern yourself, *jidoo*.'

'You tried to be there for your family, today and in the past,' Adnan added, 'and you tried to do it in a way that would not compromise your people. I am grateful. You are a noble man and Rasheed should know your worth.'

She looked at her husband, not necessarily taken aback by his grace, but he surprised her nonetheless. Was it possible to fall in love with him more?

'When all is settled with the trial, you and Lady Olive will come to me and we will talk about how much you want to tell people or how much you want to keep secret. My wife and I will welcome you in our home. Always.'

He was a sad, gentle man and as he shook Adnan's hand and turned, she thought that at least there was some good in her family. And now she knew some of what her grandmother had suffered with her own children, Olive might not mind her meekness so much the next time she saw her.

Yasser was left. 'I can take you both home in my carriage if you would like.'

'I would like,' she said.

Adnan understood. 'You walked all the way here and you will not do that again.' She could see his teasing smile and God, how it filled every bit of her being.

Seeing it, Adnan said to Yasser, 'Will you just give your sister and me a minute?'

'Certainly.'

Olive leaned into Adnan, strong, unwavering. And it felt right.

He dipped to hug her, noticed for the first time the suitcase. 'It is just the little one,' he said, with a sigh of relief.

'I had not planned on staying long.'

He kissed her long and deep. 'I was scared I drove you away. Almost immediately I returned home, eager to talk. Then my father came and it was strange with him. I found the note after he left. Otherwise I would have come looking much sooner. You walked all this way? If I'd known I would have brought a carriage to help shorten the distance for you.'

She laughed because that was exactly what she'd thought he'd do. 'Wait, your father was in Rasheed?'

He nodded sheepishly. 'The khedive came to see us. To apologize, to mourn my mother too, I think.'

She was happy for Adnan. 'At least one of us reconciled with our father. Mine turned out to be a scoundrel.'

'Tal'at may be your father, Olive. And Lord Whitmore, even if you do not share his blood, is the one who raised you. But you are your own person.'

Adnan smiled. In the darkness of the night, his eyes were intense, a coal black that she could swim in for the rest of her life. 'The khedive's judgement is good and he knew you were going to be wonderful. He wanted you for Saleem and was disappointed that my brother fell in love with Elise mostly because it meant you wouldn't be his daughter-in-law.'

She kissed his cheeks, nipped at his full lips as if they were a well of fresh water to quench the thirst that had been left unfilled. Like his eyes, Olive could sip from them for the rest of her life. 'So I was right— you did marry me to please your father.'

Adnan laughed and the music of it was the only sort she'd need to hear for the rest of her life.

'But if you want to be Tal'at's daughter, want to live unhidden from the truth, I will understand. If you want to let others know, I will stand by you. You needn't ever be ashamed with me, Olive. I am your husband and you are my wife, Olive Whitmore, or Olive Tal'at. Egyptian, English or a mix of both. A reckless young woman, but also one who is daring and brave. And with a tender heart.'

'You forget that I am also a good cook!'

'I *am* starving.'

'Oh? The housekeeper didn't make you anything?'

'Housekeeper, not cook. I have one of those and the truth is, I have grown rather accustomed to her particular methods in cuisine preparation. Even her sweets are growing on me. Perhaps she uses this great talent of hers to bind me to her side, very much like the other *things* she entices me with.'

'I am merely a domestic servant then?'

He shook his head. 'You are a lady and a princess. You are my wife, Olive.'

Adnan's tone had turned serious and she didn't want that, not now. Not after all that had happened and all that she had lost. After all that she had learned about the past, what she needed now was lightness, levity.

She traced a finger along his jaw, and he took it to his lips, held it there as she said, 'When did Mr Grump turn into Mr Poet?'

'When he almost lost the love of his life.'

'Did you say "love"?'

'I am pretty sure I heard you say it first.'

'When?'

'Earlier,' he insisted stubbornly.

She teased, 'When I was in duress? Held for ransom? My hands and feet tied up? Surely I cannot be held accountable for that.'

He lifted her off her feet, held her up as he kissed

her deeply. And even when he pulled his lips away, he didn't lower her.

While she was hoisted aloft, basking in his love, care and attention, Olive knew without any doubt that Adnan Ahmed Ali was her Nile River. Her sea on the horizon. Her balloon in the sky. Her present and future.

'Will you please take home now?' she asked.

'I will and will always do,' he promised.

Epilogue

Lord Whitmore

Dear Jane,

Finally, I am travelling for pleasure. Would you believe I am in Alexandria, Egypt, visiting our daughter, Olive, and her husband, a man named Adnan? And, were you alive to meet her, I believe you would have come to consider her like your daughter as well: Elise, and her husband, Saleem.

You will not receive this letter, but a conversation between the five of us last night on the banks of the Mediterranean in a palace they call 'the Lodge' overlooking it, has compelled me to write it, regardless. Elise says there is magic in the epistolary, the connection between souls through words. Olive says she keeps memories alive in her journals filled with favourite recipes or the anecdotes she does not wish to forget. Adnan says writing can be a contract, a bond, a way to think

*about the impact of the details. And Saleem, well,
he says he tried writing once and it worked out
quite well for him!*

*As for me, I see the truths in all of these wider
stances, but today I was moved simply to share
my happiness with you. A short note that I will
perhaps put in a bottle to watch it be borne over
the waves. Or I will toss it upon the fires that
Olive's husband is fond of stoking. She watches
him lovingly as he does it and I watch her, her
belly swollen with their first child.*

She is happy.

*You would have liked being a grandmother, I
think, as our friend the khedive tells me there is
no greater joy than being a grandfather. I have
had a taste of it already, for Elise has an infant
son who very much reminds me of her father.
Thomas was like a brother to me and I miss him.
It gives me great satisfaction that she too has
found happiness.*

*My daughters, though none of my blood, both
in love with and married to Princes of Egypt.
Fine, fine men!*

*What a beautiful world it is. This had been our
dream when we joined that London traveller's
club so long ago. While I could never regret our
daughter, I wish there had been another way to
have brought her into our lives that would have*

caused everyone less heartache, but is that not the very essence of life, with its twists and turns?

'What matters is the end of one's tale,' you often reminded me, 'the love that was gained.'

I hope you are witnessing this tale of ours, my dear, and that you too are happy with it.

Yours,
Alfred

* * * * *

Make sure to catch up on the previous instalment of the Princes of Egypt miniseries

Daring to Fall for the Prince

And why not let yourself get swept up in Heba Helmy's previous charming historical romances

The Earl's Egyptian Heiress
A Viscount for the Egyptian Princess

MILLS & BOON®

Coming next month

THE DANGERS OF DECEIVING A DUKE
Louise Allen

Celebrating Louise's 75th Book!

The kiss was not gentle, but hungry, as though both were famished.

She was not an innocent. She had been married. But this was not right. Not there, not now. Not ever.

That was his conscience, shouting at him against the thrum of his blood, the aching need and desire for her, the answering desire Cat's body was signalling. Her mouth was open under his, the heat, the dart of her tongue and the nip of her teeth acting like a shot of brandy in his blood.

They were as one in passion and, it seemed, in tune in more ways than that, because, in a split second it was over. She drew back, even as he lowered her carefully to the floor and straightened, stepped away.

'That was a very bad idea,' Quinn said, controlling his voice with an effort. 'I apologise.'

'That realisation appeared to strike us both at the same time. No apology is needed.' Cat sounded equally breathless.

She moved away a little, but not, he thought with relief, out of wariness, but to brush the dust from her skirts.

'We agreed that a cat may be friends with a duke, did we not? But friendship is as far as it can go.' Her clothes apparently ordered to her satisfaction, she looked up and met his gaze squarely. 'I am not in the market for a *carte blanche*, Quinn. And no other offer is conceivable, is it?'

Continue reading

THE DANGERS OF DECEIVING A DUKE
Louise Allen

Available next month
millsandboon.co.uk

COMING SOON!

We really hope you enjoyed reading this book.
If you're looking for more romance
be sure to head to the shops when
new books are available on

Thursday 26th February

To see which titles are coming soon, please visit
millsandboon.co.uk/nextmonth

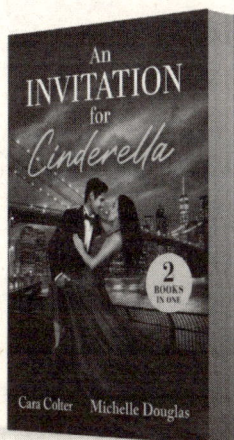

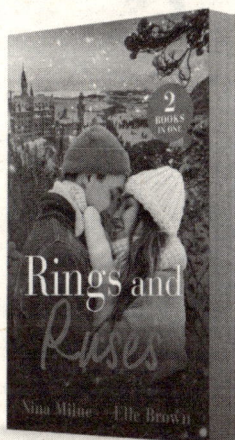

LET'S TALK

Romance

For exclusive extracts, competitions
and special offers, find us online:

f MillsandBoon

X @MillsandBoon

⊙ @MillsandBoonUK

♪ @MillsandBoonUK

Get in touch on 01413 063 232